I0684996

Dancing Toward the
Edge of Forever

Book 1

Cradle of Fire

Paul Snider

Published by Jemenon, Inc.
Naperville, IL 60564

Printed in the United States of America

For permissions, or to order additional copies of this book,
contact: JemenonMedia@gmail.com

Cover Art © 2019
Author Photo © 2017 Jonah Levy

ISBN: 978-0-9634327-2-8

First Printing, 2019

Many years ago, as a teen-age aspiring writer, I showed a story I had written to a next door neighbor, a poet who had spent much of his lifetime in travel and adventure.

He returned the story with five words of advice, which I have tried to follow for the rest of my life –

"Write about what you know."

Dedication

For all the children who had to raise themselves.

Chapter 1

It was a hot and humid midnight in the middle of June, 1931. Swarms of June bugs were flying in squadrons through the unscreened open window of the small upstairs bedroom. As large as swollen grapes and beetle-like with their hard shells they buzzed around noisily, smashing into walls and furniture, falling to the linoleum floor in a dizzy stupor. Mildred took aim at those still airborne and shushed them into stunned retreat. But one escaped her hands and landed on Andrew's forehead, greeting his arrival into the new world with the strange wet kiss of a wild and confused insect.

The big gray house on the southwest side of Detroit was already home to sixteen members of the Wheelock family. They had arrived in shifts, beginning in 1930, from Georgia and Tennessee. All had come North to find work in Detroit. The men slept three or four to a bed or on the floor, the women slept two to a bed. Big Jim Wheelock and his wife, June, had switched to a smaller bedroom alone.

The house faced Woodmere Cemetery, which gave rise to the rumor it was haunted. It wasn't, but the Wheelocks nevertheless had developed a habit of throwing salt over their right shoulders every time they left through the front door.

Outside, the air seemed thick and sluggish, heavy with smoke and acrid fumes from the giant Ford Rouge plant nearby, hard to breathe. Nothing moved in it except hope and slippery dreams.

And the weight of the Great Depression hovered over all of them, making everything seem worse. No one knew how far down the slope would go, only that it was steep and scary. The city of Detroit, like a tired old fighter, lay pounded and sweltering against the ropes. Jobs gone. Soup lines. Banks closed. Savings gone forever. The whole country reeled from the devastation of economic loss and betrayal of hope.

Desperate men and women, holding back their anger, were selling pencils, garden vegetables, anything, to sustain life. They would take any work they could find. Some would work for a hamburger, a loaf of bread, a bowl of soup, a quart of milk, a few eggs... And the lords of government and the lords of commerce looked on, seeming not to care, or personally care.

Where work was available in the big plants, men were banding together to form labor unions, most of them crushed as soon as they lifted their heads above the ramparts. But the spirit of solidarity was beginning to grow. A spirit of resilient strength was rising among them. And in the plants, men were daring to assemble, emboldened, to struggle for fair treatment and for the dignity of their labor they would claim as their birthright.

*

And it was out of these humble beginnings, three months after a hasty shotgun wedding ("the first ones are always a little early" the Wheelocks used to say), that Andrew Cameron was confronted by a new reality. The easy life was over. He would have to move on. No more of the comforting warmth of Zeedie's womb, where all his needs were supplied without struggle.

Something ancient and powerful, a mystical force, was beckoning him toward the unknown… a mysterious urge to enter into a new state of being. This would not be his last.

He threw his head forward and kicked his feet to find traction. He was ready. He found the opening. It was much too slender but it would have to do. With great effort he began the headlong plunge, down through the slippery passage departing from his former home. Now he was totally committed, no turning back. He squeezed with all his strength through the pulsing grip of bone and distended tissue, then slid the last few inches into the strong wet hands of Mildred, the midwife. She gave him a hard slap and he let out a barbaric "yawp!" to show he had entered into a new state of consciousness. He was now an air-breathing member of the human race.

And Andrew Cameron came into the world, into one of the deepest troughs of the Great Depression, the Grand Canyon of Depressions, to begin a long, difficult zig-zaggy two-step toward the deep and mysterious center of all reality, and in time to press with mind and heart and soul against the constantly expanding soft boundaries of human thought.

Chapter 2

His earliest memories (age 3) were of a world shadowed in violence and forbidden love. It was now the summer of 1934. Prohibition had ended less than a year ago. Beer and wine and liquor were flowing again.

He was conscious that he was in the rear seat of his father's car. It was cold and he had been sitting wide awake and alone for a long time. He could hear the noise of the beer garden quite clearly. A loud distant scrum of talk and accordion music. His mother and father told him to set still for a while until they returned. He wondered again and again if his parents would ever return. They had been gone forever, it seemed. But in time it was not they who returned. It was his father's best friend, Ty Gilson, who came into the front seat quietly with a dark-haired sleepy-eyed barmaid. Andrew could see her eyes glistening in the dark.

"There's a kid in here," Selma whispered.

"Don't worry," Ty said, "He's too young even to know what we're doing."

"Are you sure?"

"Trust me."

And they proceeded to do what they had come to do.

For people who were trying to keep quiet, Andrew thought they were quite noisy. From the sound of her voice he thought

Ty had hurt her. And when they finished, they left without saying goodbye.

After an agony of further waiting, Andrew heard a great increase in shouts and noise from the beer garden. The accordion had stopped. And then at last his mother and father returned. Ty and his wife Sadie were with them, and climbed into the back seat, with Andrew in the middle.

In the glare of the single unshielded spotlight that shone over the dirt parking lot, Andrew could clearly see the blade Ty was holding. An eight-inch butcher knife carefully filed down from its handle into what ended in a long, thin very sharp stiletto. Ty handed it over the front seat to Donald Cameron, who was driving.

"No, you keep it, Ty."

"That wouldn't be fair. You took it away from him."

Andrew's mother (Zeedie) spoke, taking the knife. "It all happened so fast, I didn't see it til it was over."

"Wasn't much to see," Donald said.

"Wasn't much to see, hell," Ty laughed. "Two seconds more and that thing would be tickling my liver. The guy came at me from behind. Don did it all in one sweep. With his left arm he pushed me out of the way, and with his right fist he sent this guy's jaw up in the vicinity of his ear. It was sweet. One motion."

"Why do you think he came after you?" Sadie asked in her throaty adenoidal voice.

"He thought I was making time with his girlfriend," Ty said.

"Were you?" Sadie said with some alarm. "Was it some chippie?"

"Honey, I wouldn't do a thing like that. You're my only Wahoo girl. You know me." Ty's voice was melted butter. "Besides, she was too hard boiled."

"So she <u>was</u> a chippie," Sadie said with her own sense of logic. Zeedie put the knife in her large purse.

Chapter 3

The image of the butcher knife was very much on Andrew's mind when his parents took him to be circumcised the following week. He didn't know why they were doing it, or exactly what was going to happen. And when they came for him he hid successfully for some time before they finally found him. He fought against them but they were too strong. He struggled with fear they were going to cut his penis off. Donald had to hold him while Ty drove.

And when it was over, and he found his penis intact and swollen, still bloody, he expressed (quietly to himself) his first thought of gratitude toward… somewhere in the ether, wherever such thoughts were intended to go. It was a close call, he thought.

He lay in his small bed wondering. If they had cut it off, as he feared, he imagined himself simply dying out of mortification. He would not want to live anymore. He lay visualizing the funeral, his arms outstretched across the chenille spread. He pictured himself somehow invisible and floating above them. All of them gathered around him dead in an open casket, everyone weeping.

"Now they'll be sorry," he thought. And as he watched them weeping in his mind, he imagined his mother especially distraught, saying "I'm so sorry we cut his little dickie off."

Chapter 4

Donald Cameron was born and raised in Lucknow, Ontario, a small Scottish farming community near Lake Huron, down below Georgian Bay. Donald, the only child of Kenneth and Clara, had nine uncles and aunts on the Cameron side alone. In his early years it was whispered it was a miracle he had even survived birth. Clara had barely survived as well, but could bear no more.

Donald grew up as a strong and hardworking son, the intended inheritor of his father's large apple farm. He was born with a restless and daring nature that bordered on recklessness. And by his middle teen-age years he already knew that apple growing was not in his system. He wanted a larger education than Lucknow provided, and he wanted larger horizons, some action and adventure. He needed a big city.

When he was young he once overheard the grownups discussing Henry Ford. Ford had electrified the world in 1914 by offering a five-dollar-a-day wage. In Donald's mind Detroit took on a special illumination after that. Five dollars!

And so it was that on a pleasant late September weekend in 1930 he arranged a ride with an uncle (Wilf) from Clara's side. Wilf was coming from Ottawa for a visit, then on to Detroit. The apples were picked, carefully packed in hampers, each wrapped in green tissue, and on their way in shipments to various destinations. Donald was twenty and he told his uncle he was going to the big city "just to look around." Together, they drove through the night and Wilf dropped him off in downtown Detroit very early Saturday morning.

Donald made inquiries. Then by streetcar and bus he found his way to the huge Ford plant along Miller Road on the gray Rouge River. He had not seen anything that large even in his imagination. It was enormous. The plant employed tens of thousands of workers. Smokestacks everywhere.

After walking the length of the plant, he made his way back downtown, and in a casual conversation with a fellow traveler he asked: "What are the sights to see in Detroit?" And his companion said: "Well, you've just seen the Ford plant. Next, probably you should see the Penobscot Building, especially at night—it has a big red ball on top that lights up." (Wilf had mentioned the Penobscot Building, but he had trouble recalling its exact name. He kept calling it the Mahogshot Building.)

"And after that?"

"Oh, you might try Belle Isle."

"What's that?"

"It's an island right in the Detroit River. It has a bridge. Easy to get to by bus."

"What do you do there?"

"Just walk around a bit. See the fountain. Maybe do some canoeing."

The thought intrigued Donald. He had never been in a canoe and calculated it would be fun and cheap.

*

Zeedie Wheelock was not new in town. She had come up from Chattanooga to find work, just before Black Thursday about a year ago, the day (October 29, 1929) that sent the stock market crashing and some men spinning from tall buildings into the street-fumed air to their deaths.

She was "the wild one" in the Wheelock family, addicted to dancing and Bruton's Scotch Snuff. They said she had too much Cherokee in her—too much to blend comfortably with the German-Irish-English-Norwegian mix of her heritage. One of her father's favorite sayings was: "Half your ancestors came on the Mayflower. The other half was here to meet it."

She had long wavy black hair, flashing dark eyes, and a slender figure, altogether a very attractive woman. Chattanooga was too small for her. After high school she had worked for a while in the sewing factory but grew tired of the tedium. The only other work she could find was as a waitress. But at least in that job men asked her out to dance a lot. Dancing was her greatest source of pleasure. Music and dancing.

The timing of her journey was unfortunate. With the nation sinking deeper into Depression jobs were hard to find, maybe impossible. All she could do was go back to waitressing, but this time she was able to find work in The Purple Onion, an upscale restaurant near downtown Detroit. Men still asked her out to dance but they took her to better places.

Then one day LeRoy Hunt III walked in. He showed immediate interest in her, and she in him. He took her on drives, to expensive restaurants, and dancing so much it was almost as if they were engaged. He never quite said it that way, but he spoke as if there would be a ceremony down the road. She was careful never to chew snuff in his presence because she knew he wouldn't like it. He was a little bit on the prissy side.

It was on this late September weekend when LeRoy was out of town on business that Zeedie's older sister Sarah suggested they go canoeing at Belle Isle. Sarah was rather plain in appearance, dark haired and simple, matter-of-fact in speech. She had the same genetics as Zeedie, but they were distributed differently. Upon arriving in Detroit she had rather quickly found George Hemming—a tool and die maker—married him, and allowed that her life was now all arranged.

Zeedie had been staying with Sarah and George ever since her arrival in Detroit. George had found work at Ford's.

Zeedie had just turned 22. Today was one of those rare Autumn afternoons, with all the earth at peace. Unusually warm weather, hardly any breeze, beautiful sunshine, leaves turning color, birdsongs everywhere. This would be the last canoeing of the season. The livery would close tomorrow.

Donald asked the canoe operator how to paddle, and the operator showed him the C stroke and J stroke and told him always to keep the canoe pointed into the little waves. It looked easy.

It was then that Zeedie and Sarah approached. As they came near Donald, Sarah found she had to find a restroom to attend to some immediate needs. Zeedie turned to go with her, but Donald impulsively said: "Don't go. Stay here. Talk with me til she comes back."

Zeedie hesitated, turned to Sarah: "Does he look all right?"

Sarah looked him over quickly: "Yeah, better than all right," she smiled.

And with that license their conversation began. Donald invited the two of them to canoe with him. But when Sarah returned a short time later, she said "Zeedie, yeah, I'm sorry. I can't go out with you. I have an upset stomach."

"Do you want to go home?" Zeedie asked.

"Yeah. No, I just need to sit still for a while," Sarah said, looking a little pale.

"I'll take her out," Donald said. "You need two people in a canoe anyway."

"Do you know how to canoe?" Zeedie asked.

"I've been canoeing all my life," Donald said.

"Yeah, just stay in sight," Sarah said. "Don't go where I can't see you."

"I think we can do that," Donald said, and helped Zeedie into the front of the canoe. He took the rear, the power and steering position.

It was much trickier than he had thought, Donald concluded as they ventured out into the sheltered part of the river. He found that canoes are quite tippy. Not at all as easy as it looked. But he did his best to act as though he knew what he was doing.

"I like doing spontaneous things," Zeedie said over her shoulder.

"So do I," Donald agreed. "The more spontaneous the better."

In hardly any time at all the canoe was out of Sarah's sight, and Donald was beginning to feel as if he were in control of the vessel, even instructing Zeedie on which side to paddle. They had now rounded a bend on the island and were venturing into rough water when the waves from a passing ore freighter moved across the river against them. Donald was not able to get the canoe pointed correctly. The waves hit them broadside, unbalanced them, and they were both thrown into the water.

Donald managed to hold Zeedie in one hand, the canoe in the other, kick his way to the nearby shore, then swim back for the paddles. It was an area of rather dense trees and shrubbery and bushes. He thought she would be angry, but instead she just looked at him with a warm smile.

"Well, ain't you a sight," she laughed.

"You're not so bad yourself," Donald said matching her smile.

"Thanks," she said.

"Well you said you like spontaneity," he said.

"Not quite this spontaneous," she laughed.

"We'd better get out of these wet clothes," he joked.

"You first," she chuckled again, to his pleasant surprise.

"Are you serious?"

"You first," she repeated. There was something in the way she laughed that reached into his daring nature.

"Your wish is my command," he said, and stripped clean.

She looked him over, but hesitated.

"Do you have the courage of your command?" he taunted.

"I'm not afraid of <u>anything</u>, man or beast," she taunted back.

After a time they returned in their wet clothes to the livery and to an anxious Sarah. They shook hands almost formally in front of Sarah, and assured her that because the weather was so warm, and without breeze, they would be just fine letting the clothes dry on their backs.

"By the way, what's your name?" Zeedie asked.

"Donald Cameron ...And you?"

"I'm Zeedie Wheelock. Nice to meet you."

"I really like Detroit," Donald said.

They exchanged addresses and parted. And thus was the beginning of Andrew Cameron.

Chapter 5

The Wheelock men, and there were quite a few, were suspicious of Donald at first. They mocked his Canadian accent by exaggerated pronunciations of out ("oot") and about ("aboot"). Donald never responded in kind about their hillbilly accents.

They referred to him as a Canuck and sometimes, behind his back, as "the five-cent immigrant." And they were leery of his explanation that "the first ones are always a little bit early." But finally, when they were all gathered at Sarah's home for Thanksgiving dinner, Donald had his showdown. With a smile, and in a friendly way, he offered to "fight any man in the house." And added: "I think it's high time I defended the honor of my native land." None took him up.

Thereafter they accepted him more fully, but the stigma of having come from a "foreign" country lingered and eventually transferred to Andrew. Zeedie's attitude toward the whole thing was rather casual. "Men will be boys," she said spitting a wad of tobacco juice.

Donald arrested his plans to go to school. It took more than a year to find a steady job at the Ford plant. In the meantime he worked at whatever odd jobs he could find. He asked Zeedie if she would move back to Ontario with him and baby Andrew. She said flat no. "All my relations are here," she said. "Besides, in

Canada it's hard to find a place to dance."

After a year at the plant, Donald had saved enough to buy a Model A Ford. John Henry, who ran the moving and trucking business, and for whom some of the Wheelock men worked part time as helpers, taught Donald to drive. The car gave him a new measure of freedom. But it also revealed an aspect of Donald's character he had not known he had. He loved to race trains to a crossing. He did not seek them out, but when the occasion arose, he took each situation almost as a personal challenge, quietly exulting in the victory of winning.

At first he did this even when Zeedie and Andrew were with him. Zeedie soon forced him to stop it "when the family is in the car." "I know I could do it," he would argue. "Do it when you're a dead man," Zeedie would say. But Andrew never forgot those several times when he felt he was an unwilling participant in a suicide run.

He never forgot that quickening of the stomach, that terrifying rush of sensations as he saw the speeding train screaming toward the side of the car, the battle lost, then the empty, deflated sense of relief when the adventure was over.

In 1935 Andrew saw his father come home one night quite bloodied and bruised. A pang of terror rushed through his young body when he saw the blood and wounds, one knuckle permanently pushed back into his hand. His father had been beaten up by a gang of Ford goons who were trying to stamp out the rising unionism. Donald had been helping the organizers out of a strong belief in social fairness. Zeedie washed off the blood and applied iodine where necessary, told him she was proud of him then turned to Andrew. "I married a fighting man." Her comment helped dissolve the terror Andrew felt.

During these early years Andrew spent much time battling a succession of childhood illnesses. He hardly recovered from one when the next was upon him—chicken pox, mumps, measles, whooping cough, scarlet fever. The last one almost killed him. He was hospitalized for five weeks, and placed with other children in an isolation ward. Scarlet fever was sweeping the country. Throughout these illnesses Zeedie was attentive without being affectionate. She seemed to regard his illnesses as a nuisance.

Out of the hospital, his legs were so weak he had to walk in a sinking crouch for some time. And either knee would tend to buckle unexpectedly, but he quickly learned how to catch himself in time. The fever also caused is left eyelid to droop, which took several years to fully recover.

By the Spring of 1936 Andrew was completing a truncated year in kindergarten, and falling in love for the first time. He met her playing bean bag. He noticed that whenever she got the bag she would throw it to him, with a twinkle in her eyes.

Her name was Evelyn Liska. A Polish girl with creamy white skin, sky blue eyes, and straight platinum blonde hair that fell to her shoulders. Her two upper front teeth were missing and she spoke with a lisp. When Andrew asked her name. she said "Evelyn Lithka." She spoke with a charming shyness and she did something with her eyes, a little hint of extra sparkle in his presence.

It was a mutual attraction. Andrew would walk her to school, then home again, and when bullies were near he would try to look tough, hunching his shoulders forward, dangling his arms like an ape, and if the bullies came too near, rush to defend her. They played together, explored together, climbed trees together. By summer they were almost always in bare feet. They also alley-picked together, searching for whatever small treasures they could find among the trash. It was here where Andrew began his plunge into what he thought was sin. They had come upon a brown paper bag in an alley and Andrew offhandedly gave it a swift kick, only to discover there was a brick inside the bag.

"Oh! Oh! Oh!" He tried to control the yell between clenched teeth.

"Thay it!" Evelyn said.

"Oh! Oh! Oh!" He was examining his toes, still holding back the force of the pain.

"Thay it!" Evelyn said urgently.

"...Hell!" Andrew said, beginning his descent into a new and unexpected world.

Evelyn's big blue eyes flashed with delight. "I like you," she said.

Another time as they were alley-picking, Andrew found a dead baby boy, newly born, wrapped in a bloody newspaper. The image horrified both of them. They were in tears when they reported it to Zeedie, who immediately reported it to the police.

"There's a lot of tragedy in the world," Zeedie told them.

But this was not enough for closure for their young minds. They went out in a field with high grass and tall weeds and sat down and hugged each other and cried for a long time.

[No one ever found out where the dead baby had come from, or what its name was, if it had a name.]

One day in June, as they were running across an empty field, Andrew stepped on the jagged remnant of a smashed milk bottle. The bottom had remained intact and spikes from its glass base stuck up several inches. It tore a large deep gash in his arch. As Andrew tried to staunch the flow of blood he noticed that an old man had come over to where they were. The old man had a gentle presence. He was tall and thin with silvery dark skin and a short white beard. He said his name was Skootchie-Skootchie.

He sat down with them in the grass and examined Andrew's foot. And then with long, thin fingers he scooped some black soil into his hand and began to rub it into the wound. "Whenever you get a hurt," he said, "Just take a little bit of nice black dirt and rub it in. You have to rub it and rub it and rub it, and then the hurt will go away."

"Are you a doctor?" Andrew asked.

"I'm kind of a doctor, in a way. When you get old you become either a fool or a doctor." Skootchie-Skootchie continued his gentle ministrations, packed the wound with more black dirt and stopped the bleeding.

"You're amathing," Evelyn said.

"We'll need to wrap something around this until it heals," Skootchie-Skootchie said.

Andrew took off his thin T-shirt and the old man tore part of it into a long bandage and wrapped and tied the foot.

"Thank you tho muth," Evelyn said.

"Thank you," Andrew repeated. "I feel better already."

After Skootchie-Skootchie left they walked, Andrew with some limping, through the field to a nearby tree, climbed up, and sat high in the branches talking.

"What kind of a name is Thkootchie-Thkootchie?" Evelyn asked.

"He must come from someplace really old," Andrew said.

"I love Thkootchie-Thkootchie," Evelyn said.

"So do I," Andrew agreed.

The gentle summer breeze caressed the leaves and branches and made them sway a bit. "I just thought of a new game," Andrew said.

"What ith it?" Evelyn asked.

"Come with me and I'll show you," he said. And he led her through the trees to another field with very tall weeds and prairie grass. And when he found a suitable place he looked around, to ensure their privacy, and motioned her to sit down facing him. The weeds and grass were high over their heads.

"What do we do now?" Evelyn asked.

"You just do what I do. Promise? Cross your heart and hope to die?"

"I promith, croth my heart and hope to die," she said.

He opened the buttons of his corduroy knickers. "I'll show you mine if you show me yours."

"Oh, wee," she said with a giggle, and pulled up her dress. "Are you thure thith ith all right?"

"It's just a game," he said. "Kids can play games."

"Thith ith fun," she said, as they both looked.

"I just wondered what it looked like."

"Tho did I."

"You are my real friend," he said.

"What do you call thith game?"

"Weenies," he said.

And when they had had their fill of looking, Evelyn said "Leth play Weenieth every day."

"It's more interesting than Kindygarten," he said. "You learn more."

*

They soon acquired a new friend, but they never included him in their private game. The new friend was Wiley, also going to first grade with them in September. With Wiley they would play and climb trees together. They both liked him. Wiley was sandy-haired, had a rather triangular face and a hare lip. What they especially liked about him was that he seemed to have an unusual and sincere intensity for his six years, but was so agreeable to be with. Wiley loved candy. He almost drooled just thinking about it sometimes.

In those years, in this part of Detroit, an unusual cultural pattern had developed among children. It was unthinkable for a child to go up to ring the doorbell or knock at the door of a friend's house. Instead, the culture dictated that the kid who wanted another to come out to play would stand on the sidewalk—never on the porch—in front of the friend's house, and shout loudly in a sing-song voice: "Oh John-ee!" or "Oh, Wileeey!" or "Oh Ev-e-lyn!" and so forth, until the friend emerged. Whatever the name, the call always had to be in four beats, with accent on the third beat, dum, dum, dee, dum.

On an unusually hot day in August the three of them decided to dig a hole to China. They were not sure exactly where China was, but knew it was on the other side of the world. They wanted to make friends with the Chinese.

Andrew found his father's shovel and the three began their labors.

"How big should we make it?" Wiley asked.

"Big enough for a Chinaman to walk through," Andrew suggested.

"How big ith a Thinaman?" Evelyn asked.

No one knew. But they went on with their digging, taking turns. They finally settled on a hole that would be four feet by three feet, straight through the center of the earth. After several hours they had dug down over their heads and had to help each other in and out of the hole.

During a break in their labors, Evelyn asked "Do angelth come from Thina?"

All three pondered deeply.

"I think they come from very far away," Andrew said.

"Maybe Thina," Evelyn said.

"Who knows . . .?" Andrew said.

Wiley went into his house and brought a milk bottle full of water for them. They sat around the hole sipping it for a while. All had worked up a sweat.

"Do you think we'll thurprith them?" Evelyn asked.

"I think they'll hear us digging. They'll know we're coming through," Wiley said.

Andrew pondered the question in his imagination. "I think

we'll see little boys and girls in pigtails in those little white things they wear. I think they'll be surprised. They'll say, 'you dug a hole all the way through the world, just to see us?' And then they'll ask us if we want some tea." In Andrew's mind, of course they would speak English. It did not occur to him they might speak Chinese. He imagined a simple tea ceremony with his new other-world friends.

Andrew's scenario seemed a reasonable suggestion, so they continued on for a while longer. Andrew was digging, now over his head, when water began to seep in the hole, making a wet and mucky bottom.

"I think we hit the ocean," he said. They solemnly agreed.

"How can we dig through the ocean?" Wiley asked.

"We'll have to get a boat," Evelyn said.

"I think we better fill up the hole and try something else." Andrew said. And the three of them spent another hour filling up the hole. "The Chinese will have to wait for me," he said, and by next day the whole plan had left their minds.

*

Andrew, Evelyn and Wiley all entered first grade in September. Except for private moments Andrew and Evelyn shared alone, the three had become an inseparable trio. They helped each other as they began to learn to read. They ran across the street to the store together when one of them acquired a penny. One confection especially appealed to all of them, a small chocolate wafer with coconut filling. It cost a penny. And they freely shared their good fortune, one third each.

In mid-October Wiley found a penny and the three decided to

go to the candy store. The store was located across a busy street with no stop signs or red lights anywhere nearby. All three were alert, and had become expert at timing their runs. And this time they had no reason to expect it would be any different.

They waited for an open space in traffic and all ran together. Halfway across the street Wiley dropped his penny. Andrew and Evelyn were across the street when they looked back and saw Wiley's hesitation. He was trying to decide whether to rescue the penny or get out of the way of cars. A car speeding too fast crumpled him into oblivion in an instant. And the car continued on without stopping. As other cars stopped, Andrew and Evelyn ran to his lifeless body. His limbs were in strange positions and his face was full of blood. There was nothing they could do to bring him back. He lay there in that unmistakable stillness. Their tears could not erase that awful moment.

That night, Andrew, still in shock, asked Zeedie, "Mom, where do we go when we die?"

"There's supposed to be a heaven somewhere," Zeedie said spitting a stream of brown tobacco juice.

"Must be a long way from Detroit..."

Chapter 6

By now Donald and Zeedie had begun a series of interminable squabbles. One of the problems was that Donald was not around much. He worked a regular day shift job at Ford's, and was glad to have it. In the afternoons and evenings he worked on John Henry's trucks, moving furniture. He wanted to save enough to get a better life, to go to school, to make something larger of himself and family.

All Zeedie knew was that he never seemed to be around when she needed him. "I know he's not cattin' around. He's not the cattin' around type," she said. But he never took her dancing anymore. It was all eat, sleep, chores, start again. She was becoming lovely, restless, impatient. Every time they engaged in verbal duels Andrew shuddered and became anxious, as though the foundations of the world were shaking and unstable.

Sometimes when they argued Zeedie would say, "I gave you the best years of my life." And Donald would retort: "Yes, the best six years."

"That's good and plenty!" she would fire back.

"Well, at least you got Andrew," Donald once said.

"He was the biggest mistake I ever made," she said with anger.

Andrew, in the doorway to their room, heard all that was said. He went out across a scrubby field and climbed a tree and sat in its limbs for a long time. He tried to cry but he could not. His whole body seemed numb. His brain felt numb.

The most puzzling of their arguments was one that left Andrew pondering long after the word flashing ended. Zeedie would say, "I could have married LeRoy Hunt the Third, heir to the Hunt Honey and Almond Skin Cream fortune. I could have been Mrs. LeRoy Hunt the Third."

She would always say all of those words. She never referred to him simply as LeRoy or as LeRoy Hunt or even LeRoy Hunt the Third. She always added, "heir to the Hunt Honey and Almond Skin Cream fortune."

"But you said he was a little prissy."

"I could be a rich little prissy."

"In your next life," Donald would say.

The thing that got Andrew wondering, each time she said it, was the question of his own identity. If his mother had married LeRoy Hunt, would he be named LeRoy Hunt the Fourth?

- Would I still be me?
- Would I be someone who never would be able to become me?
- Would I know that I never was?
- How could I not be me?
- But if I am, then maybe LeRoy Hunt the Fourth never was or never will be?
- Would I be prissy?"

This was all very confusing.

*

By mid-December Donald Cameron's luck had run its course.

He died violently when his car slid on a patch of ice at a railroad crossing. The car skidded off the road and right onto the tracks. There was no time to get out before the train tore into him. It took almost all his savings to pay for the funeral.

Andrew wept for days, and Zeedie did too. It was the closest they had ever been together, at least in an emotional sense. She held him a lot, which had not particularly been her habit. She talked about the good times, Donald's good qualities, his hopes and dreams. Several times she said, "He would have made it, except he slipped on the ice." But sometimes in her weeping she would turn a darker side. "We're in for it now," she would say.

Kenneth and Clara Cameron came to the funeral. A complex journey for their aging joints. They came by hired car from Lucknow to Wingham, then by bus down through Ontario and across the Detroit River and through customs. They walked some distance, each carrying a suitcase, to a streetcar, then to another streetcar, and finally on foot again to Zeedie and Andrew. They were of sturdy stock and made no complaint about the journey, but Andrew could see their emotional and physical exhaustion.

Andrew had only a dim memory of them, from his brief visits to the farm with his parents years ago. He sat at the table with them as Zeedie served bread and butter and chicken noodle soup. As they ate, Andrew studied their countenance, particularly Kenneth. There was something almost noble and eternal in the stoic quality with which he bore his son's loss, something about how he held himself and would not give in to the overpowering emotion.

"Where do Camerons go when they die?" Andrew asked.

"Same place as anybody else," Zeedie responded quickly.

Kenneth and Clara were quiet. "Grandpa," Andrew asked, "why do people have to die?"

Kenneth pondered for a few moments. "God has a plan for every person, a secret plan. And no matter how bad it looks up close, the plan has a beautiful ending. Nothing good is ever lost in the universe."

Donald's body was laid out in an open casket in a nearby Baptist church. Andrew kept returning to the casket to peer down into and touch the cold waxy stillness of his father's face. The funeral director had made him up in such a way that he did not even fully resemble himself. Donald had been lean, but the corpse was puffy. They had even put a thin coat of lipstick on his lifeless lips. When Andrew saw that, he pulled out his handkerchief in a quiet rage and wiped it all off.

The minister was a tall, heavily built man named Deeks. He had a large swath of black hair, wore a black suit, and had a thunderous voice. Andrew had never seen him before, and apparently neither had his parents, since they were not churchgoers. This would be Andrew's first impression of a Christian church.

Two months before, to attend Wylie's funeral, Zeedie and Andrew had to hitch a ride with a neighbor. Zeedie had never learned to drive and the little synagogue where Wylie's funeral would take place was some distance from home. The casket was closed, so Andrew did not feel a sense of final completeness about Wylie's death. It took a long time to work its way through the labyrinth of his mind.

Pastor Deeks began the service by reading some information about Donald Cameron. It was quickly evident Deeks had never met him. After a few perfunctory remarks, Deeks launched into a fiery sermon. He pointed with a long, outstretched arm and bony finger at the lifeless form of what had been Donald Cameron.

"That man was a sinner!" he thundered.

The unfairness of the charge shocked Andrew beyond belief. He loved his father. He knew he was no sinner. And it was clear to him that Deeks knew nothing at all about Donald Cameron. Yet, there he was pointing that long finger from his precious black suit, laying into this lifeless form. No fair, Andrew thought. His father could not rise up to defend himself.

Andrew wanted to leap up, yank his father out of the coffin, stand with him shoulder-to-shoulder to do battle with this man who was hurling insults at him, who had never even met him. But he restrained himself, except for a single tear that fell down along each cheek, and some grim clenching of his teeth. Kenneth and Clara sat stoically beside him.

Pastor Deeks went on to talk with fiery emotion about how everyone is a sinner. But Andrew never heard the rest. His mind remained in turmoil about how unfair it was to condemn what you never saw and did not know anything about.

The day after the funeral, Zeedie arranged for George and Sarah to drive Kenneth and Clara to the bus terminal for their return to Canada. And Kenneth invited Andrew to come to the farm if he could, and to go to school in Canada if he so wished. Zeedie listened to the conversation with interest, but said nothing.

Andrew had no particular desire to go to Canada. All he knew was that it was a foreign land, maybe a little strange, somewhere across the River between Detroit and China.

By January what little savings were left after the funeral were almost gone, and Zeedie had to move to the cheapest place she could find, Wonder Gardens.

John Henry moved her without charge. Donald Cameron had been a good, hard worker on the Henry trucks, he said.

Zeedie found a part-time job as a waitress, and enrolled Andrew in the remaining term of the new school's first grade. A school nurse examined Andrew and asked him: "Has your voice always been this husky?"

He did not know what husky meant. He thought it meant tough and muscular, so for some months he entertained the vision of himself as a tough kid. And this was quite helpful because, being new in the neighborhood, he had to come to a showdown quickly with the neighborhood bully, Rodney. Rodney wanted to dominate him, but Andrew had known from the earliest moments of his consciousness that he would not submit to domination.

His first fight was half punching, half wrestling, but he came away with a clear victory. An undiscovered and powerful fierceness lay within him, together with an attitude that would not accept defeat. It was the fierceness that finally overcame the bully. And when it was done, Rodney shook hands with him and said he wanted to be friends. But Andrew very much missed his old neighborhood and Evelyn and Wylie. They had been his gentle friends. He especially missed Evelyn, and knew he would never see her again.

Wonder Gardens was a ramshackle wooden tenement two stories high and U-shaped, with chipping paint, and a large brick and dirt courtyard in the middle. Zeedie and Andrew moved into a two-room flat on the second floor, a bedroom and kitchen. There seemed to be two distinct classes living there—those who tried to take care of the place and those who didn't seem to give a damn. It was a mix of hardworking poor interwoven with lazy poor who littered the courtyard with trash.

"Mom, why do they call it Wonder Gardens?" Zeedie's reply was laconic, after spitting a wad of tobacco juice. "Makes you wonder about everything," she said.

But it didn't. Wonder Gardens seem to have the opposite effect. Right away Andrew noticed there was something deadening about living there. It was almost as if the tenement, in and of itself, somehow had the power to close off horizons, to pull whatever big thoughts might spring into your head, down into little thoughts that had no destination.

Except that, for a while, big thoughts were swirling in the air, even into the kitchens of Wonder Gardens. At the end of October Orson Wells scared half the United States out of its wits when he broadcast a radio dramatization of H.G. Wells' War of the Worlds. Many were convinced an alien invasion was underway. But the ominous fears soon disappeared as the toughness emerged.

"Mom," Andrew asked, "Do you think there are people on other worlds?"

"Don't know," Zeedie said, "But it seems to me it would be a mighty big waste of space if we were the only ones."

Andrew thought about this for a long time and in his way of

thinking he agreed with his mother. There must be people on other worlds. There had to be a simple logic in the universe.

The flat was poorly heated, if at all, during these cold winter months and warm clothing was in short supply. He seemed to have a constant case of goose bumps and shivering so hard his muscles would jerk spastically. He longed for spring and warmth.

Andrew had always slept naked and he continued this habit. Zeedie would put the second blanket on the bed they shared. But she had the same habit of sleeping naked too. As he lay on his side, his legs bent forward, trying to forget the cold and go to sleep, he would feel the smell of her, and her body behind him, curling around him, following the contours of his legs, her arms folded in front of him in a warm embrace. She would stroke his chest. Sometimes her hand would drift downward as she snored. He was grateful for the warmth, but her closeness and the pressure of her flesh, and the downward drift of her hand, made him uneasy and it would take longer than usual to sink into a dream-filled sleep. Zeedie seemed to think nothing at all about this arrangement, and slept soundly, snoring into the back of his neck.

Zeedie seemed to have an Eve-like absence of self-consciousness about her physical nature. In the mornings she would emerge from the bed, stretch her arms in a catlike yawn, shiver from the cold air, then slip her sinewy legs into her peach colored step-ins, pull them up over the mysterious black forest, then find a brassiere to cover her pointed breasts, all under Andrew's watchful eye.

One time, before Donald was killed, Zeedie had just come out of bed when Andrew walked into the bedroom.

"Put something on," Donald quickly said.

"He's just a kid," Zeedie said, ignoring him.

Sometimes she would pause before pulling up her step-ins to tell Andrew a remembered joke.

"Which would you rather be," she would ask, "a bigger fool than you look, or look a bigger fool than you are?"

"That's simple" Andrew would say, his eyes fixed on the mysterious dark forest, "I would rather look like a bigger fool than I am."

"But why?"

"It would almost be like being invisible."

"What would you do if you were invisible?"

"I don't know. Don't you feel invisible now?"

"Why do you say that?"

"I can see right through you."

She laughed and pulled up the step-ins. "Nobody can see through me, even you."

*

On Valentines' Day in the new school the teacher asked the first grade class to draw names from a bowl. Boy and girl names were all mixed together. Each child had to bring a valentine for the name drawn. Andrew drew Walter Drew's name, but felt strange about it. He didn't want to give a valentine to a boy. But the teacher insisted. She said it makes no difference. Andrew knew she was wrong but felt he had to conform to the instruction.

At home he could find nothing that would serve as a valentine. And though a store-bought valentine only cost a penny, he did not have one and could not persuade Zeedie to give him one. She said she didn't have a penny.

So he found two white three-by-five inch file cards, made a paste out of white flour and water and glued them overlapping together. They made a four-by-five inch card. Not knowing what else to do, he drew a large red heart with an arrow and wrote "I love you." It didn't seem right, but he thought that's what you are supposed to write on valentines.

Next day in school he presented his valentine to Walter. All the other children were exchanging store-bought valentines.

"You made this!" Walter shouted with contempt. "You made this!" he repeated. And as he waved it in the air for everyone to see, the flour and water paste came loose and half the broken heart fluttered to the floor.

Andrew felt humiliated. He would never forget that haughty, scornful well-fed face, or the teacher's lack of wisdom in forcing him into this strange position.

Zeedie was stretching food dollars. She frequently made what she called milk gravy. Andrew would watch her put a scoop of white flour into a cast iron frying pan, stir it quickly, and heat it until the flour turned brown. Then she would pour a glass of water into the pan, a little Crisco, and keep stirring until a pasty form of gravy emerged. Served hot over Wonder Bread, or sometimes over cold soda biscuits, at least it settled the stomach for a while.

"Mom, why do you call it milk gravy when there's no milk in it?" Andrew asked.

"Half what you eat is what you think you're eating," she said.

But her other name for it was "Red Eye." He never understood why. Nothing was red about it. He asked her once. She only replied that when she ate it she saw red.

Andrew couldn't understand this at all. It made no sense to him. But she seemed satisfied, so he assumed the problem was with him.

On special nights Zeedie would make what they called Slumgullion—a stewy mixture of whatever she could find to put into the pot. Sometimes she would call it Shipwreck. But that was usually when there was some crumbled hamburger meat, mashed potatoes, and beans. It was one of Andrew's favorite meals, always different, always the same. As far as Andrew could tell, the difference seemed to be that Slumgullion was mainly liquid, and Shipwreck was mainly solid. After dinner they would each take an apple from the bushel basket hamper Kenneth shipped every autumn. Andrew loved apples and was disappointed when the supply, each year, ran out.

When Andrew needed a tooth pulled, one of his Wheelock uncles would come over with truck pliers, wipe off the grease, and pull the tooth. No one ever went to a dentist, a doctor or a hospital. You went for help when you were dying, not before. You just toughed it out at home. Hardly anyone ever called the police, no matter what. You just dealt with it in your own way.

Neither of them talked about Donald. The weeping had been done and they moved on with life. But he noticed that Zeedie found more and more things that irritated her about Andrew's actions, sometimes even his presence.

"See what you made me do!" had become one of her more

common expressions when she dropped something, or nicked a finger, or stubbed a toe.

"I didn't make you do anything," Andrew would say back. "You are in charge of what you do."

Spank. Spank.

Then later: "Look what you made me do!"

"I didn't make you do anything!"

Whack!

"You did it all by yourself! You have a mind of your own!"

Spank. Spank.

"I do not have a mind of my own! I can't afford to have a mind of my own!"

Zeedie worked almost until midnight most nights. And Andrew spent a lot of time listening to the radio. One of his favorite programs was the continuing adventures of Jack Armstrong. The announcer would introduce the program by saying with an increasingly loud and intense voice, "Jack Armstrong, Jack Armstrong, JACK ARMSTRONG—the All American Boy." Andrew thought he would like to live a life of adventure.

When not listening to the radio, he had a lot of time to think, and his mind roamed through little pathways trying to find some way toward a better life. He thought he should do something to change his circumstances. And so he became an alley picker again, but this time with a purpose.

He was a natural explorer, had a strong curiosity, and because he had so much free time, he ranged not just for blocks, but sometimes for miles in search of new treasures. When he got them home, he would clean them up and, when out of school, set up his "store" on a board set across two Sunkist orange crates in the courtyard. People in the neighborhood did not have much money, so he learned to bargain for whatever he could get.

By nightfall he would take whatever he had not sold up into the bedroom, together with the board and the orange crates.

Once when a few of the Wheelocks visited, they saw his enterprise and promptly titled him "The Little Jew." He did not know what a Jew was, but the tone of this appellation was unmistakable. "All you need is a horse and wagon," they said in derision.

He did not really like the alley picking lifestyle, always battling with the sheeny, who had the advantage of horse and wagon, to find the treasures first. Nor did he enjoy the putrid smell of garbage in the open fifty gallon rusted drum, brilliant swift greenback flies swarming by the hundreds, white maggots feasting on the rotting flesh, so thick they resembled a pulsating white blanket. He decided he would try to find another occupation, some other way to earn money.

As the weather turned warmer and warmer the courtyard scene became ever more vivid. Both human and dog feces (the children called ba-ba) appeared night after night, always populated by swarms of flies. Very small children with diapers would run loose. Andrew learned to be careful where he stepped. But there were several old women who would come out in the mornings with brooms and buckets to keep the bricks and dirt as clean as possible, talking all the while in a language he did not understand. With their hair pulled back under bandanas, and their weathered and calloused bare feet, Andrew imagined them to be the staunch pillars of the earth itself.

*

The thing Andrew wanted more than anything else, a bicycle, seemed far beyond reach of their meager circumstances. A used bike would cost ten dollars. But ten dollars might as well have been a million; both seemed that far away. His alley picking treasures brought pennies and nickels, not dollars. As much as he thought about it, turning over simple strategies in his mind, nothing seemed even remotely possible. He did not envy the children who had bicycles, rather he let his mind explore in mental companionship the freedom they must be experiencing. He dreamed over and over again what it must be like.

"Mom," he said to Zeedie one night, "is there any way you can think of to get me a bike?"

"No way," Zeedie said. "We hardly have enough to pay rent and buy gravy."

"What can I do?" he asked.

"Maybe you should pray your heart out," Zeedie said offhandedly. "I heard God likes kids."

It had not occurred to him before to pray. What little he had been taught about religion was filled with images of a thundering God who would smack you down to death in a neurotic rage if you offended him. And that somehow the only way to get on God's good side was through blood and sacrifice. It seemed so cruel and unusual and unfair. He could just imagine God yelling:

"See what you made me do! Smack! Smack! That will teach you!"

He dared not answer back in his mind.

But he could think of no other alternative, and so he began to pray in his mind. Over and over again he prayed for a bike. Going to sleep, waking up, pausing in play, he prayed and prayed and prayed, all with hands pressed in the prayer position. Nothing happened. Then it occurred to him that God was hard of hearing and could not understand these small rumblings from an agitated mind. He thought he should try praying aloud.

So he went into a field where he was sure no one would hear him. He would try to speak to God directly, man to man.

"God, I really need a bike," he would shout.

And again nothing would happen. So he thought he should pray louder or use an affected form of speech as he had heard a radio preacher use.

"Gawd, Gawd O'Mighty!" he would shout, "Listen to me! I really need a bike!"

But after many days of such proceedings, without result, he became discouraged. He had almost given up when it came into his mind that maybe God was waiting to surprise him. And so every morning he would get up at dawn, stumble sleepily out onto the outside landing of their second-story flat and look expectantly in every direction. There was no bike, ever.

Finally, Andrew decided to take matters into his own hands. He would confront God face to face about the negligence. So he went out into the field again, his private place where no one could possibly hear. It was a bright and sunny cool day. And he stood in his favorite spot and raised his right fist against the sky, and with his face against the sky, and in a trembling voice shouted:

"Your name is not God! Your name is Pisswilly!"

And as soon as the shout left his throat he crouched down and put his hands around his head, waiting for God's lightning bolt to smash him to smithereens. For a while he dared not rise again, fearing that God had got the lightning bolt tangled in his beard, or the folds of his white robe.

And after a time, when he felt that God was busy with other things, Andrew rose again and, still slightly shaken, went on with his day.

He concluded it was worthless to pray. He had tried every way he knew how.

*

By June the tar wagon would come around, drawn by a little torch to patch holes winter had left in the streets. A fire underneath the bathtub-size bucket kept the tar hot and molten. When chunks of tar fell from the wagon, Andrew and several other children would take these warm lumps and chew them like gum, the sticky blackness forming a temporary shell around the teeth. It was cheaper than Chiclets.

Then the ice trucks would come by, their rear compartments filled with twenty-five or fifty pound blocks of ice for the ice boxes. When the driver would chip the ice blocks to break them loose, small chunks of ice would fall to the street. Andrew and the other children would gleefully swoop them up and suck their stinging coolness until the ice was gone. On the few occasions when Andrew came into possession of a nickel, enough to buy a candy bar, invariably one of his acquaintances would come up to him and say "Dibs!" which meant he had to share the candy with whoever said it. Although he never once called Dibs himself, he always gave a share to a dibs-caller. But rolling around in his mind the thought recurred: Why should anyone be entitled to claim some piece of your property simply by calling for it. It didn't seem right to him, but the culture was so strong he went along with it.

*

On one of Andrew's explorations in the alleys he came upon a huge wooden rectangular structure two stories high. It was a block long, with telephone pole vertical struts holding an unbroken wall of large black boards. No windows. He went around to the front of the building and saw it was the McFadden Coal Co. He was curious to see what was inside.

On the far end of the building, where it abutted directly against a garage roof, Andrew saw that several boards were missing. He climbed onto the garage and scrambled with handholds up to the missing boards, then crawled in. All he saw inside were huge piles of various kinds of coal separated into giant bins. Having satisfied his curiosity, he clambered back up through the hole and carefully scaled down toward the garage roof.

He no sooner turned around than found he had company, two teen-age boys with a mean look in the eyes and twisted expressions in their mouths. They had him cornered against the wall.

"Sit down!" they commanded.

But Andrew did not sit down. He knew that if he sat he would become much more vulnerable to whatever they had in mind to do. He would take his chances standing up.

The boys were much larger than he, and they both sat down on the slanted roof facing him, but keeping him cornered against the wall.

"If you won't sit down, we will. We got all day," the first one said. "You are in our control. We can do anything we want to you." He pulled out a pocket knife and opened the blade.

"My name is Herman. What's yours?"

Andrew made no answer.

"And this is my buddy Morris. You better tell us your name. We have ways to make you."

Andrew made no reply. His mind was alive with strategies, trying to choose which one.

"Didja ever eat horse shit?" Herman asked.

"No."

"We're gonna make you eat horse shit."

Andrew looked at them a though they were insane. He had never encountered such weird minds.

"Didja ever eat cow shit?" Morris asked, playing with his own knife.

"No."

"We're gonna make you eat cow shit," he said. The predators laughed.

Andrew now had a strategy clearly in mind. With a fierce yell and great suddenness he bolted toward them, landing a fist in each face. He quickly moved down the roof and jumped off into the alley. It was a ten-foot drop. When he landed he instinctively threw his body into a roll to cushion the shock. It hurt, but his adrenalin shot him right to his feet. He looked back. His predators were standing on the edge of the roof trying to decide what to do. Andrew ran until he had no more breath and until he was sure at last they were not in pursuit.

He had just gotten his first pair of gym shoes the day before, and he felt fortunate that he could now run with such speed.

*

Sarah and George came over one warm Sunday afternoon to take Zeedie and Andrew to Walled Lake, not far outside Detroit. It would be Andrew's first picnic. They had come with friends, the Dubys, who had two daughters, Bonnie and Betty, who were within a year of Andrew's age. The three made an immediate friendship and went off to play and swim together, Andrew in a loose-fitting borrowed bathing suit he had tied tightly around his waist with a piece of clothesline.

Bonnie and Betty Duby were both pretty, with sand-colored curls and a sort of Betty Boop appearance, and they laughed easily and were fun to be around. They played in the shallow water for a time, and eventually began a discussion of swimming.

"Do you know how to swim?" Bonnie asked.

"No, but I've watched other people do it," Andrew said. "I think I can."

"Let's see you do it," Betty said. "I dare you."

Andrew took her challenge. He went into water up to his chest and took a few tentative strokes. He tried again, and again, until he was satisfied he could swim if he wanted to. But he had no idea how long or how far.

Zeedie, Sarah, George, and Al and Helen Duby were about a

hundred feet away, at a picnic table drinking crisp Pfeiffer's beer and roasting hot dogs, paying no attention to the children. Bonnie and Betty were no swimmers themselves. They spent their time doing handstands, splashing water, and tagging Andrew in such a way as to make him chase them and tackle them in the water. He enjoyed wrestling with girls. But their playfulness gradually took on a sharper edge.

"How far do you think it is to the raft?" Bonnie asked, referring to an anchored raft.

"I don't know," Andrew said

Betty ran up to the picnic area to consult with her father, then returned. "Dad says it's about a hundred feet."

All three studied the distance. It seemed longer than that to Andrew, but he had no way to test his sense of distance. There were no boats in the water beyond the immediate range of brown dirt beach shoreline.

Bonnie looked at Andrew again. "Do you think you could swim that far?"

"I think I could if I wanted to," he said trying to show off.

"I dare you!" she said with a challenging smile.

Andrew felt his whole identity was being challenged. Although he had gained some confidence from earlier practice swimming, when he surveyed the distance he was not sure he could swim that far. He thought about it for several minutes.

"Are you afraid?" Bonnie taunted (she was a year older).

"I'm not afraid of anything," Andrew answered instinctively.

"Then let's see you do it," Betty said (she was a year younger).

"I'm thinking about it."

"Don't think too long. I'm getting hungry," Bonnie said.

Andrew pondered the distance again. He pondered his identity disappearing into oblivion in the faces of these Betty Boop girls. And after several more moments of thinking, said "I'll do it."

"You slay me," Bonnie said.

There was a sour feeling of fear in his stomach as he moved out into deeper water. And then he began to swim with intense concentration, his arms pulling him forward through the water, his legs kicking furiously to propel him as swiftly as they could go. His mind totally focused on the task, he dared not stop or turn around. To stop or turn would mean death, he was sure. Now the sour feeling of fear was gone and he moved with a high adrenaline energy. The raft seemed even farther away than he thought. But he continued on and at last come to clutch its edges with an immense feeling of conquest and victory.

It had never occurred to him that he should have someone watching or standing by.

Chapter 7

Second grade ended in June 1939, and the next day Zeedie delivered some disappointing news.

"I'm going to move in with Sarah." Andrew instantly heard the "I" and heard no "We." But he said nothing as Zeedie continued.

"You're not going with me."

"Where will I go?"

"I'm going to send you to Canada for a while, to live with your grandparents. You'll be better off there."

"But what about school?"

"You're smart. You'll catch up," Zeedie said matter-of-factly, poking some snuff into the side of her mouth.

"Just like that?" Andrew asked.

"Just like that," Zeedie said, closing the conversation.

Zeedie persuaded John Henry to drive Andrew to Lucknow. She seemed to have a special relationship with John Henry. June was an especially busy season with too many people moving, but John agreed to do it on a late Saturday night. He could be back by Sunday night. All it meant was that he would miss a night's sleep and his regular Sunday morning services at the Temple of Zion, a group of devout Holy Rollers whose company and high energy he especially liked.

John Henry was a rough and elemental man with a craggy

personality and a warm heart, especially for a widow in distress. Zeedie said she could not pay him anything, but John said they could work things out. It would be okay. Payback was only a small thought lingering in the back of his mind. His primary motive was simple, he said. He just wanted to help.

"That's what you do," he told Andrew.

John Henry searched the side roads around Lucknow for two hours, until he found the Cameron mailbox at dawn, just in time for breakfast.

John got along well with the Camerons. He sensed some roots of similarity in their elemental nature. By late morning he was on his way back to Detroit, wondering in his sleepiness if he had been a little too soft-hearted. Maybe he could work something out with Zeedie.

Chapter 8

Your first impression of the Cameron farm would be a sense of quiet beauty. It lay several miles northeast of Lucknow in the gently rolling glaciated hills of southern Ontario. A long lane entered the farm from the Cameron Sideroad. On both sides of the lane stood a grove of tall maple trees. These extended all the way up to, and surrounded, three sides of a huge L-shaped barn on the hill, the highest point on the farm. Every autumn this great planting of maples displayed a spectacular lingering foliage of stunning beauty.

The main business of the farm was apples. There were nine different varieties. The chief varieties were Sky, Baldwin, Ontario, and Delicious. These were sold throughout Ontario, Quebec, and shipped to England. The farm had long been distinguished for its premium crops. Up near the barn, in the deep "cool water" pump house, the walls were covered with first prizes and an occasional second prize from fairs where apples had been exhibited over the years. Year after year visitors would come to the farm to see the heavily laden trees or to witness the results of new grafting and other experiments. Kenneth Cameron was noted as a quality and innovative grower. Among other things, he had introduced the Delicious apple to this region of Canada.

Long, long before this, after Kenneth had bought the farm from his parents, he had personally planted the entire grove of maples and more than 300 apple trees. In its best years the orchard would yield 1,500 barrels and more than 1,000 hampers of excellent quality apples. Barrels sold for 5 to 10 dollars apiece. In a periodic off year, when the orchard rested for a season, the yield might fall to 200 barrels, even to zero. Visitors sometimes advised that if he would pack the poorer grades he could get the count up to 2,000 barrels, but he would not. He sold the culls and "grounds' and the wind-shaken and bird-pecked apples in bulk for cattle feed.

In February 1934, three years after Donald had moved to Detroit, Kenneth saw his prized orchard severely damaged. For 22 consecutive nights temperatures hovered from 15 below to 34 below zero. More than half his trees were either killed outright or effectively destroyed. "It was the steadiest and hardest continued frost I have ever known," he wrote in his journal. By the time Andrew arrived, the orchard yield had fallen to 500 barrels and 1,000 hampers of the quality levels Kenneth was determined to maintain.

Bordering the northeast corner of the farm and on a neighboring property, tucked away over a hill and meadow and nestled singularly alone among the quiet fields, lay a substantial "Bush" of tall, dense pine trees that had never been cleared. The floor of the Bush forest was a soft carpet of orange-brown pine needles uninterrupted by vegetation. A small trout stream ran alongside the Bush.

Several large stream-crossed fields of pasture in the western and northern areas of the farm were rented out to cattlemen, who would try to add about 400 pounds of weight to each steer over a summer. Except for some wire fencing fronting the Sideroad, long and extended rows of jogjag cedar log fences lined the boundaries and separated the various fields and lanes of the entire farm. Blackberries and wild strawberries grew in the protection of these fences. Wild elderberries and choke cherries grew as well. The choke cherries, Andrew quickly learned, would make the mouth pucker and contract into dryness as the cheeks pinched shut.

The Cameron home, built in 1910, was constructed of chiseled granite blocks a foot thick, eight bedrooms in all. A very large dining room, wood-paneled and lined with chairs and couches and a "winter stove," served as the family gathering place. Eight doors led to a formal parlor (used for special occasions), a large lower bedroom, a closet, the pantry, sun porch, back porch, "summer kitchen," and to the cool cement cellar where coal and big blocks of furnace logs were stored, and all preserved food was kept. The pantry held large bins of flour and sugar, and tins of spices, and water pails with tin dippers. Off the dining room, under the second story eaves and roughs, a long metal chute funneled water from the roof down into a large rain barrel, for washing hair. The summer kitchen was actually two large rooms, a wooden structure more recently added to the main house. Off the summer kitchen, with a slightly sunken cement floor, was an all-purpose room where baths were taken, butter churned, clothes washed in big, galvanized tubs, and so forth. By 1939 a one-seat indoor toilet room had been added, with plenty of quicklime (calcium oxide) on hand for sanitation and odor control, and a huge Simpson's catalog.

Five other buildings, in addition to the barn, completed the farm—a large henhouse attached to the far side of the barn, with its own courtyard for the scratching chickens; a large workshop; a storage shed for logs and cedar; and a stone "milk house" where various chemicals were kept and mixed. Attached to the upper end of the milk house was a two-seater outhouse, complete with quicklime and huge catalog.

The fifth building, Kenneth's favorite place to sit, was the pump house at the end of the long lane, up near the barn. The pump house was built over a particularly cool water spring. Its door looked down the lane.

Kenneth Cameron, now 76, had been a powerfully built man of great strength in his youth and maturing years, but age and rheumatism had made him stiff and he now walked with a cane. He had been named after Kenneth McAlpine, first king to rule both the Picts and Scots back in the ninth century. He had married Clara when he was 37 and she was 22.

In his younger years he had once drunk six bottles of beer, and then never touched alcohol again. His strongest swear word was "By Dad!"

In his advancing years he found he had to rely more than ever on hired hands. He had always employed men to help with the apples. But now he needed their services more and more, to feed the cattle, to spread the manure, to cut the alfalfa and hay and oats. So there was always at least one hired hand working, and Kenneth paid them all well and fairly for their services.

Andrew only dimly remembered his earlier visits to the farm. Donald and Zeedie first brought him there when he was less than a year old. They left him in Clara's care while they drove into Lucknow to "see the town," one extended block in length, with two churches.

Clara decided to give Andrew a bath. In a porcelain tub full of warm soapy water she worked with diligence to keep a grip on his small slippery body. But Andrew twisted loose, fell, and hit the floor headfirst. Clara was in a state of shock as she gathered him up, carefully toweled him dry, and made all sorts of little tests to ensure she had not damaged him. She was so mortified she did not have the courage to tell Donald and Zeedie what had happened. But for many years afterward she looked at him more closely than usual. As Andrew grew, he sometimes thought she was nearsighted.

Twice after that, before confronting his last train, Donald drove with Zeedie and Andrew to the farm. But those were brief visits of only two or three days at a time.

Andrew was grateful for the relief from the intensity of the streets and alleyways of southwest Detroit. He found immediate restfulness in the peace and quiet. He loved the morning stillness of the farm—the quiet hum of the earth, the distant rooster crow, the birds atwitter in search of intimate companionship or a morning meal, the bees abuzz from flower to flower, the fresh aroma of lilacs, the whiff of roses—marigolds, zinnias, petunias, geraniums, snapdragons, hollyhocks, huge blue morning glories. But it was more than that. He had entered an atmosphere of love, conveyed in small words and gestures, especially from his grandfather.

*

The first morning after his arrival, very early as the sun was stretching its yawning rays over the horizon of a new day, Kenneth woke Andrew to take him outside. Both were in bare feet as they stepped out onto the large grass lawn. The grass, cool and wet with morning dew, gave Andrew a wonderful tingling aliveness in his feet. The air was already warm and pleasant, with only a gentle breeze. The beautiful melodic sounds of a wood thrush lingered in the trees above. From far across the fields, in the willows down along a trout stream, a wild mourning dove was cooing its melancholy cry. Andrew had never before experienced the kind of gentle quietness that was upon the land. Even in the vacant fields around Detroit, nothing had ever come close.

For a while they stood together, taking it all in, observing the bright dew upon the grass and clover. Then Kenneth led him to see the glistening splendor of a web a spider had woven on the lower pump during the night.

The sun-filled dew was strung like dancing diamonds along its silken strands.

"There is wonder and beauty in all creation," Kenneth said. "Drink it in. As long as you live, drink it in."

"It's not like Detroit," Andrew said.

"Detroit must have its own special kind of beauty. I was only there once, when your father was laid to rest."

"In all your life?" Andrew asked.

Kenneth bent down to pluck two leaves of sweet clover from a special patch he had long before planted. He broke the leaves open to release the fresh, tantalizing smell and gave them to Andrew. It had the sweet aroma of the dew of the Gods.

"All you need to grow is already around you," he said. "And *in* you."

When they returned to the kitchen Clara had several sticks of cedar flaming under the iron lids of the kitchen stove. The smell of it, the bright crackling sound as the cedar burned, added to the new sense of peace and order Andrew was coming to understand. For breakfast Clara boiled an egg for each of them and served bowls of gruel swimming in warm milk and pools of butter sprinkled with nutmeg and cinnamon. Large chunks of fresh homemade bread, with slabs of butter made Andrew feel almost as if he had lost his way and entered heaven instead of Canada. Butter, bread and milk were expensive, luxuries he had never known before in such abundance.

Andrew quickly adapted to the quiet rhythms of farm life. He willingly accepted an assignment of chores and responsibilities. He emptied and cleaned the porcelain chamber pots each morning. He brought a pail of fresh water from the cool spring of the upper pump house. He split cedar kindling. He gathered fresh eggs from beneath the warm bellies of the nesting hens, then scattered feed for them in their courtyard. He played with and stroked the fur of Moby, the great white barnyard cat, who hunted her own food—except for bowls of milk and water—and kept the vegetable garden clear of invading rabbits and other small, hungry animals. Moby often slept on the warm strong back of Charlie, the all-purpose horse.

Charlie was a very intelligent horse. He understood more than "Gee!" (turn right), and "Haw!" (turn left). He seemed to understand in advance where you wanted to go.

Andrew led Charlie to the water trough and kept it filled, then fed him oats and apples and hay and talked to him as he brushed him down. He shoveled manure onto the large gather pile outside the stable. The manure pile sat under the second story of the barn open to the air on one side.

He hoed and weeded the huge garden, picking off invading insects such as potato bugs and pulpy green tomato grubs. He brought potatoes and root vegetables from their straw-covered winter shelter in the root cellar of the barn with its cool dirt floor. He mowed the huge lawn around the house with a push mower. He brought mail from the mail box, he replenished salt licks for the cattle. He wondered how the Camerons had ever got along without him.

There were endless repairs to attend to, scythes to sharpen with Kenneth on the large stone grinding wheel. Andrew's job was to crank the wheel, spinning it through a chamber trough of water as Kenneth applied the dull blades. Then there were ditches to dig deeper to increase the flow of water in a lessening stream. He helped Kenneth pick up large rocks and boulders from the fields, load them onto the flat "stone boat" for Charlie to pull to the ever growing stone pile.

There were always fences to repair or rebuild. And in the autumn, there were the maple trees to tap for their sap, to boil it in a large tub, into maple syrup.

He helped Kenneth plant timothy to make hay, then alfalfa. Kenneth told him alfalfa has rich, strong roots that can penetrate the earth down to 20 feet or more. Both of these crops were good for the cattle—hay and alfalfa, and fallen apples.

In the lower level of the barn there was a huge, very clean apple packing room with whitewashed walls and all-day sunshine streaming through windows on two sides. The floor was smooth cement which Andrew kept clean. Kenneth showed him how to make whitewash, and he helped put a fresh coating with large brushes over all the stone walls. Andrew loved the fresh clean limestone smell of the wash, and especially the cool, sweet lingering aroma of apples that stayed in the room long after the apples were gone. There was work to do everywhere, and Andrew thrived in this new atmosphere.

Then there was the orchard itself, with its whole waiting collection of necessary chores. Field grass to cut with a scythe under each tree to make soft beds for falling apples and to nourish the trees. (Kenneth gave Andrew 10 cents for each tree bed he cut.) Props had to be placed under the most heavily laden limbs—from a selection of 1,500 fork-topped maple poles of various lengths stored in the barn along with many ladders. Branches had to be trimmed to allow sunlight to stretch its life-giving rays into all the fruit. Limbs had to be wired to the trunk to prevent too violent shaking in heavy winds. Football sized hornet nests had to be carefully cut down and bagged. And more.

Kenneth showed Andrew the king of all the trees in the orchard—a huge Spy tree that produced unusually large apples. A newspaper article had once described it as "a magnificent giant ...In the last 12 years this tree alone has produced 169 barrels of first-class apples."

Kenneth sprayed his trees several times each season to prevent apple maggot and other vermin from invading the crops, and Andrew helped him in this. They would mix the ingredients into a large drum atop a high platform in a wagon Charlie pulled. Andrew would pump continuously while Kenneth probed the long spray extension into all sections of each tree.

There was always some breeze blowing through the orchard, and the breeze would blow back some of the spray so that after a time their clothes and faces were covered white with it. Andrew found the cool, wet chalky sweet smell of the mist rather pleasant as he breathed in its vapors.

But it was not all work. Andrew found plenty of time to explore the farm and various buildings and the countryside around them.   There were no children among the farms immediately nearby. Nor were there any dogs—too expensive to feed.   So he learned to find solitary pleasures in his explorations—leaping from limb to limb in his favorite maple tree, or climbing out along a branch and riding it to the earthen floor, or laying along it and feeling the gentle sway of the wind as it moved him from side to side. On a younger tree he would climb to the top and fall gently with it as it bent to earth. On windy days he like to go under the long rows of maple and listen to the wind rush through the leaves above him. And then he would go into the Bush, where all was silent, muffled and still.

There was a large haymow in the barn, with chiseled-log supporting beams high overhead. From the center beam at roofline, Kenneth had tied a knotted rope from which Andrew would swing like Tarzan from beam to beam. But the rope swing was not quite enough sensation. And so, to heighten the experience, and to test his skill, Andrew would climb to the high cross beam and leap off in a spin, seeing how many revolutions he could make before he hit the hay. He did this repeatedly until he was certain he could do two revolutions. It was on an early Sunday afternoon when he decided to try for three. He leaped into his spin with extra force, but he had miscalculated. He landed head and neck first and found he could not move to get up. He lay there, as hour drifted into hour, fearful he had paralyzed himself. He kept trying to summon movement, but he felt numb. He worried that he was about to add new hardship to the already economically depressed life of his grandparents. He thought perhaps his life was over. He knew he could not shout for help. No one was near.

After nearly five hours of anxious, determined struggling, and the application of his utmost will, he gradually began to find movement in his limbs. Little by little he made his fingers work, then his arms and legs, and finally he was able to stand again. Still shaken, he felt his neck. It was stiff and very sore. But he was alive and could function again. He wanted to thank someone, but he did not know whom to thank.

About that time he heard the cowbell, Clara ringing it with some energy to summon him to supper. The cowbell, sounded from Clara's firm hand, was the farm communication system. Its tones would carry across the fields and through the orchard.

"Where were you?" she asked. "We looked all around." He told her he'd been playing. She made an expression of impatience. "You'll be the death of me yet," she said. But after supper he told her his neck was a little stiff and she put some liniment on it. In a way, the liniment surprised him. Clara's answer to all maladies seemed to be hydrogen peroxide.

Kenneth spent time with Andrew whenever he could. One morning he showed Andrew how to find juicy worms under rocks. Then he packed a trout basket made of woven tiny branches, long ago purchased from visiting Chippewas. The two of them proceeded slowly across a neighboring farm toward the best trout stream in the area. There was one section of the stream, a deep pool beneath a tree-shaped high granite overhang that was the home of particularly large speckled trout.

As they came near the favored spot Kenneth lay down and told Andrew to do the same. "Trout get nervous when they see your shadow," Kenneth said, "or even hear your voice." They crawled commando style up near the lip of the rock overhang, baited hooks, and pushed their poles out over the pool. The hooks were hardly in the water when they both received strikes. It was Andrew's first fishing experience and he was quietly exhilarated. In all, they caught six large trout before they went back to the farm. Andrew thought it was the best meal he had ever had as he sucked the sweet flesh off the tiny bones.

"Learn how to fish and you'll never go hungry," Kenneth said.

"I think I'm going to carry some fishing stuff in my pocket from now on," Andrew said.

Kenneth took Andrew into Lucknow, with Charlie pulling the buggy. The first thing Andrew noticed were the colorful and varying aromas that came from every store.

Birdie Button's butcher shop had a two-inch bed of clean sawdust on the floor, and its fragrance mingled with the fresh aromas of the meats. The harness shop smelled like rich well-oiled leather. The bakery pulled you into its door with the smell of deliciously warm, yeasty bread. The apothecary was filled with aromas of gentle soaps and flower essences. The dry goods store smelled pleasantly of fresh cottons and woolens. The only restaurant in town smelled like warm baking apples with a hint of cinnamon. The ice cream parlor had a clean vanilla smell. The 5 and 10 cent store smelled like maple sugar. Every smell was pleasing to the senses.

And so were the fragrances and other stimulations of the farm. Andrew had never before experienced the smell of clean sheets having dried all day in sun and flapping in the wind, the unbelievably fresh smell of captured sunlight and apple-fragrant breezes clinging within the folds of the sheets long afterward.

He liked the smell of freshly churned butter, after working long at the churn handle. He loved the taste of the buttered tarts Clara would bake afterwards.

He enjoyed the sweet aroma of newly mown hay, even the pungent earthy smell of the horse manure pile. But he enjoyed more the endlessly subtle aromas from many kinds of flowers Clara had planted, and their exotic visual beauty. Sometimes when the winds were high he would go out under the maple trees and listen to the lonely who-ooing sound as the air rushed through their leaves and branches. In the evenings he would often hear the stirring cry of bagpipes in the distance. Nothing at all like the sounds and smells and colors of Detroit. All of it was building whole new avenues of excited feeling in Andrew's brain. He had never dreamed this world existed.

And on the neighboring Struthers farm there were yet other sensual pleasures. Kenneth kept no dairy cows but Struthers did. Sometimes Andrew would be permitted to milk the cows, squeezing the milk from full udders in long quick strokes. And when young calves would assemble at the wire fence next to the barn, Struthers would let Andrew feed them frothy warm raw milk from a tin honey pail. He learned that if he dipped his hand into the warm milk and extended it into a calf's mouth, the calf would suck off the milk with its whole mouth around his fingers. It was the most sensuous experience of his young years. Afterwards, Struthers would let him crank the separator, the cream flowing out of the top portal and the rest of the milk into galvanized pails. Andrew loved the rich taste of the warm, frothy raw milk.

Nine-Mile River was some distance away, down a couple of side roads and across several fields. Andrew asked Kenneth for directions and told him he wanted to experience river swimming. Kenneth told him where it was but cautioned him. "Don't swim alone there. Five people have drowned. The river is more dangerous than it looks."

All of this made the river especially intriguing. One afternoon, vowing to be careful, he made the long hike and found the river. He stripped naked and carefully worked his way into the water, testing the rocks and current. In water almost up to his chest he began to practice. The current made it entirely different from lake swimming, and he could now see why it would be good to have a companion, if for nothing else, just to help pull you out of the tangle of fallen tree limbs if the current caught you by surprise. And after a while he got to feel the rhythm of the river and to work in harmony with it. The whole experience was rich in new sensations. There is nothing like naked swimming—the whole body feels alive and invigorated. For the rest of his life he wanted to swim naked every chance he could get.

During his long, solitary walks he had time to think. He thought often of his mother, wondering how she was, what she was doing. The decision to send him away seemed so abrupt. He knew she would not call. Although there was a party-line phone in the dining room, international calls were prohibitively expensive. He hoped that at least she would write, but as summer turned into fall, no word from Zeedie. Sometimes he wondered if she had forgotten him.

*

Angus Cameron came to visit in late October, full of concern about war that had just begun in Europe. Although now in his eightieth year, he was on his way to England to see what he could do to help.

The summer and autumn chores were done. Most of the preparations for winter had been completed. Apples had been picked, sorted, packed, shipped, each wrapped in green tissue. Manure had been spread under the trees. Hay and alfalfa had been cut, raked, coiled, dried, and taken in for winter feed. Oats had been cut, thrashed, and stored in a large bin in the barn. Cattle had been taken in from the fields and shipped to market. Wood for the winter furnace had been cut and stored, along with cedar for kindling. Some anthracite coal had been delivered for the small coal bin in the cellar.

Onions had been pulled and dried along the fences. Potatoes had been dug and stored within blankets of straw in the cool dirt-floor root cellar of the barn, along with winter squash, turnips, and root vegetables. Soon the sap would begin to flow down into the roots of the maples. Trees would be tapped to collect some of the sweet juice for boiling down into maple syrup.

For days the summer kitchen would become the special focal point of all activity as fall canning proceeded. The cast iron stove afire under all burners. Large oval-shaped tub-like copper kettles of boiling water. Corn, green beans, peas, carrots, tomatoes, and other vegetables cooling. Applesauce, raspberries, blackberries, wild strawberries. Cooked chickens cut into pieces that would fit with their own broth into mason jars. Everything sealed with a half inch of hot melted paraffin "sealer" wax, then left to cool and suction down for winter storage.

As he participated in this, and watched it unfold around him, Andrew was coming to understand that to live this life required that you practice conservation and become a planner. Conserve or perish. Plan ahead or die. That's all there was to it. No excuses. Even the life-and-death knowledge of this made him quicken and feel inwardly stronger.

He also learned another lesson, a sharp and piercing struggle with self-discipline. Five special fruit trees stood just beyond the edges of the large grass lawn—two kinds of cherry and three kinds of plum. All summer he watched the fruit grow and ripen, but the trees and their bounty were untouchable. Kenneth told him early in July that no fruit could be taken, that he had sold the yield of all five trees to a neighbor.

"What about if a plum or cherry falls to the ground?" Andrew asked.

"Not even then."

"What if it's on the ground and half rotted away and full of wasps?"

"Not even then," Kenneth answered. "Mind you, there is a huge difference between 100% and 99.9%. Huge."

"I'm not sure I understand," Andrew said.

"I sold the trees in their entirety, to be picked and gathered when ripe. We do not own a single plum or cherry, picked or fallen." He did not explain to Andrew that he had sold the trees every year, since the loss of most of his orchard had placed unusual strain on his financial condition.

Andrew almost bit his lip. The more inaccessible, the stronger became the attraction of the forbidden fruit. His mind many times raced through rationales that would enable him to at least have a taste. But he could not engage in self-deception. He would have to tough it out. He even dreamed one night of climbing into all five trees and eating his fill. The dream was so vivid that when he woke he could almost sense the lingering taste of sweet sun-filled flavors still in his mouth. But by now he had already gained such deep respect for his grandfather. This gave him added strength. "Always do what's right," Kenneth had said. And Andrew did succeed in this trial of self-discipline, which seemed especially hard because it would have been so easy to violate. A single fallen plum. Who would ever know? And finally, when the neighbor came to pick the trees, and tether every shred of fallen fruit, Andrew felt a sense of relief.

During September, as the apples were ripening to full richness, Kenneth would take his double-barreled shotgun out into the orchard and fire it into the sky when predatory birds came too close, mostly crows and starlings. And Andrew would go with him and scan the sky along with him, armed with a large metal spoon and noisy pot to frighten the birds away. Kenneth decided to teach Andrew how to fire the shotgun. He showed him the simple procedures, then lay the gun upright against a tree while he watched the sky.

This time there were no invading birds, only a small singular drama above them: A large hawk gliding overhead like a bomber on a run, searching for targets of opportunity. The hawk must have been in the vicinity of a community of starlings because they rose like fighter planes into the attack. As the big, heavy bird lumbered in a forward glide, the starlings circled in and around, darting in from all sides to strike with their beaks. The hawk seemed unfazed. It was like watching an old aerial dogfight. But as his struggle continued beyond their range of sight, and as Kenneth seemed intent on scanning the skies, Andrew picked up the shotgun.

He tried to remember the special steps Kenneth had taught him, and proceeded through them. When he was then ready to fire, he was certain he had got it wrong. The gun was innocently aimed at the small of Kenneth's back. Andrew was so sure had got it wrong he thought he would pull one of the triggers to make sure. But at the last second the thought came into his mind: What if I did it right? He pointed the gun at the ground several feet away from Kenneth and pulled the trigger.

He had done it right! The explosion was deafening. Kenneth was so startled he lost his balance and fell. Andrew helped his grandfather to his feet, then horrified at what he had almost done, fled to the barn and the haymow. And this is where he stayed until long after dark, when he came home still trembling from the gravity of what could have been a massive lapse of judgment. Kenneth was most gracious and forgiving, but the trauma would linger within Andrew.

Kenneth did not mention the shooting to Angus. There were more important things. Hitler had invaded Poland on the first day of September. Four days later President Roosevelt declared American neutrality. Less than two weeks later Russian troops invaded Poland and, in a separate battle, were soon at war with Finland as well. Events were moving out of control. England, as Poland's diplomatic ally, declared war against Germany. But Germany was beginning its quick conquest of most of Europe. Then a strange lull began to unfold into scenarios of dangerous uncertainty. For some time it seemed as if nothing was happening. It was the period later described as "the sitting war."

Angus was a gregarious man, full of stories and nostalgic recollections of the history of the Camerons. Where Kenneth was by nature more calm, disciplined, thoughtful, his older brother had a personality swirling with passions, even at age 80. He could only stay a week, but he wanted to see his youngest brother one last time before he went "off to tinker with the war."

They lit the cool oil lamp on the dining room table and sat around it talking or playing checkers.

"Kenny," Angus said, "how much have you told young

Andrew about his heritage?"

"Each thing in its time," Kenneth said. "We will get into this over the winter."

"Maybe I'm just an old man rushing into winter," Angus laughed, "but I'm of a mind to get into it now."

"You always had an impulsive streak," Kenneth smiled.

"Andrew," Angus asked: "Do you know what the Cameron name means?"

"No."

"Well it means bent nose, or wry nose—" Angus twisted his nose to one side to illustrate— "some call it crooked nose. But what it means is you follow your own nose. You don't necessarily run with the pack. You go your own way, independent in mind and thought. You don't let anybody lay claim to you if you think you should go another way."

"I like that," Andrew agreed.

"You come from a people filled with warlike passions and barbarous ways. Some call us a warlike race. But there's something you should know in our defense. No one was more set upon or harassed from without than the Camerons. Adversity forced us to become warriors. We were practically driven to live by the sword."

"Maybe Clan Gregor would be an exception," Kenneth said.

Angus thought for a moment. "Possibly Clan Gregor, I'll give you that." Angus said. "But, Kenny, I think we are running neck and neck with them in terms of harassment."

"Andrew, with the Camerons it has always been all or nothing," Kenneth explained. "We have been fierce in our passion."

Angus added, "The Camerons once fought a single running battle for 350 years with the Macintoshes. They wanted what we believed was rightfully ours."

"A Cameron can never yield!" Kenneth explained with more passion than Andrew had ever seen in him.

Andrew was fascinated by the discussion, his mind soaking it in like a sponge. He did not think to ask questions yet. Listening to his great uncle and grandfather talk was sometimes like watching a contest, Angus emphasizing more the warrior, Kenneth pointing the way more toward the romantic and spiritual side.

Kenneth went on. "Mind you, we have cherished our independence even from earliest times. We cling to it with eagle claws. The Romans could not conquer us. They thought we were wild men, so they built a wall to try to contain us… Cromwell, with all his force, could not subdue the Camerons. Cameron of Lochiel was the only Highland chief who never submitted to Cromwell… Whatever men dare they can do. And we have dared to live with independent minds."

"Hear, hear," Angus said with a gentle laugh.

"But deep down underneath," Kenneth continued, "there is something romantic, even sentimental, in the nature of the Camerons, and I think you could probably say this is true of all the Scots."

Angus laughed loudly. "The Germans didn't find us romantic at all, Andrew. With our fighting kilts a' flying, the Germans called us the Ladies from Hell. Trouble is, in the last great war, for all the killing and suffering, we only wounded them, and now they've caught their wind and they're coming at us again."

"How can they do that?" Andrew asked. "I thought they were done for."

"So did the politicians," Angus said. Looking at Andrew, he added, "There's an old Scottish saying: Never wound what you can't kill."

"Andrew," Kenneth said, "when I say there is something romantic in our nature, I'm saying we treasure unflinching loyalty to higher values. We treasure integrity and moral correctness. We treasure fairness and justice... Every Scot's child is taught to give aid and comfort and shelter to anyone who is hunted and persecuted. This becomes part of our nature."

"But on the other hand," Angus said "—I won't let you off, Kenny—the Cameron warrior reputation is that we are 'fiercer than fierceness itself.' That's what others say about us. We are committed to absolute fierceness in battle." Then Angus lowered his voice to drive home a point. "Kenny, have you told him yet of the Cameron war cry?"

"Not yet," Kenneth answered. "Go ahead."

Angus hauled back to put a deeper and more menacing timbre in his throat. Then he bellowed.

"Sons of the hounds come here and get flesh!"

The conversations continued for days, over games of horse shoes, on the sun porch, around the dining room table, over Chinese checkers, in the barn, standing in piles of glorious fallen autumn leaves. And when it was time for him to go, Angus put his hand affectionately on Andrew's shoulder. "Andrew, I must go now. You can think of me as a restless adventurer. That's what Tiny McDonald said of us. She said the Camerons have always been restless adventurers."

Then he paused. "You are now one of the Cameron men," he said.

*

In the post-harvest season of autumn, after the apple picking was done and the apples shipped, and the farm was made ready for the oncoming winter, Kenneth had developed an unusual custom, unusual for a farm community. He would arrange for thoughtful men to come to the Lucknow farm for what he called "conversations." He would lay out, in letters, the schedule and dates—Saturdays at 9:00 a.m.—and outline some ideas for discussion. His mind was too active to let these "downtime" weeks of autumn pass without some active stimulation of the minds. He was more than a man of the earth, he was a man of ideas as well, with a restless intellectual curiosity.

In pleasant weather the men would sit outside, either on the large lawn or under Kenneth's favorite maple tree, whose leaves were still falling. In rain or hard weather they would sit inside around the large dining room table. Once or twice during the day of discussion they would break for a game of horse shoes and to stretch their legs. They would park their cars along the long lane that ran in from the Cameron side road.

These conversations were particularly exciting for Andrew. It had never occurred to him that people could sit around and just talk about ideas. Over the week when Andrew was there, the men discussed Plato and Aristotle and Socrates, pros and cons of different forms of government, how to bring women to a state of full equality with men, the heavens above, the starry universe, and "what is man that God should be mindful of him." And they discussed books and stories, such as H.G. Wells' <u>The Country of the Blind</u>. Andrew listened to every word.

The range of discussions created new levels of illumination in Andrew's mind, stretching well beyond the intellectual boundaries of Southwest Detroit. And to his amazement, the men who participated seemed to treat him as an actual person rather than just another kid. They even listened respectfully to his few ideas.

One Saturday the men of this little autumn seminar had a rousing discussion of the possibilities of life on other worlds, without consensus or conclusion. Andrew contributed what Zeedie had once told him: "It would be a big waste of space if we were all alone." But their roots in the Bible seemed to be more powerful than the logic of this idea.

Every one of the men was interesting:

- Happyjack Miller (a farmer) was Andrew's favorite. Happyjack had a smiling, friendly personality, always ready with a joke.

- Rod Sterling (creamery owner) had a gung ho personality that always seemed poised to move into action, an executive in nature.

- Donald McClain (a bee keeper) was thoughtful in a way that others would describe as "deep," often reticent in speech.

- Ian Sinclair (proprietor of a dry goods store) had a smooth way of talking, but often would introduce some of the most far-out ideas.

- Gordie McDonald (a minister from Goderich) had an enthusiastic and excitable personality and a lot of intellectual and spiritual energy.

- Elmo Struthers (owner of the local flour mill) always seemed to be coated with a faint sheen of flour that would not wash off. He had a slight stutter but was a vigorous participant in the flow of ideas.

Clara never participated in the discussions. But she faithfully prepared a hearty lunch ("dinner") for the invited guests. Clara's choice of activity was "Bundles for Britain," which she formed around periodic Quilting Bees in the Cameron home, with women from nearby farms.

Kenneth attended several different churches, but the one he liked best was the United Church. With Clara and Andrew in the buggy he would hitch up Charlie and go into Lucknow. There was a huge barn near the church, shaped like a Quonset hut, where visitors could park horse and buggy. After leaving the Cameron Sideroad, a stream crossed the main road, and there Charlie would stop each time to drink the cool flowing water. Entering town, a road sign always amused Andrew. You Are Entering Lucknow! Drive Canny.

It had long been Kenneth's habit to write a summary of the essence of what he had heard in church, then pray for some time to understand its full meaning. He would do this after Sunday dinner, the noon meal. He continued this practice with Andrew, sharing his thoughts. He told Andrew he wanted him to have a variety of religious experiences, so to begin with, he took him to several churches in the area. Over the course of almost four months Kenneth had after-Sunday-dinner discussions with Andrew on a number of ideas that made a deep impression on his young mind.

- Failures are God's divine way of perfecting character.
- The compass needle rests only when it points north.
- The character of a man keeps on expanding when he gets to heaven.
- Prayers should always end with Thy will, not mine, be done.
- Duties and engagements should always have a religious aspect. Our bodies and spirits are God's and all that we have is His. We are stewards and should act as such with all that He has entrusted to us.
- Perfection is the noblest of aims.

Kenneth also instructed him in the Bible. He gave Andrew books to study such as Hurlbut's Illustrated Bible Stories. But the thing that most impressed Andrew was the <u>way</u> he taught. Kenneth taught the Book of Job as <u>poetry</u>. He said whoever wrote it was the greatest writer of ancient times. He said Job is one of the oldest books in the Bible. He said God is <u>not</u> the cause of evil. God gave men free will. Some men run amok with it. <u>Man</u> creates evil. Kenneth also encouraged him to memorize the 23rd Psalm and certain passages from Second Isaiah. And he taught him about Jesus, in long discussions about what he thought Jesus was saying in the Sermon on the Mount, and in the whole inspiration of life and teachings. "Jesus did not say the weak shall inherit the earth. He said the meek shall inherit the earth. Meek means <u>teachable</u>."

As winter set in, there was more and more time for home study. And in recognition that Andrew was missing an entire year of school in Detroit, Kenneth purchased a number of books dealing with language, grammar, American and European history, sciences, mathematics, geography, astronomy and arts, including poetry. Kenneth especially had a special fondness for Robert (Bobby) Burns, and could quote him at length.

Lucknow is rather close to Lake Huron, and winds coming from the west would pick up moisture from the lake and turn it into steady snow as they swept over cooler land. It was not uncommon to see snow banked all the way up to the crossbars of telephone poles. Sometimes in a blizzard you had to crawl out a second story window to shovel canyons for passageway to pumps, outhouse, and barn. The long lane was never shoveled. After the heavy snows began no one could come in until spring. Mail would come to the box on the Sideroad. The Camerons kept two clean galvanized washtubs full of water on hand for the worst days.

But Andrew found this to be a time of quiet splendor. On very cold days he liked to sit in the small, glassed-in sunporch and read or study. The pale and melancholy yellow light from a late winter afternoon sun would play silently across walls and windows and wicker chairs in the room, gently broken by shadows of barren twigs and branches of the trees outside. It was a restful, subdued coloration and he felt there was a touch of sadness in it.

Or he would watch the falling snow. Sometimes from the sunporch. Sometimes from the distant Bush. Before the snow became too deep, he would hike down into the Bush just to experience its utter silence. The snow fell all around but hardly any could penetrate all the way through the density of the pines. He found a deep sense of harmony with nature in the stillness of the small forest as the falling snow piled inch upon inch along the pine boughs, muffling the outside world, an atmosphere of peace and tranquility.

Afterwards, he would play along the trout creek, testing the strength of the ice, scraping areas of snow with his boots from running slides. Once he played too long and barely made it through the snow drifts up the hill. He got home just as darkness fell. He thought he would have to respect the strength of nature even more next time.

In the spring of 1940, on a Sunday morning, Kenneth, Clara and Andrew made their usual journey to church. This church had a sloping floor and was shaped in the form of a small amphitheater. On arriving, they found the regular minister was away and a substitute, Mr. Wilson, would give the sermon and take the offering. Andrew had not seen Wilson before and thought the service would follow the usual routine, but it did not. Wilson was of average height, with straight dark hair, glasses, a square face, and talked with a higher than normal pitch.

First thing he did, before any prayers were said, was make a commercial. Apparently he owned a flower shop in town, and wanted to make sure everyone could find whatever flowers they needed, for "weddings, funerals, special social occasions"—he had a good supply, with his own greenhouse.

Andrew was puzzled by this brass commercial from the

pulpit. He thought Mr. Wilson was a second-rate minister.

Then Wilson did another unusual thing. He called all the children (there was no separate Sunday school) to come forward and sit in chairs he had assembled in front of the congregation. There were eight children in all. And he proceeded for a full ten minutes to teach the children in ways specific to their understanding. Then sent them back into the congregation.

Andrew could not remember anything Mr. Wilson said, but he though the idea of teaching the children separately, in <u>front</u> of the congregation, was really neat. So he revised his opinion. He now thought Mr. Wilson was a first-rate minister.

Finally, Wilson got to a prayer, a prayer for how to use the offering. He kept saying Je-<u>sus</u> with accent on the second syllable. Then he had everyone sing <u>all four</u> verses of two hymns in a row. Andrew was revising his opinion again. Maybe Wilson was second-rate after all. Finally Wilson got to the sermon. He wanted to talk about the wedding feast at Cana. He went on for some minutes leading up to the time Jesus turned the water into wine. But when he said, "turned water into wine," he did another unusual thing.

Wilson repositioned himself and stood fully sideways to the congregation. Then he turned his head a whole quarter turn to the left so that his head was facing the congregation, his body facing the side wall. Taking a deep breath, hands on hips in a defiant posture, he then literally shouted at the congregation:

"Well <u>so</u> what!"

If anyone had been dozing, he would have been shaken out of his slumber. Wilson continued, at one point comparing Jesus to the Old West Cavalry, arriving just in time to rescue those under siege. And finally into the heart of his message.

"Jesus can do for us what he did at Cana. He can make us new again... The extravagance of God's kindness is a loving concern that never runs out. And it is offered at a time when we can't manufacture the ingredients ourselves. When we become bored to death with who we are, do what they did at Cana. Ask Jesus. Jesus will make you new again."

Andrew now made his final revision. Wilson is first-rate!

After the sermon the Camerons walked down the street for a block to visit an old friend who went to the nearby Presbyterian Church. Bertha was a very proper, conservatively dressed woman with a large white head of hair. This was the first time Andrew met her. Her first words to him were:

"A brown eyed Cameron! You're a sight to behold. Must have been the Spanish pirates way back when."

Kenneth ignored the remark. Clara shrank inward a bit. Andrew started to laugh.

As they sat for a while at Bertha's dining room table, over tea and cookies Kenneth told her about the sermon. He told her how impressed he was with the substitute minister. Then he summarized the high points of Wilson's talk.

Bertha listened, sipping her tea. And when Kenneth finished his summary she said, "But he's a queer, you know."

Next Sunday, when they came to church again, Andrew plopped 25 large Canadian pennies into the collection plate. The noise of them dropping against the bakelite bottom of the tray seemed to startle the congregation.

The experience of the first ten months on the farm raised many questions that led Andrew to begin to think about life in new ways. He had many conversations with Kenneth about God.

- Who was God's father?
- If God lives in the sky, why doesn't he fall down?
- Does God ever sleep?
- Why does God let bad things happen?

About war ...

- Why is the world going to war?
- Why don't Churchill and Hitler just get together and fight it out by themselves and leave everyone else alone?

And sometimes about himself ...

- Who am I—really?
- Why am I here?
- Where am I going?

All through the long winter months and rebirth into spring there had been no word from Zeedie. Not even a postcard. Andrew wondered if she were still alive. He wondered if she had forgotten him altogether. And then, in early June, he met someone whose companionship made him quit caring about Zeedie's indifference. Eileen Riddle.

*

By the end of June 1940 Canada had become acutely conscious of the looming war. Hitler had now conquered Denmark, Norway, and Belgium and pushed the British out of France. War fever in parts not yet affected was rising to a high pitch.

Eileen's father, Tom Riddle, wanted to move his family to a

better place, then go back to fight the Germans. So he sold his farm in Ireland and moved is wife and daughter to Canada. He thought they would be safe there until the war ended. He found a farm near Lucknow, on an adjoining Sideroad, only four large fields, about a mile down from the Camerons, and bought it with what he had gained. The farm was run down because no one had lived there for years. But Tom didn't care. His family would have shelter until he returned. This was only temporary, he thought. He would come back, fix it up, sell it, and move the family back to Ireland. They moved into the rundown farm in April.

There was some money left over from the Irish sale, which he gave to his wife, Sophie. He told her this would do her until he could send more. He said he would send money every month. Then he headed back toward the fighting.

A German U-Boat sank his ship in the North Atlantic and Tom and all hands were lost in the icy waters. By the time Sophie found out what had happened, she was almost out of the money and feeling desperate. "God invented oceans to drown people," she told Eileen. "Everyone in Ireland knows that."

Andrew first came to know of Eileen's existence on a warm, June Saturday night in Lucknow. It was the custom of neighboring farmers and their children to walk into town, or come by horse and buggy, to spend the evening walking up and down the long street, socializing and listening to the Pipers. Frequently the men brought their bagpipes and stood in a circle in the middle of the main road and played for an hour or two. In those years there was hardly any traffic on Saturday night.

Andrew and Eileen experienced an instant mutual attraction.

She had come to sit next to him as they listened to the Pipers. He felt a small thrill run through him even in the way she said hello. There was richness in her young voice—even in that single word—that portrayed a sense of maturity beyond her years.

Captured already by her voice, he liked everything else about her, particularly her eyes. Her eyes were an absorbing color of deep green and they sparkled with warmth and animation. There was something about their expression that made him feel close to her right away. They were understanding eyes. You could whisper into those eyes. You could tell secrets to those eyes.

But there was more that drew him near. She was slender, almost to the point of being scrawny, all arms and legs. Her face was freckled—many freckles—and she had an abundance of deep, rich, golden-orange hair that curled in natural ringlets. She was unlike any girl he had ever met.

"How old are you?" was all he could think to say.

"I'm nine, but going on ten."

"Well, I'm nine, going on twelve," he said.

"Close enough to be friends," she said. "You count funny."

"Your accent is fascinating," he said.

"The Scots are wearing it down," she said.

"Don't let them change you. I like you just the way you are."

She looked at him carefully, taking his measure, "Your eyes are like chestnuts, just pulled from the fire."

"I'm the only Cameron with eyes like this. Maybe there was a Spaniard somewhere way back. Or a strange Viking. Maybe some stray ship from the Spanish Armada."

"I never saw anyone with black hair and brown eyes before,"

she said.

"I think I'm a puzzle to the Camerons. But they claim me. I'm one of the Cameron men."

They laughed and briefly held each other's hand in earnest friendship.

"Are you with your family?" he asked.

"No. No family. It's me and my mum."

"Is she here?"

"Mum's not very social."

"Did you walk into town alone?"

"Yes."

"I'm going to walk you home," he said.

"That would be nice," she said. "There's one part of the road, going through the swamp, that's very scary late at night. I would love your company."

Andrew squared his shoulders. "You'll be safe with me," he said, feeling happy to be her protector.

"I think I'm going to like you very much," she said.

"I like you very much already."

The three mile walk home was like an instant. They left town. Suddenly they were at the darkened Riddle home. Time had vanished.

From the very beginning of their relationship they had an easy familiarity with each other, as though longtime friends. The shared experiences, some so similar it gave them shivers.

"Do you miss your father?" Andrew asked.

"I miss him terribly. All the time. No—the crying's done. He wasn't around much anyway... I guess what I really miss is the <u>idea</u> of a father."

"I got used to having no father. Especially because my grandfather is more like a father than my father was. I guess what I miss most is my mother, or maybe it's the <u>idea</u> of a mother. I think she left me here to grow old and die."

"Let's grow old and die together," Eileen smiled wistfully.

"That would be neat. Neat-o cool." And so they began their time together already pondering a brilliant union and eventually a mystical death together, wondering what it would be like.

The next afternoon Andrew walked over to the Riddle farm. He wasn't sure whether to knock on the door or just call to her. He decided to follow the Detroit custom.

"Oh Ei-lee-en!"

After a few tries, Sophie came to the door, with Eileen at her heels. "Why are you standing outside yapping like that?" Sophie asked.

"Then just say it! Don't stand there like a helpless dog!"

"It's all right, mum," Eileen said.

"Where you going?" Sophie asked Andrew.

"Just over to our place—the Cameron farm."

Sophie looked at him with rising suspicion but after a few moments relented. "I guess it's all right. But next time, if there is a next time, just knock on the door."

Once they left the lane, onto the Sideroad, out of sight of the house, Eileen put her hand on his arm. "Let's stop here for a minute. It was so dark last night I hardly saw you. I like your voice, but I have to study you just a little bit."

"Let's study each other," he smiled.

They stood at arm's length. Eileen looked him over with great interest.

"You look like you're trying to decide whether to buy me," he said.

"Would you like me to?" she asked. "Not that I could."

"No, I wouldn't. I have a very independent mind."

"So do I," she said.

"Good. I like that."

She was now searching deeply into his face. "I can almost taste the color of your eyes," she said.

"Your eyes are very warm green," he said. "It's easy to look at you. You have friendly eyes."

"You have friendly eyes, too," she said.

"Do they call you carrot top?"

"Some do. I used to wonder why they called me that. The tops of carrots are green. I finally realized 'top' meant my hair, not the top of the carrot. Language can be confusing. Now I don't think about it anymore."

"There's nothing confusing about you," he said.

She slapped him gently on the arm.

"Well," she said. "Inspection's over. I wanted to know who I'm going to be friends with."

Andrew walked with Eileen back to the farm. He wasn't sure what to show her first. He decided on his favorite maple, rather secluded up near the barn. He liked the way the limbs in that particular tree were arranged. Eileen was a natural climber and needed no help. She scampered easily from limb to limb.

"Are you a tomboy?" Andrew asked.

"What's a tomboy?"

"It's a girl that does things that boys do."

"I can do anything boys do."

"Good!" he said.

"Does that make me a tomboy?"

"That makes you my kind of girl. I like girls who aren't afraid of who they are."

"I don't know who I am yet," she said in a longing voice.

"I don't know who I am yet either."

"Does somebody just tell you who you are?"

"No," he said. "I think you have to find out all by yourself."

"If you find out who I am, will you tell me?"

"Yes."

"Promise?"

"Yes."

"Cross your heart and hope to die?"

"Yes."

For more than an hour they sat high in the branches, talking without pause. Her Irish accent continued to fascinate him.

"Do you want me to show you what to do?" Andrew asked.

"You climb the tree and sit. What else is there?" Eileen asked.

"I'll show you. It's one of my favorite tricks." And he selected a branch and crawled along its length until it bent substantially and began to sway slightly in the breeze.

"I've never done that," she said. "You'll die."

Still out along the branch, Andrew turned over to face toward her, and grasping branches on each side, said: "You can do it too.

I'm anchored. Crawl out here."

Very carefully Eileen followed his suggestion. "You're in the way," she said.

"No I'm not. Just crawl along on top of me. I'm holding on. All you have to do is hold on to me."

And she did as he instructed, lying full length along his body, her arms around him, with him holding branches on each side to steady their weight. And as he had told her, the branch swayed in the breeze.

"How do you like it?" he asked.

"Mother of Jesus, I've never felt like this before. Am I too heavy for you?"

"You're like a feather. Soft as a maple leaf."

"Let's stay like this for a while and feel the breeze," she said.

"You can take a nap on me if you want to."

"I don't want to. I'm too excited."

"So am I."

"Do you know what I like?" she asked.

"What?"

"I like to be wrapped and held like a newborn baby."

"Let's try it," Andrew said. We'll have to be careful so we don't fall. Just hold me like you're doing, and don't get nervous when I let go of the branches."

"I promise."

And he released his grip on the branches, adjusting his balance. And when he felt balanced, wrapped his arms and legs slowly around her. And they remained in that precarious position for some time, saying nothing. Finally Eileen spoke.

"Let's do this again sometime."

"Next windy day," he said.

When the thrill subsided they carefully untangled and resumed their seats among the branches, talking with hardly a pause. In time the cowbell rang and Andrew said, "Stay and have supper with us."

"Okay," she quickly agreed.

Andrew and Eileen came to be almost inseparable over the next few months. He didn't have to hike to her place to get her anymore. In the beginning she would be at the door at breakfast time, picking and sniffing the sweet clover that grew in the lane, and stay until after dark, when Andrew would walk her home. Sometimes they would capture lightning bugs and hold them in a jar, releasing them as they said goodbye. Kenneth and Clara were most gracious and loving as they welcomed her presence. She seemed to be becoming a permanent table guest.

But Eileen was no freeloader. She helped Andrew with all his chores, including cutting the bog lawn, so they could spend more private time together. She even learned to use the scythe and earn 10 cents for each tree bed she cut.

Andrew wanted to share with her everything he knew. He had never had a friend with whom he felt so close, even Evelyn. Evelyn was puppy love. This was mature love, he felt. There was something deeper now. He took her down to the Bush where they could sit together and ponder its awesome silence.

"It's so quiet it makes me think of death," she said.

"I think just the opposite. It makes me think of life. It makes me think of possibilities... what makes you think of death in a place like this?"

"I'm Irish. Irish think about death a lot."

"You won't die. I'll protect you." He hugged her and she responded in the same way. "Don't think of death when you're with me," he said. And they continued to hold each other in warm embrace for a while.

"I think happy thoughts, too," she said. "I'm happy when I'm with you."

"I've never been happier than when I'm with you."

Within a few days Andrew no longer waited for her to appear at the door before breakfast. He set his mental alarm clock to wake up very early. The excitement of the relationship made it work. He rose before dawn and was there to greet her as she came down the lane. They would hug and, every morning, Andrew would break two leaves of sweet clover so they could begin the day with the aroma of its gentle sweet fragrance. Sunny days. Rainy days. It was all the same. They would gather eggs from under the warm bodies of nesting chickens, then chop a bunch of kindling for the breakfast stove, then sit down to a satisfying breakfast.

Andrew took her to all the interesting places he had discovered. He taught her how to seize a bull thistle with a firm grip so that it would not lay waste to the hand. He took her to pick wild strawberries and blackberries as they ripened along the fences. They would suck the little wild strawberries into their mouths. They would test the chokeberries and make sour faces at each other.

He decided to take her trout fishing.

Andrew hiked over to Eileen's house just before sunrise. He had told her the night before and she was ready, with her mother's breakfast already prepared. He had not told her why the early morning visit, only that there was something he wanted to show her. They walked hurriedly, and sometimes ran, over to the Cameron farm.

Andrew led her to the large teepee made of maple branches. This was Clara's project. Every spring she planted flowers in abundance. The teepee was for large morning glories.

And the two of them stood there in the still dewy grass, silently beholding the natural wonder before them. The morning glories, which had been folded in a restful sleep for the night, were about to open to the beckoning warmth of the morning. And little by little they watched the flowers unfold and open to the day, large and intensely blue and glorious. And the subdued soft yellow morning sun bathed the little creatures in little halos of light.

"I didn't know they slept at night," Eileen whispered.

"My grandpa showed me one morning."

"They are so blue, so beautiful, I think I'll always remember this morning."

"I will too," he said. "I will think of you as a morning glory. All you need is a drop of sunlight. You are especially beautiful in the light of the early morning sun."

She kissed him gently on the cheek.

Kenneth had given Andrew one of his pocket knives and a compass for his ninth birthday, and they quickly became prized possessions. He even slept with the pocket knife. And because by now he always carried fishing tackle in his pocket—hooks, line, sinkers, cork—he was mostly prepared when the thought arose as they walked through a neighboring field catching frogs. He used the pocket knife to cut thin saplings into fishing pole length, then found juicy worms under some big rocks.

Following in the commando style Kenneth had taught him, he moved slowly, with Eileen crawling beside him, up to the lip of the granite rock that overhung the deep trout pool. He baited one hook for her and one for himself. The speckled trout in this pool were always hungry, and struck almost as soon as the lines were in. Both quickly caught big ones. Eileen was more excited than he had ever seen her.

They stopped at two. Andrew removed them from the hooks and prepared them to be eaten. He carried a few kitchen matches in his pocket, wrapped in wax paper. He gathered sticks, and lit a small fire on the granite shelf. The two of them roasted the trout on their fishing poles over the fire, and Andrew cautioned her to eat carefully around all the many small bones.

"They get stuck in your throat," he said.

"What happens then?"

"I don't know. Maybe you die."

"I'll be careful."

"If you know how to fish, you'll never go hungry," he repeated what he had learned.

On a warm Sunday afternoon in July, Andrew and Eileen hiked town to the 9-Mile River. He told her five people had drowned there.

"They why are we going?" she asked.

"Doesn't it make you excited knowing we're going swim in a river where people drown?"

She thought for a few moments. "Yes. One slip and you die."

"Then you just do what I do," he said.

Neither wore undergarments. He stripped off his gym shoes, shirt and blue jeans. She removed her sandals and thin summer dress. There was no self-consciousness in either of them. Their closeness made them comfortable with each other in whatever condition. They didn't even talk about it, or stare, or avert their eyes into unusual positions. They simply stood next to each other in naked skin contemplating the river and calculating the speed of the current.

Andrew went in first, then took her hand to guide her along the rocky bottom. In very cool water almost up to his chest he showed her how he had learned to swim.

"You have to swim fast or the current will carry you down into the branches of a fallen tree."

"I don't know how to swim."

"I'll teach you."

And he held her along her ungrown breasts and stomach while she practiced stroking and kicking against the rushing water. After awhile he said "I think you've got it. Tell me when to let go and try it."

"Will you catch me?"

"I'll catch you. I'll be right beside you. I won't let anything happen to you. I'll never let anything bad happen to you."

"Okay," she said. "Let me go."

And after few tries, when he did catch her and pull her back, she found the rhythm of strokes and kicks and speed and was able to hold her own against current. Then she and Andrew swam side by side for a time.

On the shore of the field of wild grass again, they stood in the sunlight drying. Eileen could hardly contain her enthusiasm.

'I feel so clean. I love the rush of it. Let's swim every chance we get," she said.

"I can't wait to do it again."

"When you know you could drown at any minute, you get the shivers," she said.

"The river is so cool you get the shivers anyway," he said, "drowning or not."

Then they lay for a while on the grassy river bank, each lost in separate thoughts.

On rainy days they would spend a lot of time in the barn. She tried to teach him how the Irish dance, but he found the position of the arms—straight down along the sides—hard to get used to. He told her it was a little bit like the Scottish girls' dance. Irish dancing required similar swift and strenuous movements of the feet and legs.

They climbed the ladder up into the haymow. First they played for a while on the rope swing. Andrew then proceeded to the highest beam and demonstrated his skill in doing two complete revolutions before he hit the hay. And after a few such trials, he lay back and she moved over to lie beside him and curl her colt-like legs over him. He pulled hay over them so that only their heads were uncovered.

"You said you like to be covered just like a baby," he said.

"I feel <u>so</u> fine," she whispered.

And they lay like that for a long time, holding each other close, saying nothing, listening to the rain falling on the barn roof above them. And after a time he began to make little kisses along her neck and cheek, and she did the same to him.

"It feels like little butterfly wings on my cheek," she said.

"It feels good when you do that to me," he said.

"Better than good. It feels delicious. Especially in the ear."

And after a time, they moved their lips to each other and practiced kissing. They kissed without movement of the tongue, only touching lip to lip. Even to the point where their lips were slightly swollen. They didn't know what to do with their hands except to stroke each other's face and through each other's hair.

"Your hair is like silk," he said. "So smooth and soft."

On Sunday mornings Eileen never came by, not until afternoon. Andrew several times invited her to go to church with his family. She always refused.

"I'm Catholic. I can't go to a Protestant Church. That would be a mortal sin," she said.

"But you said you don't believe in God," he asked with genuine puzzlement.

"Just because you're Catholic doesn't mean you have to believe in God," she said firmly.

"If you go to church, God won't have to hunt all over looking for you."

Eileen turned thoughtful. "If there really is a God, He'll know where to find me."

*

All summer the rumblings of war were growing more severe. Italy had joined Hitler in declaring war on France and England. By June, the Germans were already at the English Channel preparing ships for invasion. The United States slumbered in its belief that this was merely "a European war." England stood alone against the might of the powerful German war machine. By mid-August, the Battle of Britain was fully underway, a roaring fight to the death in the skies, terrible losses and destruction.

In early September, the British government warned that German invasion would probably come within the next few days.

On October 30, 1940, President Roosevelt made a campaign speech in Boston. An excerpt from the speech was printed in the Lucknow Sentinel.

"And while I am talking to you mothers and fathers, I give you one more assurance. I have said this before, but I shall say it again, and again, and again. Your boys are not going to be sent into any foreign wars."

It was generally assumed throughout Canada that England could not hold for long against the full force of the Germans, that Hitler would conquer England, then turn his eyes west toward Canada.

Kenneth had one luxury, a short-wave radio. To conserve batteries he would turn it on every night at 8:00 for fifteen minutes to listen to the BBC broadcast. And now as summer was proceeding into September, Andrew and Eileen had begun to listen with him.

After tonight's invasion warning, Kenneth shut off the radio and sat thoughtfully for a while. Then he stood up and motioned Andrew and Eileen to stand.

"Hitler may take London," he began, referring to London, Ontario. "Hitler may take Guelph. Hitler may take Wingham… but he will <u>never take Lucknow</u>!"

And Andrew pushed out his chest with great pride. He could stand side by side with Eileen and grandfather, one shotgun and two pitchforks. <u>And they would stop Hitler in his tracks.</u> Andrew had never felt so mighty, or so proud. He felt invincible.

Next afternoon, as Andrew and Eileen sat high in the branches of their favorite maple, their conversation took on a more serious character, reflecting the general feeling of peril haunting the country.

"What should we do first?" she asked.

"If Hitler invades, first thing you do is come over here. We have to fight him together. If we have to die, I want us to die together."

"Do you think he could take Lucknow?

"I don't know. Grandpa said we would stop him here …I think the two best men in the world are Grandpa Cameron and God."

"Why doesn't God just stop Hitler?" she asked.

"I don't know. God has his ways."

"Maybe He's playing pretend," she said.

They thought about that for a while, but neither could think of any really big thing to do. Then she added an afterthought. "It would be fun to die with you. Just us together. Do you think we would go to the same place?"

For a while he did not know what to say. "I don't know, Eileen... I think I know what I want to do when I grow up," he said at last.

"What?"

"I think the world is turned the wrong way. Somebody has to set it right again. Grandpa is too old. So I think it will have to be my job."

"Let me feel your muscle," she said. And he moved over to her branch and made as big a muscle as he could for her. She felt it. "You're pretty big."

"I know it won't be easy. I don't even know how big the world is."

"Can I help you?" she asked.

"That would be wonderful. Really wonderful."

"Where do we begin?" she asked.

"I think we both have to study and learn how to do it."

"You're thrilling,'" she said.

"So are you."

And the wind gave sway to the branches, and they held each other in an embrace of deep friendship, and they pondered the question of where to begin. And for the rest of his life, that thought would not entirely leave his mind.

*

The phone call from Zeedie came after supper while Andrew was walking Eileen back to the Riddle farm. Zeedie talked to Kenneth. She would come tomorrow about noon, bringing her husband. "It's time Andrew got some schooling again," she said.

Over breakfast next morning they talked about the impending

move. "She's going to take me back to Detroit," he told Eileen.

"What am I going to do without you?" she asked.

"Remember our plan. We're both going to study."

"It's not the same," she said.

"Nothing will be the same. Without you," he said.

Zeedie had said they would be taking him back the same day. Eileen helped him gather his few possessions. Then they went back to the barn so they could be together and talk in private.

"Will you write me a letter?" she asked.

"I don't know. I've never written a letter. I don't think I would be very good at it."

"Do you think we'll ever see each other again?"

"I'm sure we will. I just <u>know</u> we will."

They were sitting in the haymow, and Andrew was feeling miserable. He could already see a sense of loss in those beautiful sad green eyes. Then Eileen took a straight pin that she said she had borrowed from Clara.

"If we say it in blood it will come true," she said.

She pricked the pin against her wrist, drawing a few drops of blood. "Give me your wrist," she said. He did so. She pricked his wrist and drew a few drops of blood.

"If we put our wrists together, blood into blood, then we will see each other again," she said.

And they did so, and held their wrists into each other for a while as their blood mingled.

"What are you thinking?" she asked.

"I'm thinking surely you must be the most exciting girl in the world."

"What else are you thinking?"

"I'm thinking we will see each other again." And they kissed tenderly and held each other for a while, until Clara's cowbell summoned them.

Zeedie was waiting impatiently at the back door of the summer kitchen as they came down from the barn. Andrew introduced her to Eileen, but Zeedie made only a perfunctory hello and told Andrew to get washed up so he could meet his new father. Zeedie told Eileen to "go on and run into the house and wait in the dining room."

Zeedie stood nearby as Andrew washed his face for the second time that morning. Then she produced a brush and ran it through his hair. "You need a haircut," she said. "Put some water on your hair so I can brush it down. I want you to look real nice for your new daddy."

But after combing his wet hair she decided she wanted to put a wave in it. She produced a hairpin and put it in his hair to hold the wave in place.

"I'm not going to wear a hairpin," he said.

"You'll do what I tell you," she said.

"I won't do it. I won't wear a hairpin."

"I want you to look nice."

"He'll have to take me as I am."

"You <u>will</u> look nice. You <u>will</u> have a hairpin. I can't keep the wave in place without a hairpin."

"There's no way you can make me do it."

"You come with me," she said, leading him into the outer all-purpose woodshed room. She shut the door and told him sternly to leave the hairpin in place after she put it in. But each time she put it in, he ripped it out, and after the third time, he threw the hairpin into the woodpile. Zeedie became enraged.

She grabbed a heavy maple cutoff limb from the firewood pile and began to beat him with it, telling him "I am your mother! You will do what I say!" And the greater her anger the more frenzied she became. She beat him across the back with such repeated force that he eventually broke out in sobs and then she could not stop. His cries seemed to intensify her fury. The sobs deepened. Finally the sobs became so severe he had trouble breathing. It was only after she saw him gasping for breath that she ceased the attack.

As she went through the door toward the summer kitchen and dining room, she told him "You get yourself together and get into the dining room. We're leaving right after we eat."

It took him awhile. At one point during the beating he felt he was near death. He felt he was being pulled into a black room. His instinct was to strike back, to stop it. But he could not. She was his mother. And besides, she was a woman. He gradually regained his composure, washed his face again and brushed his hair. He vowed to himself never again to show when he was hurting.

He shook hands with Joe Moran, his new step dad.

Kenneth had packed all of Andrew's books for the trip, but Zeedie said no, she wouldn't take them. "We're just getting settled in a new place. More things to carry and put away. We don't have a single bookshelf."

Andrew said he would carry them, but Zeedie said no again.

"Once I've made a decision, there's no going back," she said.

Before he left Canada, Kenneth walked with him slowly around the house. Andrew told him "Please give my books to Eileen." Before they went back in, Kenneth put his hand on his shoulder. "My dear boy," was all he said.

And Eileen came to hug him as he left. "Something happened to you," she whispered.

"I'm okay," he whispered back.

She gently pressed her wrist against his. He could almost not bear to see the longing in her eyes.

Chapter 9

Zeedie had wasted no time. As soon as John Henry had moved her few belonging into Sarah's garage, she made her plan. She would find LeRoy Hunt III. "I missed my chance," she told Sarah. "I've set my cap for him. This time I'm going to land him."

She knew his habits. He always lunched at The Homewood, his favorite restaurant near the corporate offices. This was where she had originally met him. The Purple Onion had been acquired by new owners, who changed its name to The Homewood. LeRoy had always been attracted to a certain red dress she wore, and Zeedie now shopped with some intensity to replicate it. The dress she found did it one better. Her long black hair and flashing dark eyes and still-slender figure shone well against the color and the cut.

It had been nine years since their last meeting. She had no idea what his situation was, but didn't care. She knew his weak spots. There was a particular way she kissed him in the ear that always softened him and aroused him.

She held the red dress in reserve, bought another which showed her features to the fullest, then found a job again at The Homewood, lying in wait.

As she suspected, LeRoy had not changed his habits. That was one of the reasons he was so dull, so predictable. Within days of her starting her waitressing job, he walked in with several other businessmen. She saw an instant sign of recognition, then he looked away quickly. She brought menus, explained the daily offerings. LeRoy buried his face in the menu and did not look up as she talked. She noticed he grew his hair a little longer, was a little paunchier. She wondered if she still looked as fresh to him as nine years ago.

She took their orders. But since he would not make eye contact with her, she decided on a revised strategy. She returned to the table.

"Mr. Hunt," she said—eye contact at last— "There's a phone call for you ...let me show you where it is."

He followed her to the rear of the restaurant, where it was immediately apparent the phone was still on the hook. She had worn a dress that showed well from behind.

"Do you think someone hung it up?" he asked. "I mean, do you know who it was?" He was speaking so impersonally to her, she thought maybe he wasn't faking. Maybe he didn't remember.

"Well, Mister LeRoy Hunt the Third, don't you remember me?" she asked coyly.

He changed demeanor in an instant. "How could I forget you?" he asked. "I mean, I was even thinking of marrying you until you started that fight and stormed out of my life."

"Can you ever forgive me?"

"I don't know. It's been a lot of years."

"I know how I can make it up to you," she almost whispered.

"Zeedie, are you married?"

"No."

"This is all so sudden. I don't know what to do," he looked perplexed.

"I know what to do,'" she said.

"What?"

"Take me dancing at the Rondo. I'll show you how you can forgive me."

"But what if I don't want to forgive you?"

"Do you still feel the old spark?"

"Zeedie, you are very beautiful. I love your figure. How could I not feel ...how could I not feel again what I thought was gone?"

"Pick me up here at seven. We'll go from here. LeRoy, you will never regret it."

"I hope not," he said with a curious mixture of resignation and excitement.

"Seven then."

"Seven," he repeated, and returned to his table.

Zeedie served them as though there had been no personal interaction but added more smiles and charm than usual. LeRoy left an unusually large tip for her.

LeRoy met her as planned. She had gone home to clean up and change. She returned in a killer red dress. He almost gulped when he saw her. They danced until late at the Rondo and talked about old times. Zeedie was deliberately mysterious about how she had spent the last nine years, but LeRoy was too. He talked only of his business and how the looming war was cutting into his supply of raw materials.

From time to time as they danced, Zeedie would do little

things to his ear, in the guise of intimate whispers. She could feel by his body language he was aroused and melting in her grasp. She made sure he had a few drinks, but, in a secret communication with the bartender, she drank tea disguised as whiskey. And when she felt the right moment had come she whispered in his ear with a little tongue twirl, "I'm ready for a hotel room."

"Are you sure? I mean, are you really sure?" he whispered back.

"I'm going to teach you how to forgive me."

And so that night was history revisited. He seemed once again spellbound by her, and well before dawn next morning he left, promising he would call.

He did not call. Nor did he lunch at The Homewood until long afterward. Zeedie was beginning to think her plan had failed. Except for one small wrinkle. She was pregnant.

She wrote a letter to LeRoy, at his corporate office, with the word personal in big block letters on the envelope. She told him she was pregnant and must see him immediately. She wrote that he should pick her up after work the following Friday.

And as Friday came he was there as she had requested and they went for a long drive.

"Are you sure?" he asked.

"Sure as certain," she said.

"Are you sure it's mine?" he asked.

"I'll tear your eyes out if you ever ask me that again," she said. "Of course it's yours."

"I'll give you some money. I mean, get rid of it."

"How could I ever get rid of something so precious—it's part of you!"

"If you won't get rid of it, what are we going to do?"

"Have you ever thought of making an honest woman out of me?"

"Can't do that, Zeedie."

"Why not?"

"I forgot to mention. I'm married. I mean I have three children."

"You sonofabitch!"

"You didn't ask me."

"Some things you just <u>tell</u>! You don't wait to be asked!

"There was no time. Everything happened so fast. There was no opportunity."

Zeedie became silent, tears streaming down her face. "I can just see you sitting back, laughing at me—Zeedie the little fool who trusted you."

"I'm sorry," he said in a barely audible voice.

"LeRoy, I never thought you were a rat. Never once... But let's face it, that's what you are. Do you know how you make me feel? Like a piece of moldy cheese with rat slime all over it."

"Zeedie, you never talked to me this way before."

"You never deserved it before." And then her sorrow deepened into choking sobs.

"Where do we go from here?" he asked.

Finally, breaking through her sobs she said, "Just give me the money. <u>Lots</u> of it! I'm out of your life forever." She pulled out of her purse a small tin of Bruton's Scotch Snuff, and in his presence stuffed a wad of it into her jaw.

*

She used the money for its intended purpose and, still shaken from the experience, resolved to get on with her life. There was plenty left over to buy new dancing dresses. But emotionally she was in a state of raw vulnerability.

She met Joe Moran at a Harvest Moon picnic with the Henrys, along the Rouge River. John Henry had invited her. He told her he had a protective feeling and wanted to make sure she had a social life. The Henrys, in addition to their work at the Ford plant, and the moving and trucking business, farmed a large plot of land along the Rouge River. Henry Ford owned the land and encouraged workers at the plant to use these plots. Now that the gardens were emptied for the season it was a Henry custom to celebrate. They hauled everyone to the picnic in a big moving van, with the rear doors tied open.

Joe had migrated to Detroit from Dalton, Georgia, leaving his job in construction. He had lived with Betsy Blough in Dalton for several years but had become restless. He broke off the relationship. He came north to improve his position in life, a better job, a better woman. Now that the country was beginning to come out of the Depression, he soon found work at the Ford plant as a crane operator.

He was of modest height, about two inches under six feet. He was born with a sturdy frame, a strong jaw, and an easy smile. His eyes were grayish-blue and he had sandy colored straight hair. Except for the restlessness, he was an easygoing man, with a little bit more Georgia drawl in his accent that Zeedie had been

105.

used to in Chattanooga. The thing that attracted Zeedie right away was not his physical appearance, but his general character. He seemed so likeable. He seemed to be a man without malice. He seemed like a man with whom she could be comfortable.

"Do you like to dance?" was the first thing she asked him, even before she learned his name.

"I love to dance," he said. "I'm a dancing fool."

"Well hells bells, ain't we alike," she laughed. "How do you come to know the Henrys?"

"I'm a second cousin. Word's been filtering down to Georgia there's more opportunity here."

They began to date after the picnic. Joe had steady work, a good car, and knew where to park along a nearby lover's lane. But she would only let him go so far, telling him she was not the kind of woman a man can take advantage of. This, and plenty of dancing, went on through the winter and into spring, when he finally proposed.

"Before I answer, there's something you should know," she said.

"I thought I knew everything about you."

"This one you don't."

"What is it I don't know?"

"I have a son. He's nine. I shipped him off to Canada to be with his grandparents for a while."

Joe became thoughtful, and after several minutes of rolling this around in his mind, finally said, "I always wanted a son."

They were married in May and spent June getting settled in a house Joe rented next door to the Henrys. The only problem was that almost as soon as they moved in Joe concluded this was not the house he wanted to live in.

"Maybe a new paint job could do it," Zeedie said.

"It needs more than a paint job."

It was also too noisy. All the Fort Street traffic, and the constant streetcars, and the saloon next door (Mickey Finn's) gave the whole atmosphere too much busyness for him. But Zeedie almost prevailed. Zeedie didn't want to move. She had become attached to John Henry. But Joe insisted. "If you make a mistake, you fix it right away. You don't go on living with it." Zeedie decided to accede to his wishes and bide her time. It was just a rented house. She had time to move him around to her point of view.

In August they moved to Plonkatown, a neighborhood in Melvindale, into a rented house Joe found more suitable—four rooms with a cast iron stove and linoleum floors. The school year was more than a week old when they went north to pick up Andrew.

*

Andrew liked Joe Moran as soon as he met him but would not call him dad. He decided to call him Joe. Joe didn't mind.

The Melvindale school principal didn't quite know where to put him. Andrew's history showed only that he had completed second grade. He entered third grade, was quickly promoted to fourth grade and by early spring was moved into fifth grade. He also found he was repeating a previous experience. When the school nurse examined him, she asked: "Has your voice always been this husky?" He tried to joke, saying he had been a heavy

107.

smoker all his life, but the nurse did not laugh. "I'm too busy to laugh," she said.

As the new kid in the neighborhood, he found he had to fight the local bully, Melvin, an older boy. Andrew was beginning to recognize that whenever he approached a group of boys, they would become serious and subdue their conversation. After he got to know them the stiffness disappeared, but it always seemed to be this way in the beginning. In his fight with Melvin, begun when Melvin placed his body in front of Andrew and would not let him pass, he was able to win a decisive victory, but Melvin proved to be a dirty fighter. He punched him the groin. He bit him. And when it was over, Melvin vowed revenge.

Melvin did not wait long. The following week when Andrew was coming home on the long walk from school, Melvin and six other boys confronted and surrounded him. One of the boys was holding a dog. Melvin began to taunt Andrew. One of the gang of six got on hands and knees behind Andrew and when Melvin gave a hard push Andrew fell backward over the boy, and slid down into a shallow muddy drainage ditch.

The whole gang was immediately upon him, holding him down. One on each arm. One on each leg. Two holding the dog's front and back legs. The rest trying to push the dog's penis into Andrew's mouth. They were so tangled with each other they could hardly move, but they worked very hard to arouse the dog and move the beast into position.

Andrew struggled mightily, but the sum of their weight and strength held him mostly immobile. He could twist and struggle but he could not throw them off. They were dead serious about their intent, yelling among themselves, determined to do the job. Andrew twisted his head with great strength again and again. "Hold his head! Hold his head!" they shouted, but they could not hold his head in position as they attempted to maneuver the dog's penis into his mouth.

Andrew would not quit or give in. He saw the bright red prick of the dog plunging out of its wooly white hair toward his mouth. He would twist and turn and struggle so they could not fix it in position. As this great effort, which seemed to last forever, went on and on he reached a point where it became so unbearable the thought raced across his mind—just give in, get in over with. But he quickly rejected the thought. However hopeless his position looked, he would fight on and on. He would never give in. He found he could in such a moment summon reserves of strength deep within himself, reserves he did not even know he had.

Finally, the dog began to bark furiously and struggle against those who held him. And very soon they released the dog, got out of the ditch and walked away as if nothing had happened. Andrew gathered himself up, regained his composure, and walked home. But he decided to arm himself against further attack.

He explored surrounding fields and neighborhoods until he eventually discovered what he needed: a stiff and sturdy small hickory limb three feet in length. It was gnarled, like the bottom half of an old Irish walking stick. This would be his companion. He named it Guardo. He would take it with him wherever he explored. Guardo would be protector.

Next day in the school yard he confronted Melvin. "Let's go,

Melvin, just me and you." An immediate crowd gathered round. Andrew had raised his arms and fists halfway into fighting position. Melvin would not raise his fists or make direct eye contact. "I'll let you hit first," Andrew said, but Melvin would not act, and Andrew did not want to strike the first blow. "Hit 'em, Mel!" the sometime gang members yelled. Melvin would not lift his hands. "Mel, you're a scaredy cat!" the girls yelled. And finally Melvin slunk away in a diminished state. He never bothered Andrew again.

*

But that was not Andrew's last encounter with Melvin. The smallest kid in school was named Dickie Mason. Everyone called him Little Dickie. Melvin once threatened Little Dickie in Andrew's presence. Andrew said nothing, but quickly moved to Dickie's side. Melvin backed off.

After that, Little Dickie made it a point to be near Andrew as much as he could. Dickie had a distinct personality and an offbeat sense of humor. Andrew liked him. Every day in the cafeteria lunch line Dickie would maneuver himself in front of Andrew. And every time mashed potatoes and butter were served, Dickie would say cheerfully to the serving lady,

"Will you give me mashed potatoes? Will you, huh? Will you, huh?" The capturing rhythm of Little Dickie's request would never leave Andrew's memory. Andrew felt touched by Little Dickie's cheerfulness, his sense of humor, and the sincere warmth of his friendship.

After Plonkatown, Andrew never saw Little Dickie again, but many years later he read that his little friend had become a billionaire industrialist (high tech, precision-engineered engines).

*

From surface appearances, the war jitters experienced in Canada had not yet rippled across to the United States. The general mood seemed to be one of complacency, sleeping with one eye half open.

But many were poised to encounter the lurking dangers. Writing in his diary on November 25, 1941, Henry Stimson, Secretary of War, set down the following disclosure: "The question was how we should maneuver the Japanese into the position of firing the first shot without allowing too much danger to ourselves."

*

Living in Plonkatown meant renewed and broadened social activity, mostly in games and rituals with other children. And it seemed that each kind of game taught Andrew something more about his own inherent nature.

Football (no helmets) taught him that by sheer force of will he could overcome or overpower formidable opposition. They played on sand lots or cinder lots, sometimes on grassy fields. Andrew always wanted to carry the ball and usually did. And every time he went forward with the ball, he was convinced he would make it through the line. And his conviction was so strong, his will so fierce, he did often. Every time he carried the ball he drove for a touchdown with such speed and energy he very often made it. It was standard practice for his teammates to give the ball to him, or to pass it to him whenever possible.

He also learned that technique was fundamental. This lesson came in his very first game at the Melvindale School. Bozo was carrying the ball and running toward him. Andrew was all that stood in Bozo's way. Bozo was an oversized athletic kid built like a truck. Years before crew cuts became a male hair fashion, Bozo wore a crew cut that looked like a stiff black wire brush. No one ever called him anything but Bozo.

The shouts from Andrew's teammates rang through the air: "Stop him, Andrew!" And so Andrew ran swiftly toward him and plunged his head into Bozo's belly. It was like iron. Bozo was down, but for weeks afterward, Andrew's neck ached like it would never stop. He was afraid for a while that Bozo had stunted his growth. But he did learn that you are supposed to turn your head aside when you tackle.

Playing kick-the-can taught him that he enjoyed strategy and maneuver, and maybe had a talent for it. He developed a way of moving very swiftly in a wider-than-normal span so that he could come in by surprise from unexpected angles and win.

He enjoyed "Cops and Robbers." He always wanted to be the robber. He enjoyed the thrill of the chase, and the ability he found he had to outrun his pursuers.

The Halloween eve ritual was to go from door to door crying "Help the poor!" He did it once, but determined never to do it again. There was something about begging for money that seemed totally alien to his being, even if it was only the stale remnant of an ancient ritual. No one ever said, "trick or treat." Andrew never heard that phrase.

The snowball and iceball fights in winter taught him even

more about the necessity of planning and preparation. As the "enemy" gang approached, Andrew had armed his side with garbage can lids as shields. When the enemy caught on to this and did the same, in the next iceball fight Andrew divided his side in to two teams and led one in a flanking attack that caught their opponents by surprise. He became the iceball champion.

But among all the games and activities there was one he never really understood. In chanting rhyme it went like this: "I'm going downtown to smoke my pipe, and I won't be back til Saturday night. And if you touch my daughter Sue, I'll whip you black (pointing) and you blue (pointing to another)." Whereupon the chanter would put an imaginary pipe in mouth, walk ten steps away, then ten steps back, then punch a presumed culprit hard on the arm.

The only thing Andrew could figure was that something within the human mind loves to chant, that the human mind loves rhyme and poetic rhythm. But he found that he did too, even if he didn't understand it. Among other things, this deepened his love for poetry, a warm blaze his grandfather had helped ignite within him.

And, finally, he was able to buy a bicycle, to fill the aching hunger he had felt for years. He had earned some Canadian money working on the farm. Joe went with him to a bank to convert it into American dollars. Andrew was shocked by the diminishment of his earnings. The lecture in exchange rates went right over his head. All he could figure was that where money was concerned he should take nothing for granted. But he found a used bike for ten dollars, and now he felt a new kind of freedom.

He rode everywhere, exploring in all directions, with Guardo always with him.

Somehow the freedom rekindled memories of Eileen. He wondered how she was, whether she was studying, what she was thinking. Especially at Christmas, he wished he could be with her. He thought of writing but could not think of what to say.

*

The war atmosphere, which had been so dramatic in Canada, was still hardly noticeable in America. Public attitudes seemed almost indifferent to the far-off war. But the political atmosphere was a dynamic cauldron of conflicting strategies. On one hand President Roosevelt was promising neutrality. He would not send American troops to war.

On the other hand, the President was engaged in a delicate balancing act of educating public opinion, moving the consciousness of the nation toward support of an England standing alone against the forces of fascism. President Roosevelt was attempting to stimulate public thinking about the most singular reality hovering over world affairs. In January, 1941, before a joint session of Congress, he delivered the <u>Four Freedoms</u> speech.

> "In the future days, which we seek to make secure, we look forward to a world founded upon four essential human freedoms.
>
> The first is freedom of speech and expression—everywhere in the world.
>
> The second is freedom of every person to worship God in his own way—everywhere in the world.

The third is freedom from want—which, translated into world terms, means economic understandings which will secure to every nation a healthy peacetime life for its inhabitants—everywhere in the world.

The fourth is freedom from fear—which, translated into world terms, means a worldwide reduction of armaments to such a point and in such a thorough fashion that no nation will be in a position to commit an act of physical aggression against any neighbor—anywhere in the world.

That is no vision of a distant millennium. It is a definite basis for a kind of world attainable in our own time, and generation."

Andrew read this part of the speech in a newspaper and was so impressed he cut it out and pinned it to the wall over his bed. These thoughts fit perfectly within the still-hazy framework within his mind for turning the world around. If the world could get just this far, it would be halfway home. He was surprised and saddened when people didn't seem to care that much about, or even remember, what Roosevelt had said. Even in the newspapers, it quickly became old news.

Through spring and into early summer the mood for war was beginning to grow, however slowly. In March Roosevelt signed the Lend-Lease pact which "loaned" 50 destroyers to Great Britain. On June 22, Hitler invaded Russia.

But Zeedie and Joe were beginning a war of their own. Andrew began to notice a constant sniping, mostly from Zeedie. Then Joe would respond by trying to defend himself. Nothing physical. Only a war of emotions, sometimes raging out of control. When they fought, Andrew's stomach would tighten into a little ball of cold fear, which would sometimes last for hours. His sense of a future would grow dark and dismal.

In another way, their fighting was both a sorrow and relief for Andrew—relief in the sense that while Zeedie was attacking Joe, he now felt more hidden from her gunsights. But it seemed the dancing days were over for Zeedie and Joe.

*

In July Zeedie, Joe and Andrew went on an outing to an outlying township (Redford) to visit Zeedie's old friends Ty and Sadie. The screen door was open. No one seemed to hear their knock, so they just walked in. The scene they beheld shocked Andrew's mind to a state of numbing horror, then outrage.

Bobby Gilson was five years old. He was one of numerous children Ty and Sadie had brought into the world—they seemed to have one every year. Bobby had a rather round face, sandy colored coarse, straight hair, and troubled eyes. His cheeks wore a permanent scaly ruddiness. He also had something of a speech impediment.

Andrew saw Bobby sitting on the linoleum floor of the living room, dressed only in a thin T-shirt. Naked from the waist down. He was trying to pull his knees up against his chest for protection. He was trying to cry but the emotion choked in his chest. Ty, Sadie, and the other adults were sitting in chairs around him. The first thing Andrew saw was Ty reaching to Bobby's upthrust knees and pushing him into a spin where he sat on the linoleum. When the spin stopped, whichever adult was now facing him would quickly reach down and pull Bobby's small penis, then push him into another spin. Even Ty and Sadie were so engaged.

"What are you doing?" Joe was first to ask.

"We're playing Pull-the-Peter" Ty said with a casual laugh. Andrew noticed a number of empty beer bottles around the room.

"Don't you think that's a little strange?" Joe asked.

"Depends who you ask," Ty laughed.

Andrew didn't know what to do. His first impulse was disbelief. He could find no way to balance this horror in his mind. He felt urged to cry out in rage against what he saw, but the rage would not come loose. For several long moments he could only witness in anguished silence. He could not assimilate it. Finally he regained enough emotional strength to walk in the arena, stand by Bobby's side, then helped him to his feet. With his arm around Bobby's shoulders he spoke haltingly.

"I'm going to take Bobby fishing."

Bobby looked at him gratefully.

"Better put some clothes on," Sadie said, "or them fishes will bite your peter off." The adults who had been participating in this gruesome game all joined in laughter. Zeedie only looked stunned and almost swallowed her tobacco.

Andrew was glad he still carried fishing gear in his pocket. And with Bobby, he went off to find somewhere to fish. Asking a few boys in the neighborhood, he soon found the way to small nearby pond. It was weedy and had been trashed, but it was water and maybe that would be enough.

He cut poles, found worms, and taught Bobby everything he knew. After a while Bobby caught a bluegill and smiled for the first time.

"You're a good fisherman, Andrew said.

"You're my friend," Bobby said. "I never had a friend like you."

"Bobby, you will have many good friends, all through your life."

"I don't know," Bobby said with hesitance.

"Don't let anybody ever get you down." One was all they caught, but Bobby wanted to take it home and show his mom. Andrew gave Bobby the fishing gear to keep.

Andrew never saw Bobby again, but some years later, quite by accident, he learned something about the continuation of Bobby's story. Not long after the pull-the-peter "game," Bobby began setting fires. After the third event, Ty and Sadie were able to place him in a farm community home for backward children. As he grew, receiving only a modicum of education because he was classified as retarded, he became engaged in simple labor.

During the summer of his tenth year, instead of taking his vacation to go home for two weeks, he elected to spend the first of the two weeks earning money. He worked especially hard, on "loan" for the week, and earned ten dollars. He carefully folded the ten-dollar bill and put it in his shirt pocket. The Board at the farm then called Ty and Sadie to pick him up for the remaining week.

All of the second week at home he saved the ten dollars in his pocket, taking it out from time to time to make sure it was there. And on the last morning before he was to be returned, Sadie told him "Come on, get your things. It's time to go."

Bobby took the carefully folded ten dollar bill out of his

pocket and tried to hand it to her. She ignored his gesture.

"Just leave it on the table," she said.

*

By the end of 1941 the United States had become fully engaged in two simultaneous major wars. The December 7 surprise attack by Japan so aroused the American spirit that an entirely new atmosphere came swiftly upon the land. Four days later Hitler and Mussolini declared war against the United States. Since the nation was caught largely unprepared, all through the winter and spring it was mostly bad news of gruesome losses.

Andrew followed the progress of the war with ardent interest. Hitler, Mussolini, and Tojo had to be stopped. He wanted to do something personally to help, but he was too young. He gathered cans and bottles, scrap rubber, inner tubes, scrap metal, newspapers, and other things that could be converted into war materials. He took a very early morning Detroit Free Press delivery route. And he began to find the kind of odd jobs that would enable him to earn money through what remained of his boyhood—shoveling snow, raking leaves, weeding gardens, anything that would enable him to work for pay.

Zeedie seemed stunned by the war news. After three months of thinking about it she decided either she should get a job in a war manufacturing plant, if they would hire her, or volunteer to dance with soldiers, sailors, army air corps men, and marines going off to war. But she couldn't make a decision either way.

When Joe learned the Seabees had been formed, he went into town immediately to enlist.

He was told the Seabees would go in ahead of ground troops

to build landing strips, bridges, things like that. Very dangerous work but it appealed to him. With his construction and crane operating background he thought they would be eager to enlist him. But the medical examiner found he had a problematic heart. Joe was classified 4-F.

The morning he had gone down for enlistment he had left so cheerfully, and then returned so disconsolate, it was almost as if he had aged visibly during the day. Zeedie did not say anything when he told her, no comment at all. In a way her silence rang out like condemnation.

Andrew could see Joe's hurt, even the spectre of humiliation he seemed to feel. But somehow, in some wordless way, the experience brought them closer together, almost to the point of bonding. The two of them had always had an easy, relaxed relationship. There had not been a single tense moment between them. And now, as Andrew began to see Joe as an underdog, his heart went out to him, and Joe responded in kind. It was all done without specific words.

It was almost as if, for just a little while, a tenderness was in the air that seemed to reach even into Zeedie's confused emotions. For a brief period Andrew experienced a rare flush of warmth from Zeedie. One day he became ill at school, with severe pains in stomach and groin. And even though dizzy and staggering a bit on the ice, he made the long, 3-mile walk home, through a very cold and rainy February morning, just to find a place to lie down. The nurse would have kept him in school on a cot in her office, but he told her he wanted his own bed and left.

Instead of remonstrating, Zeedie received him with affection, put fresh sheets on his bed, and made him chicken soup. He was too sick to eat until the next day, but he was grateful for her attention, even the cool ministry of her hand on his forehead as she checked his body warmth. In his pain he deeply appreciated her tenderness and caring touch, and the steaming chicken soup. He wished Zeedie would stay that way. He ached for her to stay that way.

But it was not to be. As parental battles soon resumed, old tension lines were again drawn tight around each of the three of them. Joe had switched to a night shift job at the plant, unloading ore ships. His new schedule soon began to whip against Zeedie's nerves. She was not used to having him around so much. More time to find points of aggravation.

Twice following particularly furious arguments, Zeedie woke Andrew at midnight, had him pack a suitcase, then took him with her in a series of taxis, buses, and streetcars, to her sister Sarah's place. Both events caused Andrew to miss critically important tests at school. The first time he protested, but Zeedie only said "you can make it up." The second time he did not even mention it.

Each time, Joe found them right away. Sarah's place was his first call. Then after the peace-making discussions, he would drive over pick them up, and bring them home.

Zeedie had never learned to drive. Years before, Donald had tried to teach her, but she said his telling her what to-do made her nervous. In a practice run, when he was teaching her how to pull out into highway traffic, he told her "after that green car." But Zeedie somehow though he meant "before the green car." The resulting collision tossed Andrew around in the back seat, with only a few bruises. The adults were bruised as well, but all had escaped serious injury. Donald had quickly shifted himself behind the wheel to take the blame. Zeedie never attempted to drive again.

Andrew began to spend as much time away from the house as he could, and Zeedie did not seem to mind. One home in the neighborhood became a particular gathering place. Both parents worked afternoons and the boys would often assemble in the evening for stories and discussions. In one session or another Andrew and the others were told—always as <u>authenticated</u> scientific fact, that:

- If you sleep outdoors with the light of a full moon on your face, you will go insane. If you sleep inside, where the light of the full moon comes through the window on your face all night, you will wake up half insane.
- If you dream of falling and you actually hit bottom in your dream, you will die.
- If you jack off, hair will grow in the palm of your hands.
- It takes a full pint of jism to make a baby. Anything less than a pint will result in a terribly defective baby.
- If you engage in sexual penetration underwater, the girl will lock and freeze around you so tight your cock will have to be amputated ... Unless you decide just to stay that way until you both die.
- The secret ingredient that gives cream soda its distinctive flavor is made from dried camel piss.

The week following the last "authentic" disclosure, one of the more mean-spirited boys pissed into an empty bottle of ginger ale, put the cap back on, and with several other boys watching, tried to get Dondo to drink it. Dondo was a neighborhood boy with Downs syndrome, who always wore a fake sheriff's badge and in a friendly way tried to act like a local official.

Andrew came upon the group while this discussion was underway. He knew immediately what was going on. He took the bottle, pressed the cap off again with his thumbs, and offered it to Tommy, the deceiver.

"Tommy, take a drink yourself to show Dondo how good it is," Andrew said.

"No. We prepared that special for Dondo," Tommy said.

"Tommy, all your friends want to see you drink it to prove how tough you are."

"They know I'm tough without that," Tommy insisted.

"Prove it," Andrew insisted back.

"Yeah," one of the assembled boys said.

"Let's see you do it," another one said.

Tommy took the bottle and emptied it in the dirt of the alley. "I don't have to prove anything," he said.

"Tommy," Andrew said, "Dondo is my friend, and anything you do to him you do to me."

"It was just a joke," Tommy said.

"Nobody's laughing, Tommy."

With the speed and range his bike allowed him, Andrew began to explore the surrounding communities and countryside in ever-widening loops. He especially liked the pervasive scent of burning leaves in autumn, their delicate sweet pungent aroma lingering in the air like the perfume of alien beings. It was one of the things that made autumn his favorite season. It was the same in all the communities.

He found it enjoyable to fish and swim wherever he found suitable water, even into the colder months. Swimming cold and naked continued to be a rare sensual experience. Halfway toward Detroit along a secluded meandering section of the Rouge River, he discovered Naked Ass Beach, so called because others had discovered it as well. Since everyone came there with the same intent, there was no overtly conscious leering among visitors. The protocol seemed to be each to himself or herself alone. He loved the cold, clean rush of the water over his body.

He practiced riding his bike without touching handlebars, and soon began to ride from Plonkatown into Detroit without ever doing so. The worst part of the ride was crossing a big waffle iron bridge. It spanned a wide and oily gray expanse of the Rouge River after it passed along the huge Ford plant on its way to the Detroit River.

And he made other tests for himself. Sometimes he would get on his bike and decide in advance that he would, for example, ride ten blocks, turn right for seven blocks, then left for twelve more, and so forth. He had done the same kind of thing sometimes on foot when he lived in the city. The essential point in his mind was that he would make a prestructured plan without any awareness of obstacles it may present, then follow it rigidly without faltering or turning back, no matter what. In the countryside, where there were no city blocks, he would do the same kind of thing, using compass directions and minutes elapsed on the pocket watch Kenneth had given him before he'd left.

Because he regarded these as tests, never once did he turn back after the course was begun. At one time or another he had to carry his bike several blocks through a dirty sewage-infested stream, swim a river, climb up and over a building, push through monstrous thickets six feet to one side of a clear path, wade through swampy fields, or fight off attacking dogs. With Guardo at his side he could push the stick right into the snarling throat if the dog lunged at him. The important thing to him was to test his resolve once he had set a course of action. It was his way of trying to find out who he really was.

And it was at the end of one of these excursions when he came upon a large abandoned warehouse. He decided to go in. The door was half off its hinges. In a short time, in a far corner of the building, he realized he was not alone. A gang of five teenage boys had followed him in. All were smoking. They quickly surrounded him in the corner.

He did not yet know their intent, but he had Guardo. If they attacked, he and Guardo would hit their kneecaps, disable them from pursuit. He was thinking of alternative strategies when the gang leader addressed him.

"What's your name?"

"Andrew Cameron," he said calmly.

"You're not from around here."

"No, I'm not."

"What're you doing here?"

"Just looking around."

"We decide who looks around in this neighborhood."

"I didn't get your letter," Andrew said sarcastically.

"We don't write no stinking letters."

There were several moments of hard eye contact. Andrew knew the gang leader was trying to see who would look away first. Madre squinted a bit and held his challenging stare. He knew if he looked down first the gang would be upon him. But he did not. He held his hard haze and gave thought to further strategies. Then at last the gang leader looked down.

"Do you smoke?" The leader challenged.

"Sure I smoke," Andrew said in the toughest voice he could muster.

"Where are your cigarettes?"

"I don't have them with me."

The gang leader handed him a burning cigarette. "Let's see you smoke."

Andrew took a puff, blew out the smoke.

"Do you inhale?" the leader challenged.

"Sure I inhale."

"Let's see you inhale!"

A surge of inner anxiety swept through Andrew. He was carefully controlled, so there was no outward expression. His problem was he did not know what inhale meant. He had never heard the word.

"Let's see you do it," the leader repeated.

Andrew put the cigarette in his mouth again. Still not knowing exactly what to do, he took a puff and blew out the smoke without passage into the lungs. But as he blew the smoke he rolled his eyes slowly in a complete circle.

"That's not inhaling!" the leader said.

"That's the way I inhale. You should try it."

The leader looked perplexed. Andrew handed him back the cigarette. "Try it," he said again. Then the leader hesitantly followed the same procedure as Andrew, rolling his eyes completely in a circle as he exhaled. One of the gang members laughed. The leader turned on him and cowed him into submission, then made him do it, too. Very soon all five gang members were doing it, and Andrew took his time to leave with a friendly wave. "See you around," he smiled.

*

Somehow during this adventurous period of testing the boundaries of his emerging manhood, he found time to fall in love—rapturous, dreamy, excited, totally smitten. The problem was, it was not a real person, someone he could touch and hold; it was a poster, and it captured and for a time held his heart in the grip of what he saw.

Rosie the Riveter was a large poster that showed an example of women in the war effort in idealized, romantic, almost mythological terms. She seemed larger than life, but very real:

- Blonde (very blonde)
- Blue-eyed (very blue-eyed)
- Beautiful (take-your-breath-away beautiful)
- Strong (with rolled up sleeves showing the strength of her arms)
- Faithful (you could see it in her wonderful eyes)

- Resolute (you could tell by the expression of her beautiful lips)

- Hard working (you could see it in the strength of her posture)

- Heroic in attitude (her whole being projected true heroism)

- A loving partner (a full companion for all the trials of war and peace)

He knew the poster was only an idealized artist's conception. But what she portrayed told Andrew there were women in the world—somewhere—that rose above the ordinary levels of the human species, who seemed to project the warmth and courage and strength of godliness in human form, the most desirable companion he had ever imagined.

If he could ever find her, he would want to spend his life with her, to work together to build a better world. Without ever hearing her voice, or feeling her touch, he was ready to make this lifelong commitment without reservation. For a long time he would daydream about Rosie the Riveter with a longing heart. Somewhere in the world... perhaps in another time, another place. His love for her was unconditional.

*

By January 1943 Zeedie had had enough. Joe had become ill in late fall with an attack of rheumatic fever. After a brief hospitalization he had to remain mostly in bed for the following month. The cost of hospital, doctor, and medications soon exhausted their savings. Although Ford took him back on the cranes because manpower shortage was acute, Joe felt the family would have to cut back quite a bit.

"We're going to have to find a cheaper place to live, maybe farther out," he told Zeedie.

"How far out do you want to go? You already moved us into the boondocks," she said.

"Just til I get back on my feet," he said.

"I got a better plan," Zeedie said. "You go your way. I go mine."

"Does that mean you want a divorce?" he asked.

"Course it does. You got ears?" she asked.

"When do you want to do this?"

"Soon as you get your stuff out of here."

"I'm sorry, Zeedie. I really am."

"I married a fuckin' 4-F!" she almost yelled.

Andrew, in an adjoining room, had overheard the whole conversation. It was the first time he could remember that his mother ever swore.

Chapter 10

By the end of January, after thinking about it for a month, Zeedie kicked out Andrew, too.

"I'm racing to change everything at once," she said.

"Am I <u>everything</u>?" Andrew asked.

"Well, you're not <u>nothing</u>," Zeedie said, as though trying to make sense to an idiot.

Andrew paused for several moments, trying to word the question. "Does this mean I'm a fuckin' 4-F?"

"No, honey. You're 1-A. And don't use that language on me." It was the first time she had ever called him "honey." "I've got to get on with my life. I'm starting to get little wrinkles. Time's a' wasting."

"But where will you go?" he asked.

"First thing—out of the boondocks. I'll move in with Sarah for a while. Get me a job in a war plant. I heard they're pretty hard up."

"I could get some jobs, same as I've been doing. I could help you pay the rent," he volunteered.

"Too much bother. Besides, you've got to go to school. It'll be cheaper living with Sarah. I don't eat much. They can use the extra war ration stamps."

"What if I go to Sarah's with you?"

"No room," Zeedie said matter-of-factly. "She hardly has

room for me." She paused, then repeated the thought for emphasis. "Won't be any room for you there."

"Where do you think I should go?"

"Go move in with Joe. He seems to put up with you okay."

Zeedie saw the beginning of a tear in Andrew's eyes, not yet fully formed, but hovering along his lower eyelids. It seemed to drive her thoughts into a full defensive position. Now tears came into her own eyes. She raised her trembling voice to clarify her point. "I need to be <u>downtown</u>... Soldiers, sailors, marines, flying men are coming through town every day. They need someone at the USO to dance with them, show them a good time before they go off to get killed."

"Couldn't you do that from home?"

"We all have to fight the war in our own way," she said.

Andrew held the tears back. He would not let them fall. "You're very patriotic," he said quietly.

*

Living next door to the Henrys was almost an adventure in itself. I was a huge family, the Henrys, almost Whitmanesque in its elemental and sometimes barbarous passions. There were sons in all branches of the military, the oldest of whom had already been killed in action in North Africa. A gold star flag hung next to the blue star in the front window.

The Henrys came from the same southern region as the Wheelocks but were completely different. While the Wheelocks were generally hardworking, quiet, and dull, the Henrys were hardworking but much more alive with a dynamic and colorful sense of excitement that inhabited them all. Guitars, banjos, pianos, all were well used.

Their big back yard was all cinders on which were parked several moving vans with C stickers for extra gasoline. To one side there was a big chicken coop, with chopping block, whose inhabitants had no apparent sense of impending doom.

After Zeedie had thrown him out, Joe had rented one of the Henrys' now-empty rooms. But when Zeedie called to tell him Andrew would have to leave too, Joe adjusted his plans. The house next door had been empty for months, and Joe was able to rent it. It was not the place he would have preferred, but it would do for now. His only thought was to make a home for himself and Andrew. The Henrys had enough leftover furniture to make it workable without great expense. And Joe immediately enrolled Andrew in the local Detroit school.

The war effort was still desperate, but the tide was beginning to turn. The Russians had defeated Hitler's armies at Stalingrad.

In his first visit to the Henry home, Andrew noticed there were only two kinds of books—several Bibles and what seemed like hundreds of comic books.

Daisy Henry, who was three years older, took an immediate liking to Andrew and told him he could have all the comic books if he wanted them. "You don't read them twice," she explained. Daisy was a pretty girl, with dark curly hair and startled eyes. She was rather small and wiry in stature, and always wore thin, billowing dresses. She had a restless nature that seemed just near the edge of blurting out something you didn't want to hear. There was an underlying sweetness in her, together with a quality of innocence very attractive to Andrew. She also played the guitar, as did several of the Henrys, and offered to teach him how to play. "We can play together," she said.

On the mantelpiece in the Henry living room sat a small statue of three sitting monkeys, with hands respectively covering eyes, ears, and mouth. The inscriptions were:

See No Evil

Hear No Evil

Speak No Evil

Andrew questioned Daisy about it. "It doesn't make sense to have all three monkeys sitting there, like all three things are the same."

"What do you mean?" Daisy asked.

"I mean," Andrew searched for the right words, "I mean there's a big difference. You can control what you speak. But you can't control what you see or hear. You would have to live in a dungeon."

"They're just dumb monkeys," Daisy said.

"I think 'Speak No Evil' should be sitting someplace else."

"You're going to be fun to teach," Daisy said with an intriguing smile.

*

Fig Bigaro came to visit the Henrys in late March. His forthcoming arrival was preceded by excited whisper from the youngest Henry boys and a few of their neighborhood friends. Fig was a man who generated rumors about himself. The whispers said he was <u>The Cocksman</u>, that he had five hundred women, that he knew everything there was to know about women.

He was a cousin of the Henrys, from Flowery Branch, Georgia, and had come to Detroit to enlist in the Army. He wanted the word Detroit on his enlistment papers because, in his mind, that would guarantee him a job in a Detroit factory after he got out of the service.

Fig was called Big Red, but Andrew could not understand why. He was a lanky, lean, and bony man with burnt orange hair and what looked like permanent sunburn. He stood about six feet tall. His face also had a skin-stretched-over-bones look, with strangely expressive eyes. He projected an inner intensity even when he was sitting quietly, which was seldom. His speech was rather garrulous. He seemed to want to talk all the time, even about nothing at all. He wanted to make a family connection with Henrys, for after the war.

The young Henry boys made the quiet arrangements. Fig would come to a corner basement room when the men were gone and tell them everything they needed to know. On the appointed evening, ten boys assembled into the crowded room. Andrew had been invited to join them.

Fig sat on the edge of a small table, enjoying their adoring gazes. It took only one question from the boys to open him up into a rambling monologue.

"Is it true you screwed 500 women?"

Fig leaned back, in seeing delight at the question. "I don't know. I never counted. Maybe more than that I would say. After a while you forget who you fucked and who you didn't. Sometimes you fucked the same girl twice without knowing it. At a certain point, maybe some night when you're just too drunk, you lose track. You quit counting. You forget where you left off. You just keep a hard dick on you at all times, for what opportunity presents itself. You got to be a man of action. That's where it counts. You gotta be ready to get hard at a moment's notice. You gotta go in there and do the job. You gotta fuck 'em fast and fuck 'em hard. You gotta get 'em squirmin'. And I'll tell you somethin' else. Kids, you always do it from the front. Animals do it from behind. Real men do it from the front."

"How you gonna keep screwin' in the army?" a boy asked.

Fig leaned forward and spoke almost in a secretive whisper. 'I'll tell you what, kids, I'm gonna go over there and get me some German pussy. I hear that's the best. There's some way they tenderize it ...That's what you want, kids, tenderized pussy, sweet German pussy."

*

The letter from Eileen reached Andrew in April, forwarded from the Plonkatown address. She had excellent handwriting.

Dearest Andrew,

I miss you terribly. I didn't think I could ever miss someone so much. You said you wouldn't write but I can't stop myself. I've made a few friends, but there's no one like you. So I have been very lonely since you went away.

In the spring and summers mom and I made big gardens, but we never seemed to plant enough. The rabbits eat a lot. I'm up at the crack of Christ, I work my butt off, but the animals claw through the netting and eat their fill. The winters have been long and cold. I grow the biggest goose bumps you ever saw. The Camerons have been most kind to us. Year before last a bolt of lightning struck the barn and blew the whole barn clear 100 feet against the workshop. Last year a big bomber crash-landed on their farm but nobody was hurt. I fished the way you taught me until winter came, then the snow was too deep and the creek froze and I think the trout went to sleep.

I have been studying hard and learning a lot so I can help you in some way. I've been reading all the books you gave me. They are better than the books in school. I discovered I am good at figuring things out. But I have not the first idea of how to save the world. I don't even know if I can save myself. Christmas is the worst time. Sometimes I think I will never see you again, then I look at my wrist.

Please write. Let me know you're alive. Tell me you miss me like crazy, even if you don't mean it

Love from deep inside my heart.

Eileen.

The letter turned his heart inside out with fresh memories. He had thought about her many times since their parting, always with feelings of deep and warm affection. They had been so close, and the letter brought back the closeness, as though they had never parted.

He knew about the barn door and the bomber crash. Kenneth had written him from time to time and he had written back. But he had never written to a girl, even such a dear friend as Eileen. He didn't know where to start or how to begin. After thinking about her steadily for a night and day, he finally summoned the courage to put down whatever awkward words he could compose. He wanted to let her know he was alive and she was never far from him thoughts.

Eileen,

I still feel your closeness, almost like I could reach out and touch you. Your letter meant a lot to me. It reminded me how much I miss you and want so much to hold you near me again. There is probably no one in the world like you and I feel lucky we were able to get to know each other so well. Yes! I am alive. A little wounded but alive. I can't wait to see you again but don't know how soon that can be.

The war is finally starting to turn around toward our side. I read a lot about it. Ernie Pyle is my favorite writer. I heard about the bomber crash. Grandpa wrote to me. But none of us write very much. My mother never writes at all. I don't know if that's just the way we are or if we just don't know what to say. But I will tell you one thing. You mean a lot to me and I think of you probably more than you suspect. I wish there was some way we could be closer.

In your studies I hope you have read President Roosevelt's Four Freedoms. What he said makes so much sense for the whole world. That is something I think I could spend my whole life aiming for. It could be such a great starting point. I can't think of flowery language to say it but no matter what happens in my life and yours, I want you to know you are in my heart forever. I miss you like crazy too. AND I MEAN IT!

Andrew

*

By the middle of April Hitler's troops had been chased out of Africa and Andrew was deep into reading Ernie Pyle's columns from the front lines. Bill Mauldin's infantry cartoons, and more than a hundred comic books Daisy had given him.

Ernie Pyle's descriptions of battle-weary, rugged, steadfast infantrymen stirred his heart tremendously. He felt there was something heroic and noble about men who fought against Hitler's evil ambitions with such uncomplaining courage. These were now his role models. He wanted to grow up to be like them. He wanted to join with them in battle as soon as he could come of age. He imagined himself as a soldier, old beyond his years, aching from fatigue and the dust of war, slogging forward into battle, <u>knowing</u> he would defeat all forms of evil that would come against him. Oh! What momentous times! He was glad he was alive.

Andrew had read comic books before, but never in such abundance. Their stories further strengthened his feeling that the forces of good must valiantly defeat the forces of evil. The comic book view of man was that people were either good or bad, not complex beings mixed with light and dark.

And then there were the Sunday "funnies," the comics section of the big weekend paper. He read every comic strip avidly. But of them all, there was one that somehow reached down deep into his being: Brenda Starr, Reporter. Or more particularly, one story line in Brenda Starr: her relationship with the Mystery Man. From time to time the Mystery Man would appear out of nowhere, returning from some great adventure, with an eyepatch signifying he had done battle. Always clean and well dressed. Always welcomed into her waiting arms.

The Mystery Man never wrote or called. He would simply disappear from her life, sometimes for agonizingly long periods, then reappear without explanation. Because the love she felt for him was so deep, her whole life seemed to hang on waiting for him to come back to her again. In a strange way, it came into Andrew's mind that this is what true love must really be like. Once love is committed, you never had to work at it again. You could go away for years and your true love would be waiting for your return, patient and chaste. His comic book perception of reality exerted a strong influence on his mind well into his twenties.

However, one of the most invaluable lessons he ever learned came from the back pages of a comic book. It was a simple puzzle showing nine dots arranged in a square pattern, three on each side, one in the middle. The instruction was to connect all nine dots by drawing only four straight lines, without taking pencil off the paper. Try as he might he could find no way, until he saw the answer. You did not have to be limited by your apparent perception of a box. You did not have to stay inside the box. You could start outside, zoom down to angle through three dots, then form triangular lines to connect the six others, with points of the triangle outside the "box." You could not solve this problem inside the box or with rigid thinking. You could not be bound by the perception that the only solution was inside the box. He never forgot this.

*

The new school became a challenge from the beginning. Edison Elementary employed some teachers who seemed to take satisfaction in creating an antagonistic, rather than nurturing, relationship with students. The merest puzzled hard question would produce an atmosphere of confrontation rather than explanation, as though the question had been designed to put the teacher on the spot. Andrew began to feel as though a dark blanket had been thrown over his life.

In one of his first encounters, a teacher named Miss Huxley

drew a large circle on the blackboard, representing the earth. Then she pointed at two dots along its circumference, and asked the class: "What's the shortest distance between the two dots?"

"A straight line connecting them," Andrew answered.

"You're wrong," she said.

"I'll show you," he said.

"Show me," she said.

Andrew went to the board and drew a straight line connecting the dots.

"That's what everyone thinks," Miss Huxley said. "That's why you're in school, to learn."

"What do you say is the answer?" Andrew asked.

Miss Huxley took the chalk and drew a line hugging the circumference from dot to dot. "An arc of the great circle," she said triumphantly.

"You made that up," Andrew said.

"No, I didn't."

"You said shortest distance, not shortest possible distance."

"See me after school," she said, with no benevolence in her voice.

His relationship with other boys ran the usual pattern. As he approached any group they would seem to stiffen and become serious. But his friendly bearing quickly overcame the awkwardness. He made friends easily. He was gifted with a great sense of humor, which eased most potentially troubled situations into relaxed acceptance.

The old patterns were changed in one respect. Usually, he had to fight the school bully, but this time it was different. The toughest kid in school, he quickly learned, was Pete Magnuccio. However, Pete was not so much a bully as he was someone mildly feared. He was a rather amiable oversized kid who was used to getting his own way. Because of his size and strength and athletic prowess, the other kids let him have his own way whenever he wanted it. He didn't push people around. They simply cleared a path for him.

Soon after Andrew enrolled, Pete took him aside, almost in a confidential way.

"We have to fight," Pete said.

"Why? You don't even know me," Andrew said.

"I don't know. We just do," Pete said.

"Let me know when you're ready."

And that was the end of it. Pete never let Andrew know he was ready, and in a rather short time they became friends and the incident was largely forgotten.

*

By spring planting season Andrew was able to get paid work helping the Henrys prepare the big garden by the Rouge River for the new season. Both John and Ma Henry worked very hard at it. The particular job John asked Andrew to do was to help him plow up the field, then to plant and weed. John had a small hand plow with twin struts angling up to two handles at waist level. John would guide and push the plow. Andrew's job was to pull. Ordinarily this would be a job for a horse or mule or small tractor, but none of these were available and the work had to be done. John rigged a leather harness for Andrew and the two of them went to work. From time to time they stopped to rest and wipe away the profuse sweating. At one of these rest stops, John told Andrew that down home in Georgia when his plow, pulled by a mule, turned up a nest of rattlesnakes he would just stomp them to death with his bare feet. Andrew was impressed.

At another rest stop John gave him his first lesson in sex education. Wiping sweat away, he put a hand on Andrew's shoulder. "Andrew," he said, "there's playing girls, and there is good girls. The good girls are the girls you marry. Don't ever get them confused in your mind."

"I'll try not to," Andrew said.

At another rest stop Andrew was given news of his mother. Apparently, John and Zeedie had maintained some kind of connection.

"Your mother is working as a welder in the old Chevy plant," John said.

"Does she ever ask about me?"

John hesitated. "She uses all her spare time at the USO. She's very popular."

"I guess that would keep her pretty busy," Andrew said. He turned into his leather straps and pulled the plow harder than ever.

When the garden was prepared for planting, John paid him and said "I like the way you work. I like your spirit. Maybe this summer I'll try you out on the trucks. You think you could do heavy lifting?"

"I can do anything I set my mind to."

"Well said," John said, and took him home.

During this period, John invited Andrew to go with him to the Temple of Zion and Andrew did. The Temple of Zion was a basement Church with no superstructure and a flat roof. Church members were still gathering funds to finish it.

The preacher was Sister Wazzel. She was a fiery preacher with huge breasts. She would start the sermon in normal speaking tones, but as she really got into it, her whole body would rock to the cadence of her oratory. She would sometimes jump up and down, and those wonderful breasts would go up and down with her. And the whole Congregation would respond to her fervor. Some would get down and roll on the floor in their excitement. John Henry never got down on the floor but Andrew saw he was clearly moved by the passion of her sermon.

Andrew went every Sunday with John. He couldn't get enough of those giant floating breasts. He paid little attention to what was said. His mind was too much filled with sexual imagery. Sister Wazzel almost made him a convert.

Over on Vernor Highway there was a movie theater where Andrew would go every Saturday afternoon. Next door was a Woolworth's fine-and-ten cent store. The theater would show two full length movies, a newsreel, a cartoon, and a running series, Perils of Pauline. The cost was ten cents, plus two cents tax. For another nickel he could buy a hamburger. And for another nickel he could buy a large bag of gumdrops. Sometimes he would go with Daisy. She was easy to talk to.

*

With Daisy teaching him guitar, he found he was spending a lot of time in the Henry home. He enjoyed the voice of the instrument, a warm and sentimental sound. In the beginning she loaned him one to practice with. With so many Henrys off to war, there were a number of instruments laying around. Sometimes she tried to sing along as he played, but voice was not her special gift and she knew it. "I sing like a strangled chicken," she said. "I think you have a pretty voice. Very sweet," he said. When Andrew tried to join her from time to time she would put her fingers over his and say "Don't sing. Your voice is so sexy you're going to put me into a dreamy sleep."

"You do the singing," he said.

"Maybe sleep is not the word. When I hear your voice, sometimes I think you're trying to hypnotize me."

"I wouldn't do that."

"What would you do with me if you hypnotized me?"

"Wake you up, fast," he said.

She laughed. "What if I didn't want you to wake me up?"

"I wouldn't know what to do with you."

"Let's practice that sometime. I've never been hypnotized." She said.

"I wouldn't know how to begin."

"Are you afraid?" She asked.

"Not afraid. Just ignorant."

She had a way of touching him often, which he liked. It was not suggestive. But sometimes it was almost suggestive.

"You're 15 and I am 12. I think you would have the advantage over me,' he said.

"Okay, that means back to work," she said, as if turning off a switch. 'Let's start playing again."

Andrew felt relieved.

*

As he became more integrated into the Henry family culture, he learned they had some curious habits and customs. The men on reaching maturity would demonstrate their strength by lifting up the front end of a Model A Ford. Somehow, this act signified passage into full-blown manhood.

The Henrys were a hard and unforgiving family that shunned all open displays of affection. A handshake, among the men, was maximum. Nor did women get the better of it. You would never hear the words "I love you" in that family. You would never see a male kiss a female, even a wife. And yet, underneath the outward toughness there ran a strong current of deep sentiment. Like the Camerons, they would go out of their way to help someone in trouble. Their door was always open. It had never been locked. And because of the moving company sign mounted on their front lawn, men and women of color would from time to time knock on the door and ask to use the bathroom. They were always graciously accommodated, with a glass of water and a sliver of ice if they wished it. The Henrys worked hard, played hard, and fought hard, which was often.

The Henrys believed in the Bible and said they were God-fearing but only John and Ma went to Church.

On Saturday nights in the warmer months, with the Grand Ol' Opry playing on the radio inside, the Henrys would go out on the small patch of lawn in front and the men and boys from the neighborhood would do some bare-knuckle fighting. They tried to be fair, matching men and boys according to approximate weight. It was not pretend fighting, it was real fighting, with blood and knockdowns and declared winners.

Andrew had to intention of entering this fray. He thought it was stupid. But one hot sultry night in June, he was picked to fight against Bruno Selvey, a neighborhood boy his size. Daisy egged him on, almost pushing him into the arena.

Before he could throw his first punch, Bruno drove a fist in a circular direction to the rear of his left side, aimed at his kidneys. The blow landed. Andrew fell quickly into a very painful state of oblivion. He lay on the grass gasping, unable to move. The pain was severe. He felt almost paralyzed, weak and in a state of shock. He had never been kidney punched before, never even heard of it. But now he knew. Once you take a hard punch in the kidneys you never want to go through the experience again. Next time, he vowed silently to himself as he began to regain his posture, he would watch out for this. He would attack with all the Cameron fierceness against such a dirty fighter.

John Henry stepped in to put a firm hand on Bruno's shoulder. "We don't allow that kind of fighting here, Bruno, you are disqualified." And then the fights continued among those who were left. But that was all that was said to Bruno.

Nevertheless, Andrew was out of action for the night. He got to his feet, feeling weak, the pain still significant. Daisy took his arm and led him away. No one seemed to notice they were gone. "Come with me," she said. "I know a place where you can get your strength back." And he followed her around to the big cinder back yard where the trucks were parked.

She opened the swinging door of a wide-bodied van, and he followed her inside. She shut the door. It was total darkness, but she knew where everything was. She removed several thick felt moving pads from a large stack, laid them on the van floor and sat, pulling him gently down. "Lie here with your head on my lap. I'll nurse you til the pain goes away." And she began by stroking his hair and forehead and temples with her rather thin, long cool fingers. "When animals hurt," she said, "they like to crawl into a dark, quiet place to heal."

"Are you a dark, quiet place?" He asked.

"I am a dark place," she reaffirmed. "Maybe not so quiet."

Still recovering from the pain, he did what she said. She opened her legs to allow his head a comfortable place to rest. And as soon as he laid his head along her, he became aware that a thin summer dress separated his face from her flesh. He could feel the bare legs against his cheeks. He liked the sensation, and he liked the way she smelled. "I guess I'm just an animal to you," he said as she stroked him.

"I guess you're more than an animal," she said.

"I kind of like this animal world."

"You just shush," she said.

He could feel her smile coming through the darkness. Her fingers felt wonderful along his temples. It was the first time since Eileen that anyone had stroked his hair this way. It gave him small shivers. Even in the hot night, her hands seemed to have a cool and gentle touch.

And for a little while they remained in this state without further conversation, Andrew could feel the pain beginning to disappear. And Daisy's hands gradually began to comfort him around his shoulders and leaning over him, along his chest beneath his open shirt. All of it felt good and he did not protest.

"If I'm going to help you heal," she said in a voice just above a whisper, "I've got to stroke you where it hurts the most. You just be quiet."

He felt her fingers unbuckling his belt and the buttons of his pants. For a moment he stiffened, but did not stop her. She was changing his pain into a state of growing excitement. "Did I hurt you?" She whispered.

"No," he whispered back.

"I felt you wince."

"It was just more than I expected."

Again, he could almost sense her quiet smile. And she stroked the bare flesh around his lower back and sides, and in time he felt her fingers moving into the regions of his groin.

'It doesn't hurt there," was all he could whisper in a delicious protest.

"Everything is connected," she whispered.

"How long have you been a nurse?"

"Today is my first day on the job, but I know what it takes to heal a man."

He was aware she had used the word <u>man</u>. He liked that. And now he felt the sensations of her fingers along parts that were clearly uninjured, but responding quickly to her quiet touch. He was not sure what to do. He now knew her full intent, but he could not summon the will to resist it. It felt too good. He had never felt like this before. He didn't want it to stop.

"Relax," she whispered. "I'll help you heal."

But there was no way he could relax now. His whole being was aroused to a state of high excitement, mingled with terror.

His fear was mounting that John Henry would throw open the doors of the van and strangle him on the spot. He might kill then both.

"If you keep doing this," he whispered hoarsely, "I think we're going to get into trouble."

But she did not stop. "I love your voice when you whisper. I feel it all the way down." She continued on for several minutes.

"Why are you doing this?" was all he could think to whisper.

"I like to be in control," she whispered back. And she continued her tender ministrations.

"Daisy," he whispered, "I don't think I can hold it back much longer."

"Just let it go!" she said in a commanding whisper.

It seemed to blow up the world. Nothing in his experience had ever felt like this. It was the most amazing sensation he had ever imagined. He did not know the earth could contain such feelings of pure untrammeled joy. He wanted to share it, for her to experience it too. His cheek was lying against her bare thigh, and he twisted in his joyful confusion and instinctively kissed her high along the inside of her thigh. He became aware she wore nothing underneath her dress. A forest of sensations gave caress to his cheeks.

He moved up to find her lips, and to place his body over hers. But as he kissed her, she pushed him away and would not let him proceed further. "You're healed enough," she whispered hoarsely.

"I want to share the experience."

"Andrew, I'm a virgin."

"Do you want to share what you did to me?"

"Maybe some other time."

"I don't understand you."

"I think you hypnotized me," she said. "Yeah, that's what it was, for sure." There was sauciness in her whisper.

Her mood had now changed. She was done with the experience. She would not let him kiss her or hold her in an embrace. Her emotions seemed to have been turned off. Andrew composed himself and helped her fold the pads and place them on the stack. He wondered, especially with her change of emotional attitude, whether she would tell John Henry.

*

The Battle of Midway had just come to conclusion. Navy fighting planes had sunk four Japanese aircraft carriers, and the whole tide of war in the Pacific suddenly shifted in favor of the United States.

On the home front the war effort was fully mobilized and in high gear. The Russian victories against Hitler, the allied victories in Africa, and victory at Midway had all come together to solidify the larger spirit of re-conquest now illuminating the dark horizons cast over the earth. And Andrew continued in his strenuous efforts to collect all the salvage materials he could that might be recycled into the war effort—steel, iron, rubber, tin cans, glass, newspapers, everything that could be used.

Andrew tried to be as natural as possible in Daisy's presence. And her own attitude seemed to be the same. Either she was a great actress, or she could shut off emotion like a switch. He didn't know which. But from his daily interactions with the

Henrys, he could see that she had not told either her mother or father. What puzzled him the most was that her behavior toward him had not altered from its former state. They continued to play guitars together, continued to go to the movie theater together. It was as if nothing had ever happened. She was the first complex female in his experience, not counting Zeedie.

One evening two weeks later, when they were alone for a while, he ventured upon the subject of their relationship, testing whether anything had changed deeper down.

"Daisy," he ventured, "I think you just like to tease and run away." He said this in a friendly voice and with a smile.

She did not answer him directly. But on her face was an expression he could only interpret as a knowing smirk. Whatever it was, he concluded, whatever it had been, it would never happen again with her.

On the first of July John Henry gave Andrew some work on the trucks, moving furniture from a second-story flat to a third-story apartment. No elevators. The heavy lifting was strenuous work; it invigorated him. He found his natural rhythm was to take two stairs at a time when he was going back for another load. The sweat was so heavy, and his body so cool from the wind as they drove, it was altogether refreshing. And when the day was over, John Henry told him. "I charged a man's wages for you today, so I'm going to pay you like a man." Andrew walked on air as he went home next door. He looked at himself in the mirror: A <u>man's</u> wages!

*

Laura Boutin felt an immediate sense of patriotism as soon as she saw the Statue of Liberty, and that feeling never wavered in subsequent years. Born in France near Orleans, she had come to the United States while still a young girl, and her speech still bore a hint of French origins. Her father was an entrepreneur who quickly came to see the looming trouble in Hitler's rise to power. He wanted the family safe. Her mother was a deeply religious woman who had come very close to being a nun. Laura was enrolled in a private Catholic school in Dearborn. She was now 12 years old.

Laura had a strikingly pretty face and unusually large lavender colored eyes. They were knowing and intelligent eyes, that seemed to invite conversation. She had smooth creamy white skin and thick raven black hair that descended below her waistline. She usually wore it in a bun, which added an impression of maturity. When not in a bun, her choice was a ponytail.

She had a most expressive face. There was an aliveness in it that responded to every nuance of conversation or circumstance. Whatever it was, whoever was speaking, her expressions showed she was always totally involved. Her smile came easily, but could instantly change to a serious expression, even a pouting frown. And yet, underlying all of this, there was a sense of formality in her general demeanor. A sense that you could not come near her private world until she knew you very well and invited you in. She did not have any romantic attachments yet, only dreams. Even at this young age, Laura had become a person of very definite opinions. She was always so <u>certain</u> about things, never a hint of doubt in whatever she did. She had inherited her mother's deep religious beliefs, and this was one of the areas of her life in which there was no uncertainty at all. She prayed to the Holy Mother every night.

Laura was also a good organizer and had natural leadership ability. She had organized this Fourth of July party in some detail. First, she and two other girls and three boys would go to the Rouge Pools for some swimming. Then they would all go to Ford Field in Dearborn for a picnic and wiener roast. All was going according to plan until one of the three boys sprained an ankle that morning.

"Five will be enough," she said decisively.

On that same morning Andrew rode his bike from Detroit to Rouge Pools and planned to spend the day there. He had swum back and forth to the center pavilion a number of times, taken several dives, and was just contemplating what to do next when he felt her hand on his arm.

"You will come with me," she said.

"You are very bossy," he said.

"Please," she said.

"Okay. Nice bossy. Where are we going?"

She led him to her group. "We need one more horse," she said.

"Do I look like a horse?" Andrew laughed.

"To play a game, you dummy."

The two other pairs were mounting, girls with legs wrapped around the necks of the boys, getting ready to do friendly battle.

Andrew quickly sized up the situation. There was something about her that was quite attractive. And her bossy attitude intrigued him. He had never met such a girl. But his whole evaluation took only a few seconds. Laura spoke with a most pleasing French accent. Even though Andrew did not understand the language, he could feel, in the way she pronounced her words, a sense of refinement that gave her a special character.

"Okay," he said. "You picked a winning horse." And he easily mounted her onto his shoulders. She wrapped her legs around his neck tightly and with authority. Her skin felt like velvet. He held her firmly and they proceeded to play the game.

But what he noticed immediately was a sensation he had never before experienced. A warm spot of heat was radiating into the back of his neck. As the mock battle proceeded he held her even more closely against him. He didn't want the game to end. It was like a gentle, comforting warmth against the back of his neck and he wanted to keep it there as long as he could. And he had the good fortune, with his warm fighting companion, to be the victor in the three struggles in which the teams engaged. And when it was over, he was almost reluctant to help her lithe and graceful body untangle itself from his neck and arms.

"I told you, you picked a winning horse," he laughed.

"You're the best horse I ever had," she laughed in return. "I'm definitely going to run you in the next Derby."

The other four were swimming, now farther away, and Andrew continued the conversation. Whatever it was about her, whatever the chemistry of her lovely body, he did not want it to disappear from his life any time soon. It had been a chance meeting, but he felt totally hooked.

"Does the winning horse get a prize or reward?" He joked.

"Well, Mister Horse," she joked back, "I have already planned your reward."

"Tell me."

"You will come with us to our picnic at Ford Field."

"How do you plan for us to get there? It's quite a ways from here."

"My father will send a car."

"That's nice," he said. "Will there be room for me?"

"There's always room for a good horse," she punched him on the arm.

"My name is Andrew. What's yours?"

"You may call me Miss Boutin."

"How do you spell it?"

"B O U T I N. But it's pronounced Boo-tan. I'm French."

"Do you have a first name??

"I have one but you may not use it yet."

"Tell me anyway."

"I'll tell you, but you can't use it until I tell you. My first name is Laura."

"What if I just call you Laura?"

"I will kiss you until you suffocate," she said with firmness. "You will not be able to catch your breath. I will kiss you until you can't bear it any more. You will cry for help." She said these things without changing expression. Andrew did not know if she was serious. Her response was certainly unusual, and compellingly interesting.

Andrew smiled warmly. "Miss Boutin, I think I should be in exactly the right setting when I call you by your first name."

She smiled back with the same warmth. "I'm serious," she said.

"So am I," he said.

*

It was the best picnic he had ever experienced, until he did something stupid. He blended easily with her friends. Much joking and laughter. The games were fun. But about the time they were going to eat, a brief thunderstorm came over and drenched them all. Hot dog buns soaked. Potato salad full of water. Wieners only half cooked. The fire extinguished. But all of them reacted with jovial excitement and took everything in stride. The thunderstorm heightened the intensity of the experience. They all felt alive and full of laughter, bound by a new sense of comradeship.

Until Laura came out of the changing room at the pool, Andrew did not realize how beautiful her hair was, or how long. It was so black it was almost blue. It fascinated him. She let it fall straight down. And now, after the brief storm, her hair was fully wet, and clung to the lines of her body. Fortunately, the sun reappeared quickly in warm and breezeless skies. Andrew did not address her either as Laura or Miss Boutin in all this time. He was still not sure whether her remarks had been serious. He admired her physical form and was intrigued by how certain she seemed about everything. He kept thinking about that lingering warmth on the back of his neck. He wanted her in his life some way. Even though he did not yet have her, he didn't want to lose her. The source of the warmth seemed unattainable, but he wanted it near him.

The stupid thing occurred when they were all lighting Fourth of July firecrackers. The two other boys had brought some super jumbos, almost small sticks of dynamite.

"I bet we could blow that telephone pole in half," Roger said.

"Why would you want to do that?" Laura asked.

"For fun," Roger said.

"Grow up!" she said with authority.

For a while they left the super jumbos alone, until all the other firecrackers were gone. But Andrew remained curious about the telephone pole remark. He wanted to test the theory. With all of them watching, he lodged a super jumbo into a large crack in the nearby pole, then lit it. He quickly ran back to a safe distance, then waited. And waited. And waited. No one spoke.

"Must have been a dud," Roger said. They all agreed.

Andrew walked cautiously toward the pole to remove what he though was a dud. And as he came near, the super jumbo exploded. The force of it knocked him down. His eyes were full of something. They stung. He could not see.

Laura was first to come to him. She knelt over him as he struggled to regain his vision. He felt her long hair falling along both sides of his face.

"Are you hurt?" She asked with concern.

"I don't know. I can't see. My eyes are full of something."

"I'm going to get you a doctor."

"No!" he said firmly. The thought ran through his mind that doctors cost money and he didn't have any. He was raised on a culture that shunned doctors except as a last resort. You only go to a doctor when you are dying. Like an Indian.

"Are you sure?" she asked. "That was a great big huge firecracker."

"Just let me lie here for a minute. Then I need some water to wash out my eyes."

She immediately went for water. The other boys and girls were standing around him, not knowing what to do. "I guess it wasn't a dud after all," he could hear Roger say. Then Laura returned with a bucket of water. "Thanks," Andrew said. "You guys go on with the party. Don't pay any attention to me. I'll be all right." He felt self-conscious with all of them gathered around.

"Vamoose!" Laura commanded, and they obeyed her. "I will stay here til you are okay," she said. "I'm not going to leave you."

Andrew held his face over the bucket, repeatedly bringing handfuls of water into his stinging eyes. This went on for some time before he gradually regained his vision. Laura was sitting patiently at his side. And when he finally found he could see again he noticed darkness had fallen. The other four had gone to the area of the field where a large fireworks display was about to take place.

"Why don't you go with your friends?" Andrew said.

"I'm staying here with you," she said.

"You'll miss the fireworks."

"You are more important," she said. "Definitely."

"Are you sure?" He blurted. He didn't know why he said that. It was the first thing that came into his mind.

"I'm sure of everything I say."

He looked into her eyes and studied her face. "You have very beautiful eyes. Even in the dark I can feel their sparkle."

"So do you," she said. "Your eyes have a special strength."

"Well, thank you for helping me get them back. For a while I thought I would be blinded for life."

"I wouldn't let you," she said decisively.

He studied her face again. "Thank you, Laura," he said. He did not call her that name as a provocation. Rather, in the events that had followed throughout the day and evening, he had simply forgotten the "Miss Boutin" stuff.

"I warned you," she said.

She pushed him back down on the grass, then began to kiss him with great vigor. She was a wonderful kisser, with a combination of gently chewing teeth, exploring tongue, suction tender and strong, and all the rest.

"You're not kissing back," she breathed.

"I was stunned," he breathed back. And then he began to follow her lead, to kiss her in the same way.

"You're a good kisser," she said.

"You're the best in the world," he said.

They embraced fully, Andrew now beside her.

And as she continued, speaking breathlessly directly into his mouth, she told him again. "I will kiss you until you suffocate. You will be gasping for breath. You will cry for mercy."

"If I'm going to die, this is the way I want to go."

"You will not die. I will keep you for another day."

"You are always so positive about everything," he said.

"Shut up. I haven't finished with you yet," she said. "I will suck you to glory. I will suck the life right out of you." And she added even more dimensions to this ancient art. She would suck his mouth somewhat like the way you would suck on a long, large chunk of Vermont cheddar cheese—lots of squeezing and tongue action. "Are you ready to cry for mercy?" she breathed into his mouth.

"I don't want it to end," he breathed back. "I want no mercy."

It was only when the other two couples were visible in the distance that they uncoupled their embrace.

"Do you realize," Andrew said as he saw them approaching, "we kissed all the way through the fireworks?"

"What fireworks?" She poked him hard on the arm.

Just before the others were within earshot, he asked, "Who are you? Really?"

"That will take you some time to know."

"I think I would like to know the answer," he said.

"Don't start something you're not prepared to finish," she smiled.

"I think it's already started. Can I see you again?"

"I would like that. Definitely. I will give you my address."

"Why do you want to be called Miss Boutin?" he asked.

"It keeps strangers out of my life," she said simply.

"Does it really?"

"Once someone is inside the gates, who knows what will happen?"

She called home and her father sent a car for her and her friends. She offered to take Andrew home, but he declined. On the trip from the pools the chauffer had brought his bike. Andrew rode it home.

As he rode through the darkened streets he could not stop thinking about her. I didn't know anyone in the world could kiss like that, he thought. Some lucky kid grew up next door to her, never realizing what treasures lay within his reach.

And he also pondered the brute similarities. In less than two months he had found himself in intimate contact with two girls. In each case the situation arose when he was injured. In each case the girls had taken the lead and he was swept along by the emotions of the moment. He wondered about his manhood. Weren't men <u>always</u> supposed to take the lead? He did not have enough information to answer this in his own mind. The similarities—the way it had come about both with Daisy and Laura—left a troubling aftertaste. But then his mind would turn to Laura, and all he could feel was a sensation of sweetness and strength. His own. Hers. And remembrance of that special warmth against his neck.

*

The poet wrote that April is the cruelest month but Andrew didn't think so. September could do it one better. Ever since their first meeting, Andrew would ride his bike to Dearborn every chance he got. And Laura would eagerly greet him. They shared the beginning of a mutual infatuation.

Andrew often brought his guitar and would play for her. They would go out into the gazebo of Laura's parents' large back lawn and talk endlessly, in between a continuation of warm kisses and gentle touching.

"Let me know when you're ready to beg for mercy," Laura

would whisper. "I never beg. It's not in my nature to beg," he would whisper back. "Then this will go on and on and never stop," she would whisper again. "Hooray for forever," he would gasp. "I want to live forever."

*

There are anger bombs in families, underneath the manicured face of the world. They lurk unexploded below the surface of daily events. Who knows what sets them off? The Boutin bomb exploded in late September. Laura met him in tears. He held her for a while, then they went back to the gazebo to talk.

"My parents are separating," she told him.

"I thought they were very happy."

"So did I. They must be great actors. It hit me out of the blue. Surprised the hell out of me."

"But why?" he asked.

"Something that happened a long time ago," she said.

"Is it serious?" he asked.

"Very serious."

"Are they going to get divorced?"

"Catholics don't get divorced. They're separating... I think forever."

"Isn't that the same thing?"'

"Not if you're Catholic."

"This must be tearing you up inside."

"My insides are all mush. I pray to the Holy Mother all the time. I think she can't hear my prayers."

"When are they going to do this?"

"Very soon. Maybe next week. My mother is packing our

bags now."

"Where will you go?"

"My mother is going to write a book. She will get a teaching position. She is very religious. She wants to write a religious book about the stupidity of war. She says that if women had their way, we could all talk things out. There would definitely be no more war."

"Maybe," Andrew said so quietly Laura never heard it.

"What are we going to do?" she asked.

"I don't know," he said.

"Will you write to me?"

"I am no good at writing letters. I hardly ever write. I don't know what to say."

"Just write what comes into your head," she said.

"When I sit down to write, my head gets full of confusion. Then I think I'll wait til my head clears, but it never does."

"If I write to you, will you write back?"

"I'll try. I can't promise, but I'll try."

"You have to write first," she said.

The sweet, salty, strangely delicious taste of her teardrops lingered on his lips long after she was gone.

*

Edison Elementary had not changed in character as Andrew entered eighth grade. Within a month he had already become engaged in a duel of logic with his principal teacher, Gerald Pimsmucker. Pimsmucker was short, prematurely balding, wore round glasses, and had unusually round puffy cheeks. Pimsmucker one day posed this question to the class:

"You have two people sitting on the curb. They have no access to food. One of them sits there and waits. The other each day walks one block for a single peanut. Which one dies first?"

After some discussion, Pimsmucker gave the answer. "The first one to die is the one who walks one block every day for a single peanut."

"But why?" Andrew asked.

"Because it takes more energy to walk two blocks than the peanut gives back. What I am saying is you waste away faster."

"I think you're wrong," Andrew said.

"Why?" Pimsmucker asked with a startled expression.

"You forgot to include something."

"What?"

"You forgot to say the one who walked every day for the peanut was filled with hope. His hope would keep him alive longer."

"That's a dumb answer," Pimsmucker said, and closed the discussion.

But it did not shut down the process of thinking in Andrew's mind. Without having words to articulate his thoughts in neat formulations, he came to two related conclusions.

First, it had become clearer than ever that he must not take what people told him necessarily as fact. He must be prepared at all times to challenge assumptions and dogmas.

Second, he sensed that much of what he was being taught was really theory, presented in the cloak of fact. From what he had learned about the world so far, it seemed to him that much of human life is governed by theory. People call it fact to create the appearance of authority, to get their way. The truth about reality is constantly being hammered into strange shapes to fit the prejudices of the "truth pronouncer." Education is not kid stuff, he concluded. It is full of tiger traps.

*

Andrew continued to play guitar with Daisy, but she was becoming more distant, as though he had done something nameless and unforgivable to her. And as her aloofness grew, he gave back the loaned guitar. He had earned enough money working for John Henry to buy a used guitar of his own. And John continued to employ him on the trucks, so he was sure Daisy had not told him. John could be a man of wrath.

With Laura gone, he felt a kind of emptiness that would not go away. He sat down to write a dozen times, but could not begin. He kept throwing his awkward words into the wastebasket.

In the meantime, life with Joe Moran was pleasant and constructive. Joe was easy to live with, and always ready to give him assistance when he needed it. Besides, Joe was spending a lot of time away from home too. He had met a Polish woman, named Jessica, a dark haired oval-faced Canadian from Montreal, who had come to Detroit to recover from an abusive marriage. Joe was smitten with her. All signs pointed to a long term relationship. "I think she'll make you a good mother," he said.

In October, Andrew asked John Henry for the location of the USO where Zeedie was entertaining war fighters. John told him without hesitation. And Andrew decided he would visit her. On a Saturday evening he put on his dress slacks and a clean shirt, and took a streetcar downtown hoping to find her.

165.

He found the USO easily and went inside with a crowd of sailors. He had no trouble blending in with the crowd. He looked more mature than his age, and he saw several men in uniform who looked as young as he. A USO hostess gave him coffee and doughnuts, which he eagerly accepted. There was music and dancing and a cheerful atmosphere throughout the large and thronging hall. He saw no sign of Zeedie, but decided to wait, sure she would show up.

And when she finally did appear, she was so busy socializing she did not notice him among the crowd. She was wearing a bright red dress that hugged her still-slender figure. She had grown her hair longer and wore it down along her shoulders. In her eyes Andrew could see a renewed radiance. She had looked quite tired the last time he had seen her. He decided he would wait for a while until she noticed him.

One time, as she passed within three feet of him captured in conversation, he almost spoke, but thought he would wait longer.

"Look at that one," a soldier next to him pointed out to his buddy. They were looking at Zeedie.

"She looks spiffy," the first solder said.

"I'd like to have a piece of that," the second said.

"Against the rules," the first one said.

"Shit on the rules," the second said. "We got a war on. We can break the rules."

But they made no such attempt. Rather, they turned their attention elsewhere and in a short time were dancing with two other hostesses. And finally, Zeedie spotted Andrew and came over to where he was sitting.

"What are you doing here?" were her first words.

"I thought I'd come down to see where you work." He noticed she was not chewing snuff.

She pulled him aside, to a corner where they could have a more private conversation.

"You can't be down here."

"I won't make any trouble."

"Trouble's just you being here."

"I guess I'll be going then."

"You gettin' along with Joe?"

"Sure."

"I hear he's got him a new woman."

"I wouldn't know about that."

"You got no eyes?"

"I almost went blind a few months ago."

"How'd you do that?"

"Got too close to a super jumbo firecracker."

"Well, you should have better sense."

"I'm okay now. How are you?"

"I'm supporting the war effort on both ends," she chuckled.

"Do you ever get any free time?"

"I guess not."

"Even on Sundays?"

"Sunday is my busiest day."

"Well, I'll see you."

"You be good," she said, kissing him gently on the top of his hand, almost in courtly manner. He was too tall for her to reach his forehead. And he returned home. He didn't know exactly what he felt. Only a terrible yearning inside. A restless churning.

*

Mr. Pimsmucker asked the class to list their three top ambitions. "What do you hope to achieve in life?"

Andrew gave serious thought to confessing his ambition to change the world. But he finally rejected the idea. He thought anyone seeing it would simply laugh. Instead, he decided to make a safer list, things that would enable him to get through the exercise without derision. He listed: 1. Pilot, 2. Aeronautical Engineer. He searched his mind. He could not think of a third thing. Then it occurred to him that one of the Henry clan was a tool and die maker at Ford. Andrew listed this as his third choice.

On the morning the lists were turned in, he found that Mr. Pimsmucker had a further agenda. Each student would stand in front of the class, read the list, and Pimsmucker would comment. Students were called by rows rather than alphabetically, and since Andrew sat by choice in the last row, his name was almost at the end.

The routine was that a student would read the three choices and Pimsmucker would make generally supportive comments. Until it was Andrew's turn.

"The first choice I put down is to be a pilot," he said.

Pimsmucker interrupted as soon as he said it. "You don't have the brains to be a pilot."

"Why?" Andrew asked, in serious wonder.

"You are prematurely complex, you see everything in too many ways at once."

Pimsmucker spoke with a guarded excitement, as though he

were announcing the discovery of a new disease.

"What's wrong with that?"

"You can't live life that way," he said with an air of finality. "You see what I'm saying? What's your next ambition?"

"Aeronautical engineer," Andrew said.

Pimsmucker laughed out loud. "It takes even more brains to be an aeronautical engineer than it does to be a pilot." Again he spoke with authority.

Andrew asked no questions. It sounded to him as if Mr. Pimsmucker were saying: You were born defective. Just stay that way. Don't come bother us with your fairy tales of what you can never do. Don't waste our time with these foolish ambitions. Stand there and tell the class you're an idiot.

"What's your third choice?" Pimsmucker asked with raised eyebrows.

Andrew hesitated. "Tool and die maker."

Pimsmucker smiled for the first time. "Now, that would be a good ambition for you. If you work hard and attend to your studies, if you really apply yourself, I think you could become a good tool and die maker."

What was left of Andrew's mortal remains returned to his seat, still trying to recover from the shock of the humiliation.

All through the remainder of the term, and through most of the spring semester, Andrew spent more time away from school than in it.

He loved the woods, the silence and peacefulness, the little bubbling brooks, the smell of freshness in the spring, or the musty odors of autumn as earth was reclaiming its own — the sound of birds, the rustling of small animals, the crackling of ice on a winter creek.

He spent many, many days exploring on his bike, walking with Guardo, fishing, or swimming naked wherever he could find suitable water and privacy. He developed a certain pride in swimming even through the colder fall months. He swam in September, October, November, and—breaking a thin coating of ice—even into December. It was his nature to continue to challenge himself to do more and more, and not to be necessarily bound by ordinary restrictions.

Sometimes in the later hours after dark, he would bike down to the Rouge River. There was a small parking lot over by the Dix Avenue bridge where he could get a larger view of the sky. The Aurora Borealis was profoundly visible in those years, with its striking rippling curtain of green folding over the darkened skies.

October was the best month. The renewed smell of burning autumn leaves in the suburbs, the melancholy lingering of sunlight among the wintering trees, the hush of the woods and ponds—all of it brought back bittersweet memories about Laura and Eileen. He thought of them both so many times, but in different ways. He kept thinking he should write to Laura.

The Principal of Edison Elementary, Mr. Good, finally got in touch with Joe Moran to tell him about Andrew's continuing absence. The first time was in December, when Joe simply told Andrew gently, "You have to go to school." The second time was in April, when Mr. Good demanded a meeting.

After the meeting Joe and Andrew had a heart to heart talk.

"You seem to be having some kind of problem, but you won't tell me what it is."

"I'll take care of my own problems."

"But I want to help you."

"I don't need any help."

"What can I do?" Joe asked.

"Just what you're doing. Be a good guy."

"I think that's not enough."

"It's all I want."

"Andrew, you can't run away from your problems. You have to tackle them head on. I'm here to help you if you like. Don't push me away."

"I'm not pushing you away, until you lean on me."

"Well, I'm going to lean on you a little bit. You have to go to school. Will you promise me?"

Andrew hesitated. He knew if he made a promise he would never break it.

"Promise?" Joe repeated.

And finally, Andrew said "I promise."

Back in school, Andrew was summoned to Mr. Good's office. Mr. Good did not know of Andrew's promise to Joe, nor was Andrew about to tell him.

Andrew could not recall the whole discussion with Mr. Good. He could recall the stern admonitions and the serious voice. But only one thing stood out in his memory.

"You are the champion school-skipper of all time!" Mr. Good had said.

Champion! Andrew thought. Wow! A Champion! I'm a

Champion! He wrote the word in indelible ink across the back of his favorite shirt, <u>Champion</u>!

On June the sixth the invasion of Normandy began. The war was beginning to move toward conclusion. And later that month Edison Elementary graduated Andrew so that he could begin high school, ignoring his months of failure.

Through July 1944 Andrew worked alternately on John Henry's moving trucks and weeding the Rouge River garden. One of his greatest sensual experiences was to pick a big ripe beefsteak tomato, its juices still bubbling from the warmth of the sun, wipe it off, and eat it straight from the vine. He carried a salt shaker in his back pocket to intensify the lingering pleasure of its sweet warm taste.

He did not see Daisy very much, but when they did encounter each other, their discussion was brief and polite, as though no emotion had ever passed between them. Whatever it had been, however brief, was dead as a rock.

More than nine months had passed since he had seen Laura. She did not write. Nor did he. He wondered if she were just being stubborn, determined not to swerve from her command to him to write first. He thought about her a lot, but her memory was beginning to disappear from him. She was still dancing in his consciousness, but each time as she would whirl into his mind with that special warmth within her, with that long hair flowing in the wind, she would alight farther and farther away. He began to think maybe it had just been a fling, a brief summer romance, without enduring consequence. And in time he wondered if she had meant all she had said. And even as she receded more and more into the shadows, he could not help thinking: But it was so real! It had seemed so <u>real</u>!

The letter from Clara came at the beginning of August. "Your grandfather is seriously ill," she wrote. "He has been asking for you." Andrew quickly arranged to go to Lucknow. He now had enough money for the trip.

Chapter 11

Kenneth lay ill, but had rallied somewhat since Clara had written, and Andrew began immediately to help her minister to him. He kept a cool pail of water from the upper well at the nightstand. He helped her move him so that the sheets and pillowcases could be changed. He helped wash the bedding and dry it in the sun and wind. He brought warm chicken soup to sip. He emptied the chamber pot. He clipped toenails. He lit the coal oil lamp and read to him from the Bible. And when Kenneth gained a wakeful state of consciousness, he talked with him.

"I'll help get the apples picked and packed. I'll stay right here and help grandma run the farm. I'll stay here and take care of you til you're better."

"Andrew…" Kenneth said. His speech was a little more slow and halting. "Andrew, this is not what I want or need. You speak from your heart. But I want you to be wise as well."

"I can do it," Andrew protested. "I can help run things until you get better. I won't leave you."

"I've sold the whole orchard, all the fruit, to a grower in Guelph. Every apple. He will send his men and trucks to do the picking…"

"The same way you always sold the cherry and plum trees?"

"Not exactly the same. The grower has no interest in fallen apples. Only what he can pick …So you can have all from the ground you want. There will be plenty to make good applesauce and juice."

"But you will need help to get the garden in…"

"I've arranged for that. I've hired McGuiness and his son to help your grandmother."

Andrew continued to protest. "There's so much to do. I won't go back to school til you are well again."

"Andrew, everything is under control here."

"You are more important than school."

Kenneth looked at him with old, wise and compassionate eyes. "If you stay out of school, that would break my heart."

Within a week after Andrew's arrival, Kenneth got out of bed and began to walk around and do things just like his old self. Clara said his recovery was remarkable. And it was only then that Andrew thought he might have time to visit Eileen. Kenneth told him to go ahead. "I'm fine," he said. And the sense of alarm was lifted. It seemed like former times. There was no thought of calling a doctor. In this respect the Camerons were like the Henrys.

*

It was one of those serene August mornings when Andrew headed down the side roads toward the Riddle farm. Sunlight and birdsongs. Gentle breeze and gentle bees caressing flowers of the fields. He remembered the last time he had seen her, the beauty of the longing in her eyes. How much he had wanted to stay with her, protect her, cherish her young innocence. He wondered if she would be home, if she would be happy to see him. He wondered how she had been. Her letter suggested times

175.

were hard. He wondered if there were any way he could help.

As he walked up the lane he noticed the disheveled condition of the Riddle home. Two windows missing. Many loose shingles. Chipping and flaking paint over the wooden structures around the brick. It seemed to have fallen into a state of disintegration. No one was around. There was no dog. Dogs ate too much. Not even a barnyard cat.

He went up the steps. The front door was cracked open. He knocked. No one came. He went inside. He saw that half the floorboards in the living room had been ripped up for firewood. Some unburned remnants showed in the fireplace. He walked along the supporting rafters to the other side of the room. The cellar door was open. He looked down. All the steps to the cellar had also been removed. Apparently for firewood. Hardly any furniture remained. Flies and insects everywhere.

He went out onto what was left of the back porch. He saw Eileen coming in from the morning field, carrying a small basket. As she caught sight of him she ran toward him in bare feet. But halfway, she stopped and seemed to freeze. She was looking to the side of the house, where the lane ended. Andrew moved from the porch and walked to the place that had frozen her gaze.

Billy Lyons was a big and husky local boy who lived several farms away. He was fourteen, attended school in Lucknow, was somewhat retarded, but functionally capable. He had pale, blue almost colorless eyes, a thick head of straight straw-like hair, and walked with a swaggering gait.

Billy was holding a hunting knife as he approached, straight down by his side. Andrew did not yet know his intent but moved into the lane to physically block his path.

"Who are you?" Billy asked.

"Andrew Cameron."

"Oh, I know them Camerons. Camerons are okay. Get out of my way."

"Why are you here?" Andrew asked.

"To see Eileen."

"I don't think she wants to see you."

"Yes she does," he said. "Yes she does."

"I say she doesn't."

"Cock-a-doodle doo!" Billy shouted.

"What in the hell is that?" Andrew asked.

"You know the difference between a rooster and Eileen?"

"I'm sure you're going to tell me."

"Rooster say cock-a-doodle doo! Eileen say any-cock'l do! She's a cock'l-doodle-do girl."

"Billy go home!"

"You can't make me," Billy said defiantly, holding the hunting knife menacingly in front of him.

"Maybe I can."

"Maybe I can! Maybe I can!' Billy mocked.

"Go home!" Andrew said again.

Billy took a step closer, the knife in front of him. Andrew quickly removed his shirt, wrapped it around his left arm and hand.

"You think you can scare me?" Billy said loudly.

"Billy, I don't want to scare you. Go home!"

Billy took another step forward. Andrew held his left arm in front of him, positioned his feet for rapid action, then looked Billy hard in the eyes. Billy soon blinked, and Andrew knew he would back down. Which is what he did. Billy turned, his head hung low, and walked slowly down the lane, back where he had come from.

"You came just in time to rescue me," Eileen said. She had been at his side all along. Andrew saw that she was holding a big rock in her hand. "If he hurt me I was going to smash his brains out," she said.

For the first time, he looked at her, hardly seeing her, his mind still attached to the drama of the scene. "I guess I should say hello," he mumbled.

"This isn't the way I wanted to see you," she said. "I had a whole different picture of our first meeting in my mind ...I feel so miserable."

Why does Billy come here bothering you?"

"It's not just Billy. There's almost a gang of them. They think I'm easy pickings because I'm different. In school they will tape a sign to my back that says, 'Kiss me, I'm Irish.' Dumb things like that... but I'm afraid of Billy. He doesn't seem to have a normal mind." She saw Andrew looking at the basket.

"I've been picking berries for mom's breakfast, she's not very well. I make her some oatmeal and berries in the morning and fresh cow's milk." Eileen told him. "I guess I should say hello back." She seemed to wait expectantly for a moment, then picked up the basket. "Since you've already been inside, why don't you come in with me."

After preparing the oatmeal, using a small stick of cedar to heat the water, Eileen went upstairs to ask Sophie if Andrew could come up with her. "Can't do any more harm than's been done," Sophie said.

Eileen explained to him that Sophie was very sensitive. She would never let her bring any friends to the house. "I don't want them to see how poor we are," Sophie would say.

Sophie sat propped up against several pillows, eating the oatmeal slowly. What are you doing with yourself?" she asked Andrew.

"I'm going to school. High school now."

"So is Eileen. She graduated top of her class. Smart as a whip."

"I wish we lived closer together." Andrew said.

"So do I," Eileen agreed.

After breakfast, she took him into her spartan bedroom and told him to lift her pillow. He did. The letter he had written her lay neatly folded underneath.

"I sleep with your letter under my pillow. You'll have to write me another. This one's almost worn out."

The sentiment moved him deeply. He touched her tentatively, then hugged her for a long time.

"I am so deeply honored," he said.

"I meant everything I said," she said. "I have felt very isolated and lonely since you went away. I missed you like crazy."

"I missed you too," he said.

"Do you really mean it?"

"Yes, I mean it. I never met anyone like you. No one has

ever been as close." He thought for a moment about Laura. "No one," he said again.

"Can we go for a long walk together?" he asked. "Will your mother be all right? It's a beautiful day. Maybe we can swim."

"I'd love to walk with you. A long walk. Mom will be all right... swimming would be fun. I've been to the river since you left, but I didn't swim. I didn't want to swim alone. It's time we got acquainted again. Yes, it would be fun."

*

It was almost noon when they came to their favorite spot along the wild-grass shore of the 9-Mile River. The sun was high and a warm summer breeze blew softly across the field. The river had not changed in four years.

"I thought you might be swimming every summer," he said.

"I come here sometimes on warm days like this. But I only sit and look at the water, get my feet wet, and think about you."

Now that they had passed through the initial awkwardness of their reunion, all the stiffness quickly disappeared. It was as if no time had passed since their last summer together. Such was the strength of the bond they had made. It leapt across the bounds of time, holding them again in its nurturing grasp. And now they were together again, hurried and unhurried at the same time.

"Ready to go in?" Andrew asked.

"I've been ready for four years."

Andrew removed shoes, socks, shirt, blue jeans—all that he wore—without thought or hesitation, his mind operating on old reflexes. They were standing side by side, but she hesitated. "Are you sure you're ready?" he asked.

She slipped off her thin summer dress and sandals—all that she wore. And Andrew beheld her for the first time. The effect of her new appearance jolted him to the gravity of his bones. There was a certain untamed wildness in her beauty that quickly aroused a deep, almost animal instinct in him. Four years ago she had been thin, almost scrawny, with a hairless body, no hips and undeveloped breasts.

What he saw before him now was a powerfully moving vision of young womanhood, slender and colorful, full of new mysteries in her compelling beauty. She had never applied a razor to any part of her body, and the rich, golden orange hair grew in abundance in its absence.

"I look a mess," she said hesitantly.

"There is so much <u>abundance</u> in you… you are the most beautiful thing I ever saw."

For a few moments the faced each other with an innocence like the birth of creation, without self-consciousness. But then self-consciousness came roaring into their minds like a whirlwind, and nothing would ever be the same again. Almost in the blink of an eye, they passed from innocence into awareness.

"All I can think to say is… you are like a mountain, rising out of the forest," Eileen said. "What a gollywhopper. I can't take my eyes off it."

"I can't help it," he said.

"Can you swim like that?" she asked. "You'll die."

"I'm sorry. I can't help it."

"Andrew, I think we have become sexual beings."

"This changes things, but I'm not sure how yet."

181.

"What's to become of us?" she asked.

"I don't know. Maybe we are children of destiny."

"Why did you say that?"

"I don't know. It's just the first thing that popped into my mind. I was trying to think of something dramatic."

"Mother of Jesus, I enjoy looking at you," she said. "That's the first thing I thought of. You are one glorious beast. Do you think that's a mortal sin?"

"Sin is for grownups,'" he said. "I think we have to learn about sin. That's what the teenage years are for."

"It's scary just the same.

"It's hard to tear my eyes away from you," he said.

"We came here to swim," she reminded him.

"Okay. Let's go in."

"Are you sure you can swim like that?"

He smiled and took her hand, leading her into the water, helping her brace against the current.

"This is so cool and delicious," she said. "I don't know why I had to wait for you to do this."

Andrew plunged in, swam for a short ways against the current, then let it carry him back to her side. He held her by the waist, leaned her forward, and she began to stroke. But when he let go the current began to carry her away and he had to catch her. After a few more trial runs, they were swimming together side by side, just like old times.

And when they had had enough of swimming, when he could bear it no more, he swept her into his arms, holding her as though ready to carry her. Her arms swept around his neck and he stood with her in water up to his chest. The feeling of her bare body next to his own electrified all his circuits. He brought her face close to his, looked deeply with new awareness into her eyes, then kissed her on her parted lips, a long and lingering mutual exploration of their new being. "Even the cold water doesn't seem to affect you," she murmured.

He became so lost in the sensations of her response he forgot for a moment they were in a moving current in a dangerous river. The water knocked him down and her with him. And they tumbled in the cool rush several times before he could catch her and take her in his arms again.

"Now I know why five people drowned in this river," she said breathlessly.

"You will never drown with me."

"I love the rush of it against my skin. I feel so cool and clean."

And he held her against him and carried her over the rock-strewn bottom to the shore again, lying side by side against the grass, letting sun and breeze slowly dry them. Eileen took his hand, stroked his fingers, "I feel good again," she said. "This is so fine."

"Everything feels so natural with you," he said, as he moved his lips to the firmness of her breasts. "The sun has warmed you to perfect ripeness . . .My mouth feels a brilliant warmth. Can I hold you in my mouth forever?"

"You can try," she murmured stroking his hair.

He kissed her on the mouth, lingering in the warm sweet taste of her lips. "I feel a wildness in you. I guess it was there all along and I didn't notice it. I can't tell you how attractive it is."

"One of the things I like about you is ...nobody has ever tamed you," she said. And he began to stroke her gently, exploring, testing, bundling with new sensations. "This is what it must have been like on the first day of creation," he said.

"If you make me feel like Eve, I am going to start thinking about sin."

"Don't."

"I can't help it. It's my nature."

He moved his lips to hers again to hush the expression of thought. And then he moved his body over hers, but she pushed him away. "Not here!" she said with sudden alarm. "Not under God's sky!"

"Do you think he's watching?"

"I know he's watching."

He paused. "Let me know when you're ready," he said softly.

"Will you be all right?" she asked.

"I'll be just fine," he said.

*

On the way to the Cameron farm, she led him across the field where the bomber had crash landed. The airplane had been cut in sections and removed. Only ruts and furrows remained, now grassed over, the sharp edges gone. The fences had been repaired.

On the way to the house, they stopped under what had been their favorite maple tree and stood looking at it for a while.

"I don't climb trees anymore," he said.

"I haven't climbed a tree since you left."

"Well, I guess that part of our lives is gone."

"I think of us up there, lying in the branches, bending slowly in the wind. It was a good feeling," she said. "It would be wonderful if grownups could learn to do that."

"The best of all," he smiled, "was when you lay across me and I wrapped myself around you."

"I guess we're too big for that now," she said.

"I guess," he said.

Clara made a simple supper, homemade vegetable soup and chunks of freshly baked bread, lavished with butter from the pantry crock. Kenneth sat with them but only sipped a small amount of soup. He didn't say much and left as soon as supper was finished, to return to his bed.

After they washed dishes and cleaned up, Andrew and Eileen went outside again.

"Should we bring some soup to your mother?" he asked.

"She's all right. She can move around okay. There's food in the house. She just likes to stay in bed a lot."

"If she can't work, what do you live on?"

"The government gives us a little money every month. Not enough to live on, just enough to keep us alive."

"Come back to Detroit with me," Andrew said impulsively. "We don't have much, but we have plenty to share. Joe is a nice guy. He won't mind. You can go to school there. We can go to school together."

"I could never leave my mum."

"Bring her too. We have heat and shelter and food enough for all of us. I've been working after school. Your mom could get work. There's plenty of jobs. Most of the men are away at war."

"Mum would never do it. She's quite fearful. She thinks the Yankees don't take care of you when you get sick. They just leave you alone to die."

"Will you ask her anyway?"

"I'll ask but she'll say no."

"Then you come back with me."

"Andrew, I'm serious. I could never leave my mum."

"You're very brave," he said.

They talked through the remaining light of the day, into dusk, and finally when darkness fell, he walked her home. In a bedroom window he saw the light of a single coal oil lamp. All else in the house was dark and spooky.

"Maybe you and your mom could come live with the Camerons. There's plenty of room. And they both love you. I know they would say yes if I asked them."

"Mum's too proud. She wouldn't do that."

"There's so much work to do around the farm, with both of you helping, it wouldn't be a burden. More of a relief. Would you ask her?"

"I'll ask, but I know what her answer will be." Andrew held her close to him and she held him tightly in her arms. "I hate to leave you," he said.

"I hate to leave you too, but this is the way it's got to be," she said.

"I can't come over early in the morning," he said. "Too much to do first thing."

"I'll come over soon as I've taken care of mum."

And they held each other, neither one willing to let go. And they kissed for a long time. "Even by the stars of the night I can see your beauty," he said. "I can see little sprinkles of starlight in your eyes."

"You feel so strong and manly," she said.

And as he held her close, she whispered, "There you go again. Good Lord, what am I going to do with you?"

"Sorry about that," he said. "I can't help it. But I have a suggestion," he laughed softly.

"It feels good," she said. "It tells me you really care about me… can you walk home like that?" she murmured.

"I think this will get me through the side roads," he joked.

*

Next morning, after early chores were done, he saw her coming down the lane, and went to meet her. He picked sweet clover and they smelled the wonderful aroma.

"What a beautiful way to begin the morning," she said, kissing him gently. And he kissed back the same way.

"Let's just spend a quiet day together and talk, he said.

"I would like that."

"I have to go back in a few days."

"How can you come into my life, sweep me off my feet in the middle of a dangerous river, then leave?" she asked with a pouting frown. She added, "You know I'm kidding. I know you have to leave."

"Have you talked to your mom?"

"I talked to her. You know what her answer was?" Eileen

tried to imitate Sophie's expression, put her voice into a low throaty growl. 'Eileen,' she said, 'he's only thirteen! Thirteen!' But he's an old thirteen, I tried to tell her. 'Nobody can be that old,' she said, and that was the end of it," Eileen said.

"So the answer is no?" Andrew asked.

"The answer is no, but thanks for asking."

He caressed the golden orange ringlets in her hair. "You feel like silk," he said. "Natural silk."

"What you're doing to my head feels like heaven."

"Going home without you will be hell," he said. Andrew told her he had not been to the Bush since he got back, and they walked over the high ground and down the sloping field. The quietness of the countryside continued to impress him, after the steady rhythm of noise in Detroit. And where the field began to slope up to the Bush again, Andrew tagged her on the arm. "Race you to the fence," he said, and took off.

It was no contest. Even with her sandals off she could not keep up with him. "You like to run, don't you?" she said.

"Yes, I do."

"You run like the wind. You almost glide."

They moved in among the dense pines, over the floor of pine needles, almost the color of her hair. Even from the distinct quietness of the fields around them, once within the trees all sound seemed to vanish. No buzzing insects. No murmuring frogs. No sounds of tractors in the distance. Nothing at all except that sense of stillness he had always felt there. "I used to come here to think," he said.

"What did you think about?" she asked.

188.

"Sometimes I would think about you… sometimes I would think about my mother. But other times, what kept going through my mind is how messed up the world is, and trying to figure… there must be some way to fix it."

"When you thought about me, what did you think?" she asked.

"To be truthful, I was trying to figure out how I felt about you."

"What did you figure?"

Sidestepping her question, he said "My grandmother asked me if I have the sweets for you."

"What did you say?"

"I said that was my private business."

"Do you?" she asked abruptly.

"I think the answer would be yes," he said. "But I'm not sure I know what sweets means."

They were sitting now on the soft blanket of pine needles on the floor of the little forest. When Andrew mentioned his mother Eileen's face turned sad. "I remember what she did to you. You never told me, but I could see it in your eyes."

"She has some peculiar ways," he said.

"Last year my mum told me—this is exactly what she said— she said, 'This is a hard thing for a mother to say to a daughter, but things would be better if you had never been born.'" Eileen's eyes were rimmed with tears.

"Oh my God," he said, and brought her close to him, and held her in his arms. "My mother said the same thing about me, in different words."

189.

"Maybe all mothers have peculiarities," she said. He kissed her gently around the eyes, taking her salty tears into his mouth. "I feel so close to you," he said.

"I want to say don't ever leave me," she said in a whispering voice. "But I know you have to. Maybe there is something to this destiny business... why did you use that particular word when we were at the river?"

"Don't know. I said it without thinking."

"Do you believe fate and destiny are the same thing?" she asked.

He pondered her question. "I think fate is something trying to overtake you and bring you down like a wounded animal."

"...and destiny?"

He pondered again. "I think destiny is something you have to grab by the nuts and hold on til it hollers your name."

"You're very colorful," she said. "I like that. But what if destiny is a woman? What will you grab then?" She laughed a warm throaty laugh. She stroked his cheek. "You see with different eyes from other people."

"I don't know if I'm right. It's just the way I think... what does destiny mean to you?"

Now it was Eileen's turn to ponder the question. "For me, destiny is like a beautiful lover, with arms outstretched and waiting. Come home my lover is saying."

"Interesting how differently our minds work," he said.

"Do you remember four years ago you promised to tell me who you think I am?"

"I remember."

"Who do you think I am?"

He smiled. "You are a gift from the gods."

She punched him. "Be serious."

"You are a <u>serious</u> gift from the gods."

"Andrew, what am I going to do with you?"

"Something you've been doing, but more of it."

*

The day before he left a fierce thunderstorm lay headstrong, hovering in the clouds. Eileen had come all the way to the farm before it broke out. Before tornado-like winds and rains swept against the barn, where they had gone to talk and be alone. The powerful thunder seemed to rattle the foundations of the structure. And the rain fell hard on the roof.

"Feels good to be inside," she said.

"Feels good to be anywhere with you," he said.

They climbed up into the haymow and lay back listening to the storm, Andrew's arm around her at his side. "I love the smell of the hay," he said, "even when it's old."

"You haven't done a single somersault from the rafters," she said with a voice of understanding.

"I don't do that anymore. I almost killed myself doing that. I could even see my tombstone as I lay there wondering if I would ever be able to get up again."

"What did it say?" she asked.

"Here lies Andrew Cameron. Died of stupidity at the age of nine."

"But you couldn't do that," she said quickly. "Remember, our destiny is we are going to die together."

191.

"I forgot," he said.

"Don't ever forget who you promised to die with."

"You're being very Irish again."

"I can't help it. It's in the blood."

Eileen rolled over on top of him. She felt so light. She had a relaxed sexuality about her that made every movement easy and appropriate. "You have me in your power," he said.

"I think it's the reverse," she smiled ... "you know you have me in your power ...What are you going to do with this wild Irish beauty you've captured?"

"I'm going to set you free," he laughed. And she giggled.

By now they had begun to kiss and caress each other. They shed their clothes. And Andrew quietly began, without words, to teach her everything he had learned from Laura.

"I want to learn everything about you," he said.

"Don't hurry," she said. And he began his explorations.

"See what you're doing to me." she said in time.

"I want to taste you, too. You're like silk everywhere."

"I dare not touch you," she said. "I'm afraid to touch you."

He took her hand, held it within his own as he guided it.

"Andrew, I'm still a virgin. No one has ever got anywhere near me before."

"So am I," he whispered. "Sort of."

"Please stop me," she whispered.

"I don't want to stop. Your hand is so beautiful. Your body seems so warm. It's saying to me: Andrew, come here. Come home. Where have you been?"

"We <u>have</u> to stop," she said.

"If you want me to stop, I will."

"Oh, I want you to stop, I don't want you to stop. I have so many thoughts in my head I can't think them all." She paused... Don't stop."

In time her breathing pattern changed. She moaned, "Don't stop now! No matter what I say!"

After awhile she whispered, "Now you've really worked me up. You've got to finish me off. You Scots have a saying: Never wound what you can kill."

He laid his body on hers, propping himself, so as not to crush her. And she moved to bring him to the tree line at the edge of the summit to paradise. "Eileen..." he began to say. But suddenly she seized him. She gripped and held—that strong Irish grip—he could feel himself throbbing against her firm and slender fingers.

"First, say the words!"

"What words?" he asked.

"You know. Just say the words!" Her mouth was flushed and open.

"I don't know what words you mean."

"Say the words!" she said again. But again he said nothing.

She pushed him away gently. "I can't let you do this. Not this way." A single tear ran down her cheek.

"I don't understand," he said, still prepared. "What words?"

"I love you, you idiot!"

He pulled back, felt himself lying alongside her, his mind swirling with confusion.

"I'm not used to those words," he said slowly.

"Some things you just <u>know</u>," she said.

"I never grew up with those words," he said. "Those words were never spoken in my home or in any home I've been in. I would have to get used to words like that. I can't just blurt them out of the blue... If I said them now, it would be a lie."

"I don't care," she said, still in tears. "Make believe would have been enough... Needing someone is hell."

"I hate to see these anxieties in you."

"Andrew, I'm at a time in my life where things get really big."

"You're closer to me than anyone I have ever known, except my grandpa."

"How can I make you love me?" she asked.

"I don't know how much closer we could ever be."

"I want to be better for you... I don't know how."

"I told you, you are a gift from the gods. I meant it."

"Am I more to you than just a friend?"

"So much more. So much, much more."

"Then why can't you tell me?"

"I thought I did."

They untangled themselves. Andrew knew it was over now. He became conscious of the power of the wind and rain against the barn. They both put on their clothes.

"It's just as well," Eileen spoke with sadness. "If I allowed you to have a sexual relationship with me, you would just fall in love with me on account of it and want to marry me as soon as we come of age... I don't want it to be that way."

"How do you know I'm not in love with you already?" he asked.

"You wouldn't say the words."

"Why is it different when you say three words?"

"They're very important, she said.

"But why?"

"It would tell me you are committed to me for all time."

"I told you in my letter you are in my heart forever."

"It's not the same."

They waited until the storm had passed before he walked her home. On the way Andrew asked: "You want to know a secret?"

"Yes," she said.

"This is the second case of lover's nuts I ever had. Hurts like hell. The first began on the banks of the 9-Mile River, with you." He began to laugh.

"Oh," she moaned. "I hurt you. I keep leaving you alone to die. I owe you one. Maybe two." She kissed him in apology.

"I won't die," he said. "Just feels like I should."

"How can I make it up to you?" She kissed him again.

"Someday maybe we will find a way," he said.

Every time he brought her back to that spooky house, he felt a sense of dread for her. If only she would listen, move to Detroit with him. And Sophie, too. It would be so much better for them. And for his peace of mind.

*

Kenneth managed to get up from bed and join them at the breakfast table. Eileen had fed her mother early and arrived in time to join them. It was a glorious morning after the storm, the air clean and bright and freshly washed. Even the fragrance of the grass and flowers seemed renewed again. The open windows of the summer kitchen let it all flow through.

After saying grace, Kenneth said, "Eileen, it would be a blessing if you and your mother could come stay with us. At least until the war is over."

"Andrew's been talking to you," Eileen chided.

"Only what you would say in his place," Kenneth said.

"Mum and I will survive okay. Thank you for your kindness, now and through all these years. I'm a survivor," she laughed.

Kenneth reached over, took her hand. "There's an old Scottish saying, well known to the Camerons: 'Keep your sword up.'" He smiled with warmth and graciousness. "Keep your sword up, Lassie!"

"I hope you live for a hundred years," she said.

"Whatever time I have," he said, "is of little matter. I have lived in Christ. I will die in Christ."

Andrew and Eileen helped Clara with the cleanup, then went outside. Andrew had arranged to hire a neighbor with a car to take him to the bus line, and it was almost time.

Eileen took him aside and showed him a straight pin, looked at him questioningly. She drew a drop of blood from her wrist, held it for him to see. And he followed her lead, holding out his wrist to her. She did the same with him and placed their wrists together. "This will keep you in my life," she said. "For how long, God only knows. I don't want to let you go."

"If you can find a way to come to Detroit, what I told you is a permanent offer. I want to be near you, too."

"You know I can't."

"Maybe things will change. Maybe Sophie's heart will

soften."

Kenneth and Clara assured Andrew they would be fine, and encouraged him to resume his studies.

"Just call, or write. I'll come back," Andrew said.

Eileen walked Andrew to the car and they kissed with great tenderness. "Til we meet again," he said. "Maybe God knows when or where."

"Til then, my sweet love," she said, but the words were so soft no one heard them, not even Andrew.

And as soon as the car left the driveway, Kenneth took to his bed, exhausted by the visit, instructing Clara that no matter what happened, she was not to tell Andrew anything about his failing condition.

Chapter 12

On the way home, Andrew contracted a severe case of food poisoning. He had eaten at a diner in downtown Detroit, near the bus terminal. The symptoms struck him on the way home. Twice he had to leave the streetcar to puke his guts out. He arrived home ashen and weathered. Joe was at work and the Henry house next door was quiet. He was grateful to have a place to lie down.

The next day, still recovering from the food poisoning, Joe brought him up to date on the local news. First, that he and Jessica would marry as soon as the divorce from Zeedie was final. Second, that Andrew had a job to do. "Your mother is giving me a hard time about you living with me. I don't know if she's trying to punish me in some way, or whether she doesn't want to let you go... I have a letter from the Friend of the Court saying I have to get written permission from her."

Two days later, after calling Sarah to ensure Zeedie would be there, Andrew put on a white shirt and tie, dress trousers, and made the journey to see her, not knowing what to think. He felt somewhat self-conscious about the formality of his appearance but reasoned that if he had to persuade her to write the Court, he should look his best. He wasn't sure what he would say to her. One thought kept recurring: make up your mind. <u>Mother, make up your mind!</u>

Zeedie had a pleasant bedroom in Sarah's home, cozy and

well lighted rather than large. She had not yet found a suitable place of her own. When Andrew came to the door, Zeedie did an unusual thing. She hugged him briefly. Zeedie was not given to displays of affection, so this surprised him.

"How've you been?" he asked.

"Been supporting the war. Welding and dancing. That's what I know how to do."

"How did you learn to become a welder?"

"Easy. They teach you everything when they're hard up."

"Is it hard?"

"Matter of fact, I'm pretty good at it."

"How's the USO?"

"Keeps me really busy. And the dancing keeps me young. They think I'm ten years younger."

"Well, we've got Hitler and Tojo on the run, so you won't have to do that too much longer."

Zeedie frowned and turned thoughtful for a moment. "Don't know what I'll do after the war."

"Joe said we need a letter from you for the Friend of the Court."

"Oh, that! Why can't he just handle the paperwork and keep me out of it?" Zeedie asked annoyed.

"He's trying to. This one has to come from you."

"Everything has to come from me!" she said with an exasperated sigh.

"Will you write it?"

"I don't know what to say."

"Just say what you think."

"I don't know <u>what</u> I think," she said. "I've got no time for thinking."

"What if I help you?" he asked.

"Would you do that, honey?"

Two displays of affection in one setting. Andrew was feeling a mild sense of confusion. She hardly ever called him honey. They were in her bedroom. She was sitting at her vanity, Andrew standing. There was no other chair. She had not offered to find one. She searched through drawers and found a writing pad, pen and ink.

"What should I say?" She asked

"What do you want to say?"

"You tell me," she said.

Andrew was now becoming annoyed. You're the mother! His mind was saying. You know what must come from a mother's heart. I can't go into your heart and drag the words out of you.

"Maybe you should begin: Dear Friend of the Court," he said at last.

She wrote that and stopped, waiting for him to continue. Now his annoyance was turning toward impatience and anger.

"You have to say it's okay for me to live with Joe."

"Is that what you want?"

"I thought that's what you wanted," he said, holding back the impatience within.

"It's what I had to do," she said.

And into his mind swept a whirling of all her old recriminations. See what you made me do! See what you made me do!

"Well, I'm here now," he said. "Where do we go from here?"

"Honey, you can see there's not much room here."

He paused for a few moments. "Dear Friend of the Court... I Zeedie Wheelock Cameron... being of sound mind and body..."

"I'm not going to say that. They have no business going into my mind and body," she said impatiently.

"Let's start over," Andrew said. "I, Zeedie Wheelock Cameron write this letter that you requested..."

Zeedie now wrote as he dictated, "to give my permission for my son, Andrew Cameron, to go live with my divorcing husband, Joe Moran..."

"What else?" she asked.

And somehow, her question opened up a flood of thoughts. He continued. "This is what I think is best... I am in no position to take care of him..." His mind awhirl with emotion, he went on, hoping in every word she would reject what he was saying, tear up the paper and tell him this is all madness, I will never let you go... that she loved him and somehow they would make it together, no matter what, fighting the battle shoulder to shoulder.

Zeedie looked up at him. "Is this what you think is best?" she asked.

It was the closest Andrew would ever come to pleading with her, he said quietly "I can earn a man's wages on John Henry's trucks. I've already been doing it."

"I know honey. John told me."

"It's not too late to change your mind," he said.

"Everything's already getting too late for me," she said. "Forever will have to wait."

Outwardly he maintained a stoic expression. Inwardly his mind was beginning to rage with passionate intensity. "I guess we should continue," he said.

"I guess," she said, taking pen in hand again.

"I realize... in doing this..." Andrew was struggling to find the words, "...that I am giving up my rights to this child... forever." He watched her write what he dictated, hardly willing to believe she would put such words on paper. He waited for her at every moment to stop, throw the sheet away, and begin again. But she did not.

As he watched her write the word <u>forever</u> the full storm of emotion blasted through him like a reckless tornado. She is giving me up forever! Abandoning me to the winds and wild dogs of fortune! Why can't she say No! I will never abandon you! I will never leave you!

The questions surged against the borders of his mind. What did I do? Why could I never gain the fullness of your love? What is it about me that makes me so unworthy of your love? You are giving me up forever! Why? Why? Why? Look at me! I am your son. You are throwing me away like discarded trash! Does my life have meaning? Did it ever have meaning? Where are my foundations? Am I a gnat you simply swat out of your life? Why? Why? Why? What more could I have done to make you love me?

If there is a God in heaven, tell me what I could have done! Can the stars descend from the skies and sit in a circle of light to bear witness to this awful event? God in heaven, if there is a God in heaven—she is throwing me to the wild dogs of fortune! She does not want me in her life! To share! To struggle together! To succeed and cherish together! She wants no part of me! Mother, you are giving up your only son! Why? Why? Why? As if all the Whys in the universe could give sufficient answer!

"You are being very quiet," Zeedie said, breaking into the maelstrom of his emotions.

"Just sign your name," he said quietly. She signed her name and handed him the sheet. He noticed there was a single tear in her eye.

"God gave you big shoulders because he knew the load you would have to carry," she said.

A drop of coldness came into his heart, which for the rest of his life he thought might not entirely disappear.

*

He missed Eileen more than ever. The vision of her natural loveliness played across his mind like tantalizing etchings. He held her eyes, her voice, her new womanliness close to him. He wondered again and again how his life might have changed if he had said those three little words. I was so close. She was so ready. What would she have been like when I lit the flame within? What would she have been like when it was over? Would she feel as close? Would I have felt as close? He wondered. How would our destinies have changed, if at all? Why does so much of the world, so much of life itself, hang in the balance of three words? Her sense of mysticism was most touching, and perhaps a little contagious—he felt, too, that they would see each other again. And what then? He thought of writing, but could not lift his spirit out of its depressed state. It seemed too hard. But then, she had not written to him either. The thought bounced around recklessly in his mind—maybe in the cool light of day she had changed her mind. Maybe she was embarrassed by how open they had been. Maybe she did not want him in her life. Maybe no one really wanted him in their life.

Chapter 13

Southwestern High was an experimental school, 1700 students, one of two in Detroit. But none of this mattered to Andrew as he settled in. He had promised Joe he would not skip school again, and he kept his word. He was dispirited, lonely, confused. He had never done homework in all his school years, and had no plans to break this habit. He wasn't sure he knew the difference between a noun and a pronoun. All that Kenneth had tried to teach him was beginning to fade from his active memory.

The school had set up three tracks of study—college prep, general studies, and vocational. During his first week, when choice of curriculum had to be made, a friendly senior, Daar Freel, took him aside and talked to him for more than an hour about why he should choose college prep and also advised him to learn to type. Andrew quickly rejected the typing suggestion. Typing class was all girls. He thought typing was for girls. Andrew thanked him but had no interest. He would choose general studies. His world view, his hopes to help make a better world, had faded into the shadows of his mind. He felt listless. The future looked dim, horizonless. He would just take each day as it comes.

The new teachers didn't lift his thoughts any higher. One, in particular, Mrs. Strange, began right away with what would become an endless refrain—"My mother loves me, my husband loves me. God loves me. I don't care if you don't love me." She would repeat this every few days.

Once, she broke the class into convulsive laughter when she said to one of the athletes "you're not going to pull any boners on me." At least she wasn't dull, not for a time anyway.

He spent a lot of time in sports, mainly track and football. He enjoyed their requirements for maximum energy. He could still do that. His buddies for much of the fall term were the two Petes—Palucci and Magnuccio. He jokingly called them Peter and Repeater. Both were among the top five athletes in the school. Both were girl magnets.

Which is how he met Kuki Holland. She was in the same grade as Andrew, but was one year older. Almost everyone was one year older. Somehow, he had entered high school a year ahead of normal age. Knowing this, he carefully concealed his age from his peers. He had already learned that girls do not like to go out with younger boys.

Kuki was stunning in appearance. Of Dutch and Swedish ancestry, she was slender, had straight-down silver blonde hair, a permanent and very attractive rose-colored blush in her cheeks, a black velvet eye-patch, and breasts that resembled two love torpedoes shot out of paradise. As a young child she had pulled at a tablecloth on which a hardcover book was sitting. As the book fell, the corner struck her in the center of her right eye and blinded her in that eye.

Kuki came from a family that had fallen on hard times during the Depression, moved to a poor neighborhood, and had not yet found a way to improve their condition. She was strongly drawn to athletes. She frequently wore black velvet to match her eyepatch. Black velvet seemed to stimulate boys to want to caress her.

Kuki was addicted to danger and liked to live on the edge, sometimes not knowing exactly where the edge was. She also had a masochistic streak that demanded to be punished from time to time, even if she had to engineer the punishment.

Andrew did not see these things in her at first. What he saw in her face was a look of startled innocence. What he saw in her body was a vision of exquisite beauty. The eyepatch drew him, unfurled his protective instinct. And those breasts—he had never seen anything like them. They excited his imagination. He wondered what they would look like unleashed with their torpedo-like love power.

He met her at a small party for athletes, the same day she happened to witness a rather spectacular touchdown he had made in pouring rain. She came near him to offer congratulations. "I like the way you run," she said.

"Good things always seem to come in pairs," was all he could think to say.

"Did you say good things or good times?" she said with a teasing smile.

"What should I have said?"

"You'll figure it out." She leaned back a little to show the full effect.

He didn't know what to say. It took some effort to keep his eyes off her breasts.

"You can look at my bosoms if you want," she said. "You

can look, but you can't touch. You know?"

"Sorry," he blurted. "I didn't know I was looking."

"I can tell when a guy is looking from fifty feet away."

"I guess you get a lot of practice."

"Are you a wolf?"

"I'm not sure."

"I like wolves."

He growled. She smiled.

"You didn't ask me my name yet. Are you shy? Or backward."

"Maybe a little bit of both," he confessed.

"I never went out with a guy who's shy, you know?"

"No. I'm not shy," he said, regaining his composure. "I was just thinking."

"Oh, you're one of the brainy ones. You think."

"Everybody thinks. Depends what you think about."

"I never went out with a brainy guy either, you know?"

"I'm not shy and I'm not brainy. In some ways I'm still a little backward… So what's your name?"

"Kuki. Kuki Holland." She paused. "Do you like me?"

"Hubba, hubba. There's something about you I really like."

"The same thing all the boys do," she teased.

"What does everybody like?" he responded to the tease.

"You know," she teased again.

"Tell me," he smiled again.

"Something nobody can have," she said.

"Never? Ever?"

"Not til I decide," she said with finality.

He was intrigued by her whole persona. He liked her and felt protective, but his attraction to her was more fascination than infatuation. They talked easily together, mostly about school and sports. They began to see each other regularly, whenever they could after that first evening.

Concealed within the innocent appearance she projected, Andrew soon learned she had an experienced passionate nature as well. He discovered this right away, on their first date. She was especially adept in use of the tongue, and a thousand little nibbly kisses she planted everywhere there was exposed flesh. What she did to his ears, one after another, aroused him to an unbearable pitch. And he gave back in kind.

"What are you trying to do to me?" she whispered breathlessly.

"Same thing you're trying to do to me," he said.

"It won't go anywhere. Don't get your hopes up."

"They're already up."

But she quickly taught him she had rigid boundaries with regard to placement of the hands and how far they could go. "Bosoms" were okay, but anything in the region of the groin was taboo. "You can't pet the monkey," she said, even as she held herself up to his searching mouth. From things she had said at their first meeting, Andrew assumed she was still virgin. He also assumed she was building up her appetite. Sometime soon would be a feast.

He began to understand the more complex, darker side of her nature soon after that. Sitting alone in the bleachers of the football field on a moonless late October night, after an extended period of kissing and fondling, she suddenly turned to him and said, "Hit me!"

"Why would I want to hit you?"

"I want you to hit me."

"I don't hit girls."

"Chicken!" she taunted.

"Why do you want to get hit?"

"Because."

"Because why?"

"Just because… because I need it."

He took his open hand and gently slapped her on the cheek. It was more of a caress than a slap.

"You don't hit very hard."

"That's as hard as I'm ever going to hit you. Maximum."

"But I didn't even feel it," she pouted.

"Let's change the subject," he said.

Then she hauled off and swung her small fist into his cheek. He looked at her but did not respond.

"Hit me back!" she cried.

"Kuki, what are you really looking for?"

"I'm looking for something important," she said immediately in a tearful voice.

He took her in his arms, held her close. "I really like you," he said. "I like to be near you."

"I'll make you hit me," she said. "Just you wait and see."

Whenever they were together, Andrew always walked her home. When it was not late, she would invite him in. This is how he met her younger sister, Mienda.

He was instantly fascinated with Mienda's eyes. They were the strangest, most beautiful color of blue—like blue from another world.

In his first conversation with her, he learned she was only nine, which surprised him. She looked twelve. She had long silver blonde hair like Kuki, had Kuki's slender form, but all else was different. Where Kuki was edgy, Mienda was soulful and quiet in nature. A sublime sense of peace and harmony had already begun to radiate from her young being. Kuki's main interests were boys and risky adventure. Mienda's main interests were scholarly learning and music. She was taking violin lessons and saw the violin as her great career goal. She longed to have her own instrument, but the Holland family was still too poor. She did not pout about it. She accepted their current condition with philosophical understanding. All she could do in the meantime was practice on the rather beat up violin in her music class at school.

Andrew almost immediately found more comfort with Mienda than the uncertain relationship he had with Kuki. Because Mienda was only nine, he dared not show his affection or touch her in any way. But when he played with the numbers he let his imagination roam into realms of a prolonged future romance.

Mienda 13, Andrew 17. No.

Mienda 15, Andrew 19. No.

Mienda 18, Andrew 22. Possibly.

Mienda 21, Andrew 25. Yes. That would work. He wondered where she would be when he was 25. He would wait if he could.

"Do you ever wonder what you'll be doing when you're 21?" he asked.

He saw her retreat into thought within her soulful eyes. He could almost see her mind at work. She put her hand on his arm, as though to help him understand.

"When I am 21 I will be finishing my third world concert tour," she said with confidence.

"You really have thought about it."

"I think about everything," she said.

The touch of her gentle hand, simple and innocent as it was, deeply moved him.

"You are a very intelligent girl. You think."

"What will you be doing when you're 21?"

Even though he had initiated the conversation, the rebound question caught him by surprise. He had never thought about it. He had thought vaguely of somehow saving the world from itself, but never specifically about what he might be doing in any given year. Startled for an answer, he blurted:

"Saving the world from itself."

"Do you think you can do it?" she asked, as though it had been a perfectly rational answer.

"Maybe we could do it together." They both laughed.

Andrew now made up his mind. He would buy a violin for Mienda for Christmas. He would work after school and on weekends on John Henry's trucks whenever work was available. Maybe even get a steady job somewhere. He would save everything he could to do this for her. Mienda had now become part of Andrew's attraction to Kuki. Kuki's desperate need for love made her seem greatly in need of a protector, and this reached into his heart. They continued dating as often as they could. They spent a lot of time talking over phosphates at Brenda's Ice Cream Parlor. Kuki loved cherry phosphates. She told him he was the only boy she was seeing. "I want to make you love me," she told him. "Really love me. I want you to be the first." "Is that a promise?" he asked jokingly. "I can't wait."

"Yes you can. Yes you will. You have to do it my way. You know?"

On Christmas Eve, Kuki had agreed to go out with Andrew, walk in the snow, see the Christmas lights together, then go to a party with some of the school athletes.

But Christmas Eve morning, when school was only half a day, she took him aside and told him she could not go out with him that night. "My mother's in the hospital. I have to see her."

"I can go with you," Andrew volunteered.

"No. I have to do it alone. Me and my dad. But let's do New Years' Eve for sure."

"Will Mienda be going with you?"

"She is too young. The hospital won't let her in."

Andrew had now saved enough money. He had bought a violin the Saturday before and decided to take it to Mienda. He wanted her to have it under the Christmas tree. So when he arrived that evening after dinner, he was shocked when Kuki's' mother answered the door, a glass of wine in hand.

"Are you okay?" he asked.

"What do you mean?"

"Kuki said you were in the hospital."

"Well, here I am. I never get sick. Andrew could once more see where Kuki and Mienda inherited their beauty.

"Is Kuki here?"

"She went out."

They were still inside the front doorway. "I brought something for Kuki, and something for Mienda. Can I put them under the tree?"

"Yes, of course. Kick that snow off and come in."

And as Andrew put his gifts under the tree, Mienda came downstairs to thank him. She put her hand on his arm—that innocent warmth again—and said, "I think this is going to be the best Christmas ever."

If only she were older, Andrew thought.

"Please ask Kuki to call me as soon as she gets home," he asked her mother.

"What's the latest time she can call?"

"However late it is, ask her to call. I'll be near the phone."

He walked home wondering what had happened. On the way, he decided to drop in briefly at the party they were to attend. Maybe Kuki had gone without him. But no one had seen her. The curious thing was that Roger Drummond, captain of the football team, had not shown up yet. No one knew where he was. Andrew did not have a suspicious mind and gave it no thought.

The parents were out and the teenagers had been drinking beer since late afternoon. One of the girls, Georgeann Wilcox, a girl with a large and pretty face with too much lipstick, took Andrew aside.

"Looking for Kuki?" she asked breezily. Andrew could see she was quite intoxicated.

"We were going to come to the party together," he said.

"Well, whaddayaknow?"

"Have you seen her?"

"Whaddya see in her, anyway?" Georgeann asked.

"We're just good friends. I like her."

"I bet you'd like me better. For sure."

"Why?"

"I got more to give."

"Must be the spirit of Christmas," Andrew joked.

"No. Really."

"I like you just fine, Georgeann. But Kuki and I are okay together."

Georgeann pulled back a bit, to fix him more exactly within her wavering eyes.

"She laughs at you in the locker room! She says you're too dumb to know what's going on!"

The sword of Kuki's imagined laughter cut through his heart. He was stunned. "How do you know?"

"Ask any of the girls," she said, then collapsed into his arms. He rushed to a phone to call an ambulance, but as he was dialing she came to her feet again and told him she was alright.

Kuki never called that night. Not until next afternoon, saying she was sorry, there must have been a misunderstanding.

"I want to see you. Now," he said. "Can I come over?"

At her door, Andrew told her to put on her coat he wanted to take a walk. "What happened last night?"

"Do you really want to know?"

"Yes."

Kuki paused. "I blew Roger last night. He said it was the best blow job he ever had. It was a Christmas gift."

"But you won't let me close to you," Andrew said, trying to recover from surprise. "You keep my hands in sort of a prison."

"That's different. I'm still a virgin."

"Kuki, I don't know what you are."

"Aren't you going to hit me?"

"I couldn't hit you any harder than you hit yourself."

"Bastard!" she yelled, and walked away and out of his life.

That was the last they officially saw of each other. Whenever they met accidentally at school, they both remained aloof, not showing any emotion. Their studied aloofness was, in itself, a display of emotion, and soon Andrew recognized this and began to relax about it. And Kuki found other close companions among members of the football team, and at school dances came to be known as the Jitterbug Queen. What he missed most was Mienda. There was no way he could see her now.

It seemed she was out of his life forever.

*

Andrew joined the Civil Air Patrol as a Cadet. Now he felt he was becoming a tiny part of the larger picture. As the war continued, he had visions of himself learning to fly, patrolling borders, intercepting saboteurs slipping across from Canada. In reality, it was not dramatic at all. There was the beginning of some military discipline, a lot of homework, and occasional rides in an old open-cockpit Ryan PT-22. But it was as close as he could come to enlisting in the front line war effort. He loved to fly and decided he would take flying lessons as soon as he could earn enough money. All the pilots he met were mature, friendly, generous, and responsible. He liked their company.

*

In the meantime, he came to know Jessica Lavenda and found her a welcome addition to his life. Joe married her as soon as the divorce from Zeedie was final. It was done quietly by a Justice of the Peace. There were no witnesses except as required by law.

Before she met Joe, Jessica had known only six lovers. First was a high school sweetheart in Montreal whom, in a moment of intense passion she let go too far. Second was an abusive husband whose emotional and sometimes physical torment left her self-esteem in shreds. Third, fourth, and fifth were part-time sequential lovers whom she stopped seeing after a few months of concluding they were not right for her. Sixth was a man she lived with for two years, and who shared with her a strong chemistry of attraction. Until now, this had been her greatest love. But it could not culminate in marriage because of his need to drink too much and too frequently. To make it worse, he became abusive when drunk. She didn't want to be hooked up to a loser. She left him and moved to Detroit.

Jessica was Montreal–born, pleasantly attractive, and spoke English with an unusual combination accent that was part Polish, part French Canadian. She had dark hair, brown eyes, and more weight than she preferred to carry, which she was always trying to lose. She would not tell her age, but Andrew guessed it was somewhere near Joe's, maybe a little older.

Jessica's personality projected an immediate sense of down-to-earth common sense practicality. In this respect she seemed to be a mirror image of Joe. But she was much more uninhibited than Joe. Where Joe was rather bland in speech, Jessica's comments often sparkled with color and earthiness. She spoke her mind freely, swore when she had to, to get a point across.

Andrew's introduction to Jessica was a bit unusual. Joe took him to meet her, for the first time, where she was still living in an upstairs flat on Vernor Highway. As they shut the front door Joe called out "Jessica," then opened the bedroom door. Jessica was in bed with only a sheet covering her. At the opening of the bedroom door she moved her legs to kick off the sheet. She slept naked and for a few moments Andrew was introduced to all of her at once. A large, bushy black forest seemed to extend halfway to her belly button.

Joe quickly put the sheet over her. "I forgot to say we have company."

But Jessica was not bothered. She seemed to be comfortable in her sexuality, not at all fidgety, and Andrew liked that about her. None of the stiffness of Zeedie.

"I heard a lot about you," she said.

"I guess we'll be okay together," Andrew said.

He liked her earthiness. Soon after Jessica moved in with them, he overheard a brief conversation she was having with Joe, about a mutual acquaintance. "He's so tight," Jessica said, "he squeezes his shit twice."

Another thing Andrew liked—Jessica did not try to build walls around his relationship with Zeedie. She did not say or do things that made him feel he was in the middle of complex adult relationships. And Jessica and Joe seemed to have an easy relationship, none of the tension he remembered when it had been Joe and Zeedie, or even his father and Zeedie.

Next door, John Henry suddenly died of a heart attack.

Andrew felt great sadness at his death. John had always had a fatherly relationship to him. Zeedie did not come to the funeral. Andrew expected she would be there and was disappointed when she did not come. But in the back of his mind, John's death caused Andrew to wonder—what had been his <u>exact</u> relationship with Zeedie?

*

With Kuki out of his life, Eileen marooned in Canada and maybe not interested anymore, and no word from Laura, Andrew felt lonely for female companionship. His mind seemed preoccupied with sex, now more than ever.

The war in Europe had accelerated to a feverish pitch. The Allied forces were pounding Hitler's armies into oblivion. On April 12 President Roosevelt died. It was a warm and beautiful spring afternoon in Detroit. Even the gentle setting sun seemed to have a touch of hushed sadness, none of its usual noisy spinning.

On April 28, in Italy, Mussolini was caught by partisans as he was trying to escape with his mistress. He had been traveling in disguise as a woman. The partisans killed them both, stripped them naked, and hung them upside down for all the world to see.

On Aril 30, in a deep bunker in Berlin, Hitler blew his brains out.

VE day, Victory in Europe Day, was celebrated on May 8 after Field Marshall Keitel signed the document registering Germany's capitulation. Unconditional surrender. No ifs, ands, or buts. Germany was crushed. It was a day of great exuberance, overflowing joy. People dancing in the streets, kissing strangers, feeling their bonds as a community emerging victorious against great odds. Japan had yet to be conquered, but these thoughts were put on hold for a while as the celebratory mood expressed itself.

Andrew was swept up in the great emotion of victory, the same as everyone else. And his high emotion led him into a desire to express his gladness in creative channels of thought. For months he had been admiring the view that one of his teachers unknowingly presented as she worked the blackboard. As she faced the blackboard, he composed a poem.

Miss Whittle's Ass

There was a young teacher named Whittle,
Who had a magnificent ass.
Each time she taught mathematics,
Each time she went to the board,
This trooper would sit at attention,
No part of him ever got bored,
His heart fixed on things not to mention,
To behold such rare beauty and class—
For all of the gods had assembled,
Perfection they tried to surpass—
And they did it, they did it at last
They fashioned that glorious ass.

Pete Palucci, sitting at the desk next to him, glimpsed some of what Andrew had been writing, and snatched the paper away while Andrew was looking out the window thinking of what to write next. Pete smiled broadly and quickly passed the paper on to someone else. Soon it was floating around the room, to gleeful expressions, out of Andrew's control.

Miss Whittle saw what was happening, told its current holder to bring it up to her, read it silently, then said, without any show of emotion, only a cool gaze and level voice, "Andrew, I want to see you after class."

Sandra Whittle was 24, a strawberry blonde with tantalizing brown eyes, voluptuous lips, and a thin waist. Your first impression would be that she could win any beauty contest she entered. She would be Miss Everything. Your immediate second impression would be: She looks so well balanced, clean and wholesome, in great physical condition. She was also a gifted teacher. Mathematics was her specialty, but she also taught English. She had a bouncy, positive, fearless personality and a compelling wit that enabled her to reach into the minds of those she taught. She was full of life and had a smile for everyone around.

As instructed, he came to her classroom after school, sat on the chair beside her desk, and braced for trouble. But she disarmed him with her first comment. "You're the cat's pajamas." Her smile softened his tenseness. She unfolded the poem.

"I started to write about a pet donkey," he said, "but the words got away from me."

"You'll have to work on your innuendo, and your ability to

give a straight answer."

"I'm sorry if I offended you."

"On the contrary. You sparked my imagination."

"Mine is on fire all the time," he said.

"You will also need help on your poetic structure."

"I'll take any help I can get."

"I could tutor you."

"I wouldn't be able to afford you."

"No charge," she smiled warmly.

"Thanks. I know I need help."

"How old are you?" she asked.

He thought quickly. He didn't want to tell her he was still 13. "I'll be 15 in June," he lied. It startled him that he could lie so easily, so casually. He had only added a year, but a lie is a lie, he thought, and wondered if he were destined to become a liar. The thought raced through his mind and gave him pause. But he was careful to show no outward sign of his inward agitation.

"So you're still 14. You look 18."

"You look 22," he said. Her smile and general bearing gave him what he felt was the freedom to say that.

"Twenty-two will do," she said.

"How old are you, really?"

"Twenty-four," she said without hesitation.

"That seems so old," he said without thinking.

She changed the subject. Looking at his poem again, she asked: "What does sitting at attention mean?"

He blushed. "You know..."

"Have you always had that husky voice?"

He didn't know what to say, or where she was going.

"You really like my ass, don't you," she said with a smiling boldness that quickened the play of images in his mind.

"Especially when you wear those tight belts."

It was like a roundhouse to the jaw, waking his whole consciousness, when she added: "Do you think you could handle the real thing?"

"I can handle anything that comes along," he bragged.

"Meet me in the parking lot tonight at eight o'clock. This is a very special day. You can help me celebrate. I'll show you who's old."

"I think you're very, very beautiful."

She handed him the folded poem. "Eight o'clock."

"I'll be there. It's a happy day."

"I always end wars my own way," she said enigmatically.

Andrew came to the parking lot at eight. She put him in her car and drove about a mile to the flat she rented. All over the city the sounds of celebration filled the air.

"Quickens your blood, doesn't it," she said.

"Mine's pretty quick already," he said.

Inside, she poured herself a glass of red wine, but only offered him a sip. "Wet your lips," she said. She let her hair down and slowly removed all that she wore. Andrew began to do the same, but she stopped him. "I want to do you." And she did, item by item, kissing him gently, lingeringly, all the way down. "You're big for your age," she said casually. Her lips were as voluptuous as they looked. And her slightly rippled abdominal muscles were most sensuous to touch.

Everything about her was sensuous to the touch.

They began without preliminaries. And as they lay in close embrace, he was surprised at how slippery she was. It happened slowly, like rolling thunder. Holding him tightly within, Sondra brought him way beyond anything he had found with Daisy. She made him feel the world disappear into sweet oblivion.

"So this is what victory feels like," Andrew whispered when he regained his breath."

"I told you. I end wars my own way."

Outside, all through the city the joyful noises continued. Car horns. Fireworks. Banging pots and pans. Laughter. Joy.

And after a little while, as they held each other close, she said: "Can you do that to me one more time?"

"In about ten seconds."

"This time I'm going to teach you how to slow down."

"You're the teacher," he grinned.

And all through the second time she held him wrapped in a way to guide and control his rhythm. Slower, unhurried, more undulating. She seemed to like the lingering unbroken kiss as she rose breath by breath into the heights of her own sensual awareness, until in time she could only whisper "Don't stop. Don't hurry. Just keep doing what you're doing." In time she stiffened and gave out a sharp sweet cry filled with joy.

They lay back, Sondra running her fingers through his hair, caressing his face and chest, saying nothing for a while. Then she moved on top of him, and as she sat astride, bringing his hands to fondle her, she said: "Can you do that again? Just as slowly? But this time from behind? That's my favorite position."

"That's what dogs and horses do," he said, almost as a question.

"We are all part animal." She smiled in return.

"I want an A plus from you," he smiled in return.

She rose to her knees along the edge of the bed. It was the first time he actually saw fully what her clothes had hidden. Her natural self was more beautiful than he had even imagined. The softness of her flesh, the soft small contours fit so well into his hands. She arched her beautiful back so that what she offered was fully available to his ravenous eyes. The lusciousness of her offering stimulated every pore of his body to an almost animal— spiritual state of rapture as he entered her again. His poem took on a new reality. He never wanted to stop. He felt he could go on forever.

Over the years Andrew had seen young women in ads in bathing suits or something skimpy, so often with their butts waving toward his face. He thought they were merely trying to look cute. What he now began to understand was that those sexy pictures of stuck out butts were really intended to signify something else—an invitation to come in out of the cold.

She taught him how to rest in between episodes, gently stroking while never leaving her. And when at last they fell into bed again, her limp flesh molded to his own, she whispered: "A plus."

"What a teacher you are. I think you're the best in the world."

"How's that for an old woman?" she whispered.

"Old is good," he whispered back.

"What do you think of me now?" she asked.

"You're too beautiful to be a teacher."

"Why?"

"I spend too much time looking at your beauty. I don't hear everything you say."

"Do you still think I'm old?"

"You didn't feel old. Nothing about you feels old."

"You're just trying to butter me up."

"Miss Whittle…" he began, but she immediately put her finger over his mouth. "You can say Sondra, but never in school."

"Sondra… Why did you pick me? Was it the VE day? Was it the poem?"

"Some of both," she said. "VE Day aroused my spirits. Victory was almost shouting in my ear: <u>Do</u> something! <u>Do</u> something to celebrate."

"…And the poem, crude as it was?" he asked.

"The poem struck my imagination. It reminded me how long it's been since I felt a man… there was a hint of some mysterious religious quality in what you wrote. You spoke of gods, plural. The thing that really attracted me was that you seem to see something almost spiritual in me. Are you religious?"

"I'm not sure what I am. Sometimes I feel very religious. Most of the time I just forget about it. Religion and sex are so mixed up in my mind, I can't get them separated right now."

"But you seem to think of me almost in a religious way. That gives me a real rush."

"Right now I have no religious feelings at all. All I feel is intense passion for you. Even after the third time, my desire is as strong as ever. It doesn't go away."

"Andrew, you are so sweet I could eat you up... maybe I will." She kissed him gently.

"I'm a little hungry too," he responded, not knowing her intent.

"Do you want to know another reason why I picked you?"

"Tell me."

"I wanted to see the expression in your eyes when you blew my socks off."

"But you couldn't see me the last time."

"I could <u>feel</u> your expression! All of it!"

"So now what do you think?" he asked.

"You'll have to buy me a new pair of socks."

"Beginner's luck," he laughed.

"Do you realize we have made love for more than three hours?"

"I wasn't looking at the clock," he said.

"I wasn't either. It just jumped into my head." They took a shower together with lots of sudsy soap, and it was evident his passion for her was easily renewed. "There's plenty of life left in you," she said. "I'm not done with you yet. VE Day calls for prolonged, lingering celebration."

She poured another glass of wine and let him have a glass of his own as she dried her hair. She threw a fresh sheet on the bed and they lay back again, folded in each other's arms. "Do you know the word <u>engorge</u>?" she asked. Andrew had never heard it.

"This is an English lesson. When I'm done with you, you will never forget that word. Don't you do a thing. I'll do everything. Relax and enjoy."

She was right. He would never forget that word. She had a way of timing him, bringing him near then backing him down, bringing him near again, until it came out like an explosion. "You almost blew the back of my head off," she pouted.

And after they lay together for a while again, Sondra sipped some wine, then kissed him, sucking at his mouth.

"Now it's my turn. I'm going to teach you about preliminaries... Andrew, there are many other ways to satisfy a woman. Many ways. Let's do the whole thing. Are you game?"

"I'm not sure I know what you mean."

"I'll guide you. First your fingers. Follow my lead. You have strong fingers so keep the pressure gentle. The secret is to keep doing the same thing until you know when to stop." And she guided him with her gentle fingers. Every sensation seemed new. And she was as fresh again as in the beginning.

What she taught him to do with his hands seemed to create mysterious new fields of arousal.

In an almost lazy voice, she complimented him. "You're a quick study."

"I have a great teacher."

"Now for something extra, the bubbly at the end of the celebration ...Are you willing?"

"I'm willing to try anything."

"This time I want you to practice some gentle suction. Make sure it's gentle. Like an all-day lollypop. Let me hold your head in my hands."

This was beyond the boundaries of all his sexual dreams. He

accepted her leading, kneeling at the edge of the bed as she opened herself to him, fingers stretching.

"See that little red rosebud? That's your target. No, not there... higher... Yes. That's every woman's sweet spot. You can lick it and move your tongue around it for a while. Then you suck it—remember to be gentle—you hold it in your mouth and suck it until something wonderful happens. The sweet spot is small but very powerful. And when I come into your mouth, stay with me. Let it rest a little bit, then do it again, and keep doing it, again until you're tired. I don't want to wear you out. I want you to become the best lover in the world. Remember to be patient," she whispered.

He wondered how the hair below could be so stiff when the hair above was so soft and luxurious. He saw again and again the little muscles of her belly ripple before his eyes like a series of waves rushing to a waiting shore. And as he paused for a short time in between, he reflected on those rippling waves. It seemed like the beauty of the universe was unfolding before him.

And as the final ripples began to subside, he rose and moved boldly into a final communion, strong and powerful.

"That was beautiful, beautiful," she sighed at last. "Two beautifuls. We were really together. You shut down my whole brain for a minute. What a victory celebration."

"You are unbelievable," he whispered.

"So what do you think?" she whispered.

"I think I started at the top," he smiled.

By now it was five o'clock in the morning. The city noises had died, and only the energy of a victorious emotion lingered through the streets. She said she would drive him home, but he declined. He wanted to walk, to stretch his legs, to think, to gather himself. To feel the total saturation he had just experienced. Where does the brain go when it's shut down, he wondered?

Before he left, Sondra took him into another room in the flat to introduce him to her pet iguana, Mortimer. It was so unexpected, Andrew did not know how to react. Mortimer was more than five feet long. She introduced him to the beast as though it were the most natural thing in the world. He mumbled a hello, but wanted to get away from the animal as fast as he could.

At the door, after a lingering kiss goodbye, she said, "I would like to see you again."

"To continue my education?"

"To do what you want with me. Practice makes perfect."

"…Sondra, every part of you is beautiful; I don't think I could ever get enough of you."

"I'm already counting the minutes to next time. Tell me when you're rested and ready," she smiled.

She paused. "I want you to continue writing poetry. I think you have promise. I can help you… Come see me again," she repeated. Then added, almost casually, "My husband won't be home til October."

Her last statement was like a bullet in the stomach. She had not told him she was married. She wore no wedding ring or golden wedding band. There were no pictures. Now he felt terrible. Engaging with a woman whose husband was off fighting a war. How low could he sink? How could he dare celebrate victory when he had violated the spirit of trust her husband had left behind? He felt unpatriotic. The fact that he did not know her situation only somewhat dispelled the waves of guilt that now rushed through him. What beast have I become? His soul cried from within.

As he walked the five o'clock streets, verging on sunrise, now so quiet, a cauldron of emotions poured liquid hot into his mind. Sondra's beauty and her sensuality and her sexual prowess were stunningly attractive, but the fact she had chosen an oversize iguana as a pet made her seem a little strange. That, and this new information about a husband. How could she do that to him? How could he, Andrew, do that to them both?

No, he thought. I will carry this no further. What's done is done. It was tremendous while it lasted, but now it felt almost empty. Her last statement sucked all the life out of it, all the beauty. He wished she had not told him. He wished she did not keep strange pets. But as he thought more about it, he was glad it was all out in the open. He would not want to carry on with her with that dark secret hovering in the shadows.

"Where were you?" Joe and Jessica asked over breakfast, on VE Day morning plus one.

"Out celebrating," Andrew said. And left it at that.

He kept thinking of that awesome night with her. "You shut down my whole brain for a minute," she had said. He couldn't remember what he had said when she said, "come see me again." He did not recall making a promise, or mumbling anything, only expressing a hope. So in the days that followed, he did not do anything that would suggest continuation.

Next day in school, Pete and several kids who had seen the poem, gathered around him. "Did you get in trouble?" they asked.

"Yeah, big trouble," he said with a serious face.

"I think he's got suction with Miss Whittle," Pete said.

Andrew thought to himself. Pete is not even aware of how close his statement came to the real truth.

For the final few weeks in her classroom Andrew tried to betray no emotion as he answered her teaching questions or otherwise interacted with her. But each time he left her classroom he would have to hold his books I front of him to hide the large protrusion in his pants. Once he saw her looking at it, with a faint smile. On his report card she did give him an A Plus.

*

Then, in the last week of freshman year, as though springing out of ambush, Andrew heard six words that changed his life.

It was in Mr. Stone's English class. Andrew—as was his habit during this period of his life—was sitting in the last row of classroom seats, and when Mr. Stone was not looking playing slap-the-hands with Pete Palucci.

When the ambush came, Andrew was paying only casual attention to the proceedings of the class. Then Mr. Stone asked Aram Kanajian to stand up. Aram always sat in the third row, was very personable and a straight-A student, well-liked by teachers and classmates. Andrew hardly knew him. They traveled in different worlds.

"Aram, would you conjugate the verb *to be* in Latin?" Mr.

Stone asked.

Latin! This was an English class. What's this about Latin?
Andrew thought Latin is for sissies. Maybe Mr. Stone must be
trying to get him to show off.

Aram rose.

"Sum…

Es…

Est…

Sumus…

Estes…

Sunt," he said, and sat down.

The six words struck Andrew like a bolt of lightning. My
God, he thought, he is speaking another language! He is my
age—well, a year older, but close to my age—and he can already
speak another language! What am I doing here, in the last row,
playing slap-the-hands? What am I doing with my whole life?
He is my age and already speaking another language! Where
have I been? What have I been doing? How much time have I
wasted up til now? Andrew! He thought to himself, time to wake
up!

How far had he fallen from his dream of who he ought to be?
The thought rolled through his mind again and again. He now
realized he had been failing for much of the last year, maybe
much of the last two or three years. And waves of discouragement
swept through him. I am on the floor, he thought. How do I pick
myself up, kick this sense of discouragement, become stronger
than ever? How?

And to compound his misery, his thoughts turned again to Miss Whittle. Here I was, doing everything in creation with her! And she a married woman all along! Shame! Her husband off fighting the war, maybe getting wounded, maybe getting killed, trusting her all along! Defenseless against a cheating heart! Shame!

And as the semester ended, he gathered the remains of his bruised and battered psyche off the floor and vowed—he did not yet know to whom—that he would climb out of the pit of darkness into which he had fallen, renew his quest for something still beyond his horizons, and try to rebuild his life.

Chapter 14

After ten days and nights of agitated confusion, a trainload of agonizing thoughts, Andrew woke one morning to a dawn that seemed limitless. It was as though a pleasant wind had swept through his life and blown away the fog. It was like the freshness of a spring morning after a storm-inhabited night. He became <u>aware</u> of the life force within him, strong and restless, surging toward accomplishment, victor over the darkness that had held him unawares in its grip. He felt brand new.

So many thoughts were rushing through his head, he had to sit quietly in his room for a while to sort them out, give them priority, make a plan, organize his actions. Work and study. No play for now. One of his football buddies who was leaving an after-school job with a nearby newsprint distributor, took Andrew with him to meet the boss and Andrew got a full-time summer job. He learned to maneuver 500-pound rolls of newsprint around the warehouse almost effortlessly (if he got the balance right) using thick rubber pivoting strips. On Saturdays he continued to work on the Henry moving trucks for $1.25 an hour. With John gone, one of the sons, Lee Henry, had taken over. Lee had been exempt from the draft because of a mangled foot. Andrew was not particularly fond of Lee, but a job was a job. Not a lifetime commitment.

In almost every waking moment when not at work, Andrew

read. His mind was like a giant sponge he could not saturate. All through the summer he began an enormous effort to catch up, to go beyond. He mastered the lessons of his former schoolbooks. He studied history, biography. He bought an out-of-date set of encyclopedias and began systematically to work his way through all the fields of knowledge. Beyond his preoccupation with sex and religion, he now wanted to study <u>ideas</u>.

He attempted to memorize the dictionary in alphabetical order, and came to know a lot of words that begin with A. He memorized <u>The Prophet</u> by Kahlil Gibran, and Fitzgerald's fifth translation of <u>The Rubaiyat</u>. He memorized many poems— <u>Invictus</u>, <u>Thanatopsis</u>, <u>The Chambered Nautilus</u>, Edgar Guest's <u>It Couldn't Be Done</u>, Kipling's <u>Annabel Lee</u>. He found he had unusually strong retentive skills. He could adjust his reading speed to the value of the material. He did not have a photographic memory, but he remembered most of what he read and could recall it quickly. He felt alive in ways he had never sensed before. His drive to learn seemed to fill every corner of his mind. He began an adventure in lifelong learning that would never stop, grow dim, or lose its excitement.

And all during this time the war was coming fully to a brutal end, but he was hardly aware of it. On August 6, 1945, the American fighting forces dropped an atomic bomb on Hiroshima, an important Japanese military command and communications center. On August 9, Nagasaki followed. Kyoto, the cultural center of Japan, had been the first designated target for the atomic bomb. Japan fought hard to have Kyoto spared, and was only barely successful.

President Truman told the world of the new reality in the history of warfare during his radio broadcast of August 6, 1945.

"Sixteen hours ago, an American airplane dropped one bomb on Hiroshima, an important Japanese Army base. That bomb had more power than 20,000 tons of T.N.T. It had more than two thousand times the blast power of the British 'Grand Slam,' which is the largest bomb ever yet used in the history of warfare.

The Japanese began the war from the air at Pearl Harbor. They have been repaid many fold. And the end is not yet. With this bomb we have now added a new and revolutionary increase in destruction to supplement the growing power of our armed forces. In their present form these bombs are now in production and even more powerful forms are in development.

It is an atomic bomb. It is a harnessing of the basic power of the universe. The force from which the sun draws its power has been loosed against those who brought war to the Far East."

Hundreds of thousands of lives were lost, but several million lives were saved. It was the only way. Japan had determined to fight on until the last warrior was killed, then continue with an aroused and determined civilian population, engaged in guerilla warfare. But the two bombs persuaded Emperor Hirohito that further resistance was both futile and unwise. Japan surrendered on August 14. Andrew took some moments from his studies to wonder how Miss Whittle was ending the final war (VJ Day), and with whom. He toyed with the thought of calling her but resisted its horny urging.

On September 8 the United States and Russia divided Korea into two parts, North and South along the 38th Parallel, Russia's prize for coming into the war against Japan at the last minute.

Andrew took time to write to Kenneth and Clara. He told Kenneth of his rekindled love of learning and thanked him again for planting the seeds in his mind. He told him he would come up to see him over Thanksgiving holiday. Kenneth was too ill to respond, and Clara wrote just a brief note telling him that. "I read your letter to him, and he smiled."

Upon entering sophomore year, Andrew immediately changed his curriculum from General Studies to College Prep.

With the war over, he dropped out of the Civil Air Patrol Cadet Corp. He dropped all sports activities. He wanted nothing to take away time from learning. And without conscious thought or effort, he found he was changing his circle of friends. It was almost like a <u>mind gravity</u>, drawing him nearer to the smartest, most well-adjusted kids in school. In less than two months into tenth grade, he was quickly becoming friends with a number of boys and girls he found both fascinating and highly intelligent. Only months ago he had casually assumed they belonged to another world that had nothing to do with him.

In the meantime, he signed up for what was then regarded as the toughest club to get into—the Boys Dramatic Guild. He had no special interest in dramatics. He signed up only because of its exclusive reputation and rumors of how hard it would be to get through the brutal physical initiation.

All he had heard was true, and worse. The hazing was vicious and prolonged. It lasted three days. Designed for intense humiliation, and stretching past the ordinary borders of pain, the initiation attempted to sort out the sissies and the half-hearted, leave them in the dust outside of the club's exclusive bounds. Initiates were called worms and were for these three days—according to initiation protocols—required to obey all commands from any member of the club, and call them sir, whether on school grounds or outside. Furthermore, initiates were required to submit to paddling on the ass by any club member, on commend.

"What is lower than a worm?" a club member would ask.

"Sir, the answer is, nothing is lower than a worm."

"Worm, assume the position."

Bend over. Whack. Whack. Whack.

"Worm, what do worms eat?"

"Dirt, sir."

"Therefore, you will eat dirt!" (The member had learned the word <u>therefore</u> only the day before.) "Let's see you eat dirt."

Eat some dirt.

"You're not a worm," the club member would say, "You're a pissant. Pissants are lower than worms—what do pissants eat?"

Andrew quickly calculated. "Dirt, sir."

"Wrong answer. Assume the position." Whack. Whack. Whack.

"You are my lackey. Carry my books."

The worst day was the last day. Worms were required to submit to crushed raw eggs and flour and ketchup scrambled through their hair, faces marked with different colors of paint, and to go through classes all day that way. After school came paddling night. All former club members were allowed to return and to engage in the paddling. No time restrictions. Two or three members returned year after year for this, with thick oak paddles in which one-inch holes had been drilled, to allow for swifter air passage to the targeted ass.

Martin Scarf was a particularly ominous former member. Now, at the age of 25, he continued to return year after year. He swung with merciless cruelty and counted his hits. Every year he would paint the new member's name on his paddle, as though a fighter pilot posting his kills. His face had a rather puffy angular quality. His eyes were posters for mental illness campaigns. He slicked his dark hair with Brilliantine. Driving downtown for further humiliation, in the same car as Andrew, Scarf would lean out of the open side window whenever passing a girl and yell "Hey! Pig!" Andrew vowed that if he ever came into administrative control of the club, he would ban former members from these strange and sick returns.

Paddling night went on for hours, both on school grounds, then downtown, then on school grounds again. Most of the paddles were oak and heavy. After hours of this the buttocks would become extremely painful and greatly swollen. Three initiates quit at this point, going home in tears.

But Andrew had his own reasons for submitting—to gain entry into an exclusive club, to prove to himself that he could take such an initiation, and—as the night wore on—to place himself in a position to bring an end to the most sadistic and senseless parts of it.

A year later he endured a second and similar initiation, into the Young Men's Club. As always Scarf was there too. He seemed to have no other real life (he had never become an actor). But Andrew vowed he would end this menacing presence. Which he eventually did, in both clubs.

*

News of Kenneth's death, although not unexpected, came nevertheless as a shock. He died October 24, a month before Andrew had planned to visit him. Clara made a rare telephone call to the states and gave Joe the news. Andrew left for Lucknow immediately.

Seeing Kenneth there, laid out in an open casket in the parlor of the Cameron home, brought the reality of his death into sudden focus. For several minutes Andrew stood just inside the door, hesitant to approach. And then he came next to the body. He tried to peer down into his death, to search its meaning. All he could sense was the reality of mortal finality. He stroked the cool, waxy lifelessness of Kenneth's hands, kissed him on the forehead, then wept for long time. He could not hold it back. Something beautiful had died in the world.

It seemed to him as he thought about it that Kenneth had determined not to release his grip on earthbound life until the war was ended and the apple picking season gone. He thought back to the time in the orchard when he had almost killed him with the shotgun, and wept again. He comforted Clara as best he could. She was weepy but stoical. She said it was a merciful release. Andrew hardly heard anything the minister said at the funeral.

Only one thought continued to linger in his mind. The minister said Kenneth had "lived in Christ, died in Christ, and would rise in Christ." And was "beloved by all who knew him."

Kenneth's remains were buried in Greenhill Cemetery in a cool, drizzling rain on October 26. And when it was done, a winter pitch came into the wind and blew even the drizzled leaves across the carpet of lifeless grass.

The next morning, before he was to return, Andrew decided to walk over to the Riddle farm. He had not seen Eileen at the funeral and wondered if she had heard. The cool rain continued, with gusts of a hard wind. A gloomy day from beginning to end. Little patches of sunlight occasionally tried to coax their way through the gray-blue clouds.

As he walked up the lane to the Riddle home, he noticed several boarded-up windows. No sign of life at all. The place had deteriorated to a much greater extent than he last remembered. Out of habit he knocked on the front door. Without response. He walked in. Nothing had been repaired since the last time he had seen it. The atmosphere was singularly depressing. It was obvious no one lived here anymore.

He went up the stairs and looked into Sophie's room. The bed and nightstand were there, nothing else. Then he went into Eileen's room. A bed and nightstand, nothing else. But on her bed he saw a pillow. Something was embroidered on it. He picked it up, and saw the one word she had left him, embroidered in the pillowcase.

Kismet

Nothing else. She must have known I would return, he thought. He wondered what had happened. Then he left the house, into the gloomy cold rain again, and walked down to a neighboring farm.

"What happened to the Riddles?" he asked. "I went over to their house. It's all empty."

"Oh, they're gone. Left after the war. Went back to Ireland, where they belong... The place is up for sale. Needs a lot of fixing."

"Where in Ireland?"

"Nobody knows."

Andrew expressed thanks for the information. As he walked back to the Cameron home to say goodbye to Clara, his mind crowded with thoughts. What had happened to them? Why did she not write? I had a thousand things to tell her. And what about that one word she left on her pillow? How did she know I would be back? What did she mean in that one word?

He was certain she left that word for his eyes alone. The rest of the world could look on if it wanted to. But the message was for Andrew. What was she trying to say? He wondered. One thing is clear, he thought. Our relationship is not yet over. That's what she was trying to say? Or was it? He instinctively looked at his wrist.

*

Back home, he devoured books like a consuming fire. He plunged into schoolwork with great energy. He studied. He began to get the highest grades on all his tests. And his new mode of behavior drew him naturally even deeper into a new circle of friends and acquaintances, especially a small informal social group known around school as the "Wheels." They seemed to be at the center of everything important that was happening, excepting sports.

He found them highly intelligent, friendly in nature, hardworking and progressive in spirit. In general, they had a level of curiosity that almost matched his own. Without conscious effort or plan, Andrew rather quickly became a full-fledged member of the new crowd. He felt a real attraction to all of them, and he sensed, they to him. Their acceptance and companionship was warm and relaxed. Once he had expanded his mind to this surrounding new reality, it seemed they were all there to greet him with welcoming arms. He was one of them now. His heart was opening to happiness. He felt rich. Five especially became the new center of his relationship—Aram Kanajian, Brundi Nasudovitch, Jiggity Winkers, and Glendeen O'Deneman and then later Cynthia Downing.

*

Aram Kanajian, the Latin whiz, was the first to whom Andrew was drawn. Aram was firstborn of the first generation of his family to live in the United States. Those who became his parents, as teenagers, had barely escaped the massacre of a million Armenians by the Turks in 1915. They made their way to Canada, then on to Detroit, with memories of the slaughter still burning in their souls. His father became a doctor, and with Aram's birth, began a family in 1930.

Aram was born with a gregarious and generous nature, a happy disposition, cheerful personality, a tawny complexion and friendly brown eyes. The thing that struck you most about him, in addition to his obvious intelligence, was the sincere and open innocence of his character. He knew all the stories of the massacre, but would not let them weigh him down.

He also had a special love of music. He did not play, but he was a connoisseur in matters of musical taste. Shortly after they began their friendship, Aram invited Andrew to stop in at his home nearby on the way home from school. He wanted to introduce Andrew to a new musical discovery, a recording of Rachmaninoff's Second Piano Concerto (in C Minor), played by the New York Philharmonic.

In all his growing up years, Andrew had never heard a piece of classical music, not once that he could remember. His musical vocabulary was more or less limited to country (especially Grand Ole Opry), folk music, popular big band songs, love ballads, Be-Bop, regular jazz, and jive. He did not know classical music existed. He did not know what to expect. Aram placed the needle on the 78-rpm phonograph record.

The music was like nothing he had ever heard. A certain passage in the concerto came into him so powerfully beautiful in its sweep, it almost brought him to orgasm. Without the slightest thought or arousal of his penis, there it was, wanting to pour itself into the music, wanting to join in. It was all he could do to hold it back. And the strange thing, he wasn't even stiff. But he kept his outward composure. Looking at him, you would never know the depth or excitement of the response within.

When it was done, Aram asked him how he had liked it.

"You just changed my musical life. I didn't know music could have such intensity."

"I'd hoped you would say that," Aram said. "I could tell by the expression on your face you really loved that music."

"More than you will ever know," Andrew smiled.

Aram's steady girlfriend was Anna Manoogian, daughter of a local businessman. Dark haired, quiet in nature, she had friendly eyes and a great sense of humor. One of the superior students in school, Anna was totally devoted to Aram, and had no plan for her life other than becoming his wife and bearing his children. Andrew felt a warm affection for her as soon as they were introduced.

Anna also shared Aram's passion for music, and played piano with great skill. In a very short time the two of them helped stimulate what was to become Andrew's lifelong love of great music. He especially liked the rich melodic themes and cared little for music that seemed composed primarily as a technical exercise. But the love affair had really begun in those delicious moments with Rachmaninoff and the experience of near-orgasm.

*

Brundi Nasudovitch, also from the beginning, became a very close friend and confidant. He and Andrew seemed to be on the same wavelength. Brundi was also a brilliant student and had given up athletics to concentrate on his studies and his quest for knowledge.

To look at him, your first impression would be football linebacker, which is what he had been. He had played left halfback, while Andrew had played left end. Brundi had the power, Andrew had the speed. Brundi was strong as a bull. His nose had once been kicked in and was still a little bent in the middle. He had a broad forehead, prominent cheekbones, naturally wavy hair, gray-blue eyes, and a friendly countenance.

Brundi projected a generally serious demeanor but was gifted with a quick sense of humor. As soon as he spoke, you would notice his earnestness and sincerity. He sincerely wanted to learn everything there was to know. He was frank and straightforward in speech, honest in mind and heart, and as Andrew would learn in experience after experience, utterly reliable.

He also had an unusual problem with self confidence that expressed itself in relationships with girls. To ensure he would know what to say, he had a habit of listing the things he wanted to talk about before calling a girl on the phone.

Although they had played football together, they had never had much of a personal discussion, until now. Andrew came to know him in some depth quite early in their new relationship. It happened in an unusual way. On a long walk after school one late afternoon, Brundi confided that he faced a serious problem, one that might wreck his life.

"But you're only 15. What could wreck your life so early? You haven't even got started yet."

"That's the problem. I got started. I didn't see it coming, but I'm off and running."

"What happened?"

"You know Gretchen Sperling?"

"Sure, I've seen her around."

"Gretchen and I went out for a while. We started going out when I was still playing ball."

Andrew recalled to his mind Gretchen's appearance. She was well built, of average height, sandy colored curly hair, pretty but not beautiful, and she had large, puffy lips. Andrew remembered her eyes especially. They were intelligent eyes, but seemed to harbor a lingering pain somewhere deep within.

"I never saw you together."

"We weren't going steady. But we were going at each other. For a long time she wouldn't let me get near. We would get real close in some ways, then the gates would shut. I was getting frustrated more and more. What was driving me out of my mind was, she would tease me along in a way that made me feel next time would be it. I started carrying a pack of Red Top rubbers. Every time we went out I thought this will be it."

"So far it doesn't sound like anything that would ruin your life."

"Andrew, the sad part is, we finally made it. Last August, the week before school, I took her to Bob-Lo on the boat. We had a swell time. And on the way back she whispered in my ear that her parents were out of town that weekend. She pretty much let me know the time had come... Well, when we got to her house we went at it for a while and she told me she was ready now. 'That's great,' I said. 'I brought a rubber.' She just looked at me. 'One or two?' 'Three,' I said. 'I don't want you to use it,' she said. 'But what if I get you pregnant?' I said. 'I'm OK,' she said. 'I just had my period.' But I was reluctant. 'I think I should use it,' I said. 'No!' she said. She told me twice. 'No. No. No.'"

"That's three times," Andrew laughed.

"Don't laugh. This is serious stuff."

"OK, no more laughing."

"…So we did it."

"Was it worth the wait?"

"I can't even remember that part. It was sort of a blur."

"So what happened?"

"She got pregnant."

"I think I saw her around last week. She didn't look pregnant."

"I'll get to that part. What happened next was turning my life upside down. I reminded her of our conversation. She tried to convince me it was all a big misunderstanding. She said she didn't mean to get pregnant. I asked her to get rid of it. I would work to pay for it. She told me she was going to keep the baby… And do you know what she said?"

"What did she say?"

"She said, 'I've always wanted something for my very own.'"

"Wow!"

"I saw my life in ashes, burnt up. I didn't love her, and I never told her I loved her. Come to think of it, she never told me that either. The love word never came up between us."

"What do you think she was trying to do then?"

"I don't know. It's still too fresh. It's still churning inside."

"Seems like it's not over yet."

"Oh, it's over. Really over. When she insisted on keeping the kid, I was desperate. I thought the only honorable thing to do was to marry her. I thought we could take a bus down to Kentucky or someplace like that. Someplace where they don't look too closely at your age."

"What did she say?"

"She didn't give me an answer. She told her parents instead... They insisted I come over. So we had this tearful meeting at her parents' house. And do you know what she said?"

"No, what?"

"I swear to God, she just sat there and told them a boldface lie. She started crying. 'I told him to use protection,' she said. She just sat there and said that. She could lie to Jesus."

"What did her parents do?"

"They took her to get an abortion."

"So it's over."

"I don't know. She never said yes or no to my offer to marry her. I don't know if I'm still supposed to do that."

"Have you seen her since?"

"Only in the hallways. She sticks up her nose and walks right past me."

"Sounds like she's saying no."

"I think you're right. I think I'm off the hook. Unless her parents want me to pay them back."

"Doesn't sound like it."

Brundi paused in their walk so he could face Andrew directly to make a point. "Andrew, beware of German girls."

"How can you generalize on a single incident?"

"There's something about them," Brundi said solemnly.

The gravity of his adduce was so strong, the thought would linger permanently somewhere in the back of Andrew's mind. <u>Beware of German girls.</u>

*

Jiggety Winkers took the lead immediately, the first time Andrew met him.

"I know first thing you're going to ask me is how did I get a name like Jiggety. Well I'll tell you," he went on without interruption. "When I was born they said I came sort of bouncing out. I was so jiggety they found me hard to hold, so my Cherokee grandmother stuck that name on me."

"Do you call yourself Jiggety?"

"You can call me Jig for short."

"What else was I going to ask you?" Andrew joked.

"I'll save you the trouble. Let your mind rest. I'll tell you about myself all at once." He paused. "Just think of me as a simple gutbucket Arkansas hillbilly. But I should tell you right away, I take a lot of pride in my hillbillyness. So don't underestimate me. People tend to underestimate me. My mother never raised any dumb hillbillies."

"Well, you live in Detroit now," Andrew said.

"My body lives in Detroit. My mind hunts across the world."

"What are you looking for?"

"I'll know it when I see it," Jiggety said.

"You have a colorful personality," Andrew smiled

"I speak in epigrams, maxims, axioms, thermos, proverbs, allegories, aphorisms, plagiarisms, even adverbs. In a pinch I may resort to onomatopoeia. My mind roams the world looking for illumination. I am given to statements of wondrous sweep."

"And I sense you can't wait to illuminate others."

"I shine the light. It's up to them to raise the blinds."

"Jig, I think I'm going to like you."

251.

"That would make me happy as a pig in mud."

Jiggety had an outgoing personality, not a hint of shyness. He was one of the most self-confident individuals Andrew had ever met. He was a little shorter than average in height, had a strong, wiry frame, and greenish-brown eyes that seemed always on the verge of dancing. He spoke with a deep southern drawl and wore an easy smile. He also had a photographic memory. His whole mind seemed to have some of the quality of a squirrel cage, with interesting facts and observations tucked into every cranny imaginable.

His constant companion, whenever the two could arrange it, was Poppy Gander. The two of them made a fascinating couple. They were as close to soul mates as one can get at age 15.

Poppy, her given name, was smuggled out of China by daring southern missionaries during the confusion surrounding the rape of Nanking in the winter of 1937-38. Nanking had fallen in December. She had been only seven. Later, through the missionaries, Poppy learned her mother had been raped and murdered. She felt a deep guilt and sadness that she had not been there at her mother's side to help fight off her attackers.

Poppy was adopted by the Gander family in Tupelo, Mississippi, and grew up with one of the richest southern accents you ever heard. The richness of southern accent, coming out of such a pure Chinese face, created moments of substantial incongruity until some adjustment in perception reframed the conversation. Poppy grew to be a healthy and well balanced teenager, the perfect foil for Jiggety's picturesque speech. Poppy had a quiet, shy sense of humor, and often referred to men as

Yangs and women as Yins. "I keep Jig anchored to earth," she would say. "Without me, he might go flying off into space."

Jiggety and Andrew came to know each other quite well some months later, in the spring of 1946. From the beginning of his new quest for academic excellence, Andrew had worked closely with Mr. Holtzen, Director of the experimental Citizenship Education Program. Within a few months Andrew was appointed Coordinator of the program.

With the wider latitude he now enjoyed, he set out on a number of new initiatives. One of the first of these was to form a chess club. He had just learned to play chess by reading a book, and discovered what he thought to be an impregnable defense. Since no one else in school played chess, Andrew rounded up nine other students, taught them to play, taught them the "impregnable" defensive moves, and, in a cocky mood, promptly challenged Northern high school to a chess competition. Jiggety was one of the nine.

Northern accepted. They had the strongest chess club in the city, with 59 players. Andrew and his nine took on Northern's top 10. Andrew, as president of the club, played Northern's president.

The defeat was decisive and brutal. Andrew lost all his matches rather quickly. So did the others, all but Jiggety. Jiggety won all his matches. Back home, Jiggety beat Andrew too. In no time at all he had become a superior player. Andrew asked him to take over as president of the club.

In a post-mortem meeting Andrew's team tried to assess what had gone wrong. Jiggety was the most instructive. "First," he said, "You have to control the center of the board. Control the center and you control the game. It's the same way with ideas—control the metaphors and you control the evolution of the idea."

"Do you think that's the most important lesson?" Andrew asked.

"No. Not on your life. We went in there with a superb defensive strategy. That was wrong. There's nothing wrong with defense, per se, but to make it your basic strategy won't win many games. A purely defensive strategy, no matter how brilliant or well executed, will always lose to the assault of a skilled player determined to win. Always. Only a strong attack can win. Attack! Attack! Attack!"

It was a lesson Andrew remembered for the rest of his life. The humiliation of losing so quickly, so thoroughly, burned it into his soul.

But there was one other thing said in Jiggety's explanation that struck a chord in Andrew's mind. "I am an excellent judge of character," Jiggety had said. "I studied my opponent before the game. I looked at all kinds of signals and reactions he was giving off with his eyes, his hands, the way he was sitting—everything—I was playing against someone I already know a lot about, things people are not even aware they're doing, signals that tell you what kind of character you're dealing with. I especially look at the parts that lie in hiding. I look at the psychological makeup. I almost knew how he would make his next move."

Andrew decided Jiggety was one of the people he wanted to know for a long time.

*

Glendeen O'Deneman was also one of the most brilliant students in school, but she made no show of it. She was a curious mixture of shy and outgoing, shy in her intelligence, outgoing in her music. Deannie, as she was called, played folk guitar, and had a voice of Celtic purity that arrested even your inner thoughts. She could find the guts and heart of a song. She could pull you inside of it with her, make you feel its edges, guide you through its spooky hallways, linger with you in caressing every soft curve of it. Someone said, in describing her, "she has a way of climbing inside a song, making herself comfortable, make you feel you are visiting her in her room on a lonely night. She sings like she's wearing pajamas." Hours afterward, sometimes days afterward, her voice would linger in the grassy meadows of your soul.

She had a rather square and sturdy face, wore thick glasses, and had auburn colored hair. Her eyes were Morning Glory blue and had a hint of impishness. With her glasses off you could see more clearly a quiet electricity, a warm current of caring and compassion. She was a strangely attractive young woman—strangely because most of her features were not individually beautiful, but taken together she projected an attractiveness that was magnetic and alluring. Even more so when she sang.

Andrew had seen her around school from time to time but had never paid any attention to her. He first became conscious of her at a party that Aram and Anna had arranged. It was late November. Thanksgiving had been done, and the whole country and much of the world was coming into the first Christmas season in years unsurrounded by an atmosphere of war. Even the wounded were coming home, except those very badly wounded. There was a generally joyous spirit in the air. Andrew had brought his guitar to the party, but put it discretely aside when Aram asked Deannie to play and sing. She was many classes above him in talent, especially her voice. He saw her with new eyes.

No one knows what produces the chemistry of attraction between two human beings. Whatever it is, it seems to arrive with an almost magical atmosphere, except there is no illusion. It is like the coming together of two pieces of a living and organic jigsaw puzzle, of a larger spirit—touching at all points, fitting together perfectly, alive everywhere they touch. It is rich and satisfying in the way it nourishes the souls of each. Whatever it was, Andrew felt it with her the first time they said hello, and knew she felt it with him. He knew he had to see her again after that night.

But for all that he felt, he began their first conversation with considerable awkwardness. He had just discovered the humor in puns and was trying out this form of humor every chance he got.

"If I told you you had a beautiful body, would you hold it against me?"

She slapped him gently and smiled. "Then I would know you're lying. I have a body like a beer can. Promise you'll never lie to me again." She almost caressed him with her voice the way she said it.

He took her hand. "Maybe we can begin by making the same promise to each other."

"Deal," she said. And they were off. Even though they had spoken in smiles and jest, Andrew knew he had made a solemn vow. Somehow it seemed to move them both right away into deeper realms of a new relationship. The vow of honesty created an almost immediate sense of homey comfort.

She noticed his guitar propped against the wall.

"Play for me," she said.

"I'm not in your league."

"The angels will decide that. I want to hear your voice...You have an unusual voice. When you speak, there's something in your voice that does things to me."

"I sound like a dying frog."

She handed him his guitar. "Okay, mister frogman, do some croaking."

"Can I play you something I made up?"

"I would love it."

"Promise you won't laugh."

"I want to hear you."

He strummed:

"Old mister gui-tar-eo

said to miss banjo-eo

come marry me-oeo

come marry me-o…"

He stopped. "That's as far as I got. It's a poem in progress."

"You're creative. Do something longer."

So Andrew sang, "Can I Sleep in Your Barn Tonight Mister."

"I never heard anyone sing like you," she said, "especially when you sing 'It's Cold Lying Out on the Ground.'"

And then they tried duets, but found their voices did not harmonize well.

Andrew walked her home that night. And they stood in the wintering air for an hour talking, reluctant to say goodbye.

"I like your name," Deannie said. "Everyone calls you Andrew naturally. You're not an Andy. No one would think of that. You seem to rise up to fill your name ...do you know that Andrew was Jesus' first apostle?"

"I didn't know that."

"Now you will know it forever."

He kissed her softly, feeling the gentle innocence of her lips. "I don't want to barge into your life like a runaway truck driver," he said. "But I already feel as though we have known each other for a long time."

"Andrew, I already feel very close to you." They kissed again, gently as the first time, with only quiet exploring, as though they had all the time in the world.

*

Andrew began to spend every spare moment he could with Deannie, even studying together. They seemed to exist in the same rhythm. It was unlike anything he had ever experienced. He told her that, and she said she felt it too. They had already begun to share their innermost thoughts. For Andrew, it had been a long time, not since Eileen. Laura was not the kind of girl he felt he could share anxieties with.

"We've only known each other for a few weeks," Deannie said as she kissed him goodnight before he walked home, "and we're already as comfortable as an old pair of shoes."

Andrew brought her home to meet Joe and Jessica. It was at the end of an aggravating day of work for Jessica. During the war she had worked at the big Fisher Body plant a short ways north on West Fort Street, building tanks. When war ended, when men were coming back to their jobs as the plant re-converted, Jessica stayed on. She was a good productive worker and no one attempted to ease her out. But with all the changes involved in the conversion, she was shifted to a new department, under a foreman she didn't like, one who hadn't been drafted because he had four children. It was a personality conflict she bore the brunt of within herself, but at home she was tempted to open the emotional pressure valve and let off steam. This night it happened Deannie was there. Jessica didn't care. She had to blow.

"He was up my ass and to the left," she said.

"You're sure it was to the left," Joe joked.

"Damn right, honey. That's where it hurts the most."

Andrew and Deannie were silent as Jessica continued about the new foreman. "He has his head up his ass and he doesn't even feel it."

"Let's get out of the hind end," Joe joked, trying to divert Jessica's line of thinking.

"Okay," she said. "As far as that's concerned, he lacks something in the mental department, too."

But the general mood was relaxed. And afterward, as Andrew walked Deannie home, she told him she really liked his parents. "Your stepmother is fearless. She's not afraid to say anything. I like that. I think I could learn a thing or two from her."

"Don't learn too much." Andrew joked, "I like you just the way are."

It was a warm and beautiful Christmas that year, with blossoming love and close friendships, the warmth of a world now able to begin anew the search for peace, everything ...The group ("The Wheels"), ten of them, decided to go caroling in the snow of Christmas Eve, which they did. No guitars. Only voices. Over warm punch later, they described themselves (echoing Tonto) as the kemo-sabes, "faithful friends forever."

There was no word from Zeedie. No card. No call.

*

In January Andrew bumped into Miss Whittle, almost literally. He was rounding a corner in the hallways as she was doing the same. In the almost-collision he instinctively put his hands out to catch her if she fell, and in so doing momentarily held her upper arms. It was the first time he had come face to face with her since he had left her class after VE Day.

"Sorry," he quickly apologized, releasing her. "I wasn't paying attention."

She smiled warmly. "Still writing poetry?"

"I'm on to other things now. Did your husband get home safe and sound?"

"Safe," she laughed. "But sound—I don't know." Andrew was puzzled by her statement. He wondered if the war had bashed in her husband's brains.

"Hope you had a nice Christmas," was all he could think to say.

"Andrew," she responded, "You really do seem to have a

poetic instinct. If I can be of help to you in any way, let me know."

"I think you're the best teacher I ever had, except for my grandfather. He taught me the Book of Job, <u>as poetry</u>. You taught me things I didn't <u>know</u> I didn't know."

"Hooray for him. I can take you to the next level… if you're interested," she teased.

'I have very specific interests right now."

"Let me know if things change," she smiled.

But he knew things would not change in their relationship. They made their brief goodbyes.

*

All through the spring Andrew was so preoccupied with extracurricular activities, he began to neglect his studies. He was still pulling straight A's in all his classes so he did not feel the sting of misplaced priorities. Not until two incidents arrested his attention, stimulating him to realize he was off track.

The first was in an English class, on a quiz. The sentence was: "If Fred was/were more tactful, he would not criticize Ellen's hat." Andrew chose "was" as the answer. Because he was now known as one of the "brains," several students who had been discretely looking at his paper changed their answers from "were" to "was." They had studied. He had not. They thought he knew something they didn't know.

But his answer had been dead wrong. The lesson dealt with the subjunctive mood, and he had not read the preparatory explanations. He just <u>assumed</u> he knew. Those who had copied his answer, or changed their answers because they thought he must be right, castigated him. He read the lesson plan and apologized. He experienced chagrin. He felt dismay, shame, humiliation.

The second incident followed soon after, like a one-two punch. His remarkable memory had made him one of the last still standing in a spelling bee. It was Andrew against Marjorie Andorian. Marjorie was a very intelligent, diminutive and chirpy little creature with an excellent memory. Darkly pretty, with expressive eyes, she talked with a rapid and interesting cadence. She spoke several languages and bore an accent hardly easy to identify. There was an almost birdlike quality to her. It seemed that at every moment she might just fly away. If Andrew had not been so preoccupied, he would have ventured to know her better.

The word was <u>all right</u>. He spelled it <u>alright</u>. Mrs. Goodwin told him that was wrong. The spelling lesson, which he had not studied, showed it was two words. "But," he protested, "I've seen it spelled <u>alright</u> in novels." Mrs. Goodwin reluctantly accepted his protest and let him continue. He went on to spell down Marjorie, win, and go on to the finals in the auditorium the following week. He took second place, a loss.

But the whole episode led him into a lot of thinking. He reviewed the lesson plans and found Mrs. Goodwin had been right. Two l's was, of course, the proper spelling. He much regretted his protest. He felt he had brought dishonor to himself, first for protesting at all, second for being wrong in a stupid way. He had not studied. He should have simply accepted the consequences. He thought Mrs. Goodwin should have held her ground, disqualified him. He thought she had let him get away with it only because of his growing reputation. That was wrong. He felt the bite of shame again, remorse. How could he undo it? There was no way.

Then he thought of Marjorie. Innocent Marjorie. He had taken advantage of her. She should have won. She would have won in the finals. He thought of the look she had in those expressive eyes, a quiet sorrow intermingled with a hint of betrayal. He wished there were some way to make it up to her but he did not know how.

Both experiences had trimmed his feathers, taken the lift from his soaring flight. He vowed never to let such things happen again. From this point on he would make sure he did his homework. He would not coast on assumptions. He would not go into situations without having done his homework. And this lesson etched itself so deeply into his consciousness it guided his actions in many ways for the rest of his life. In later years, he became noted for having "done his homework."

*

Cynthia Downing came into the group during the spring, when Brundi began to go steady with her. She did not fit the group dynamic well, except in brainpower. There seemed to be more craft and cunning in her behavior than Andrew felt comfortable with. He was a bit wary of her. But Cynthia had exceptional emotional intelligence, seemed to be strongly intuitive, and seemed to sense right away that she was quite different. She sometimes joked that Brundi had "smuggled" her into the group. He was, at least for now, quite enamored of her.

Cynthia's parents were Hungarian, from "way before the

revolution." Her father saw the impending instability in Europe and moved with his wife to London, then to Detroit in the 1920's. Cynthia was born on the same day as Andrew, but one year earlier. Not knowing his true age, she thought they were born at the same time. "Do you think we might be soul mates?"

"I don't think so," he said.

It would be many years before Andrew would let her know of the one year difference in their ages.

When in London, Cynthia's father decided he no longer liked his Hungarian name—Pooschkie—and decided to change it. He liked English names and took the name Downing. It had a regal quality that appealed to him. It would better serve his business interests. He began a manufacturing company in Detroit, supplying certain auto parts to General Motors. The stock market crash in 1929, then the Depression, put his plans for growth on hold for a while, so he was not yet able to move the family to a fancier neighborhood. This would come soon, now that the war had ended. He had his eye on Grosse Isle, on the Detroit River.

Cynthia had warm, mink-brown sparkling eyes, an easy smile, beautiful features, and a pleasant figure. She had straight platinum blonde hair which she wore at shoulder length. Her hair was almost the same color as Mienda's, which made her instantly attractive to Andrew. But he would not show it. He was fully committed to Deannie.

The thing you would notice right away about Cynthia was a subtle undertone of bawdy amorality in her expression. You could see traces of Hungarian spitfire in her face, quickness and aliveness, but there was just a hint of decadence, even at this young age. As he tried to read the expression in her eyes, Andrew saw something almost lurking within their beauty that told him she could betray you without looking back. But all of this was quite subtle, fleeting nuances that he put way in the back part of his mind. The problem was, he really liked her. There was an appealing aliveness in her presence. He was glad she was not part of the crowd.

Brundi had asked him: "Andrew, what do you think of her?"

"Five things. She's bold, beautiful, intelligent, a little cunning, and…"

"And what?"

"You've got your hands full."

"Hubba hubba, I can't wait to get my hands full," Brundi said.

"I think it will come sooner than you think."

Cynthia had a way of making private comments to Andrew when no one else was within earshot that always carried a suggestive tone. She seemed to enjoy being provocative but shielded by ambiguities of nuance and double meaning. She had a habit of saying, when they were alone, "What's up?" with the hint of a saucy smile. "Nothing," he would say. "Too bad," she would say with a wistful smile. "Make yourself useful."

She was also given to speaking in abbreviations and acronyms. She once said to Andrew, when he was wearing shoes with soft spongy soles, "I see you're wearing your B.C.'s." He bit. "What are B.C.'s?" She smiled, "Brothel creepers, you idiot." She would point out another girl's "V.P.L." Andrew bit again. "What's a V.P.L?" "Visible panty line, you idiot." She was fond of calling him an idiot. But she always did it in such a relaxed and friendly way, the word had no bite. Once she pointed out to him a D.O.M. (Dirty Old Man).

Cynthia's most poignant venture into abbreviations came during a June outing the group was having at Ford Field in Dearborn—the place, Andrew remembered, where he had almost blown his eyes out. This time it was a shish kabob roast. Aram and Ann had cut the lamb into small chunks and soaked it overnight in a salty brine. Andrew and Deannie brought charcoal, skewers, onions, peppers, tomatoes, and others brought pita bread, coke, ginger ale, and chips.

But about the time the shish kabob skewers were roasted to perfection over the charcoal, a soft rain enveloped them and made a mess of the food. Andrew thought back... he had only been to Ford Field twice, and both times it had rained. And as in his first experience like this, the group took it with laughter and excitement. The rain somehow deepened the pleasure of everyone involved.

There was only one thing. Deannie had such firm and prominent well-muscled breasts she never wore a brassiere. She also liked to wear peasant blouses in warm weather. It was her favorite outfit, and she looked unusually attractive when she dressed that way.

After the rain, which soaked everyone to the skin, and while everyone was devouring the soaked kabobs, Cynthia pointed to Deannie's wet blouse, shaped around her breasts, and said, "Now don't any of you guys get your hots up looking at Deannie's T.E.'s."

"What are T.E.s?" Andrew asked.

"Tit erections," Cynthia laughed.

Deannie immediately got up and ran to the protection of a large tree. Andrew followed.

"I'm so embarrassed. I wasn't paying any attention to myself. Now, that's all they'll think about."

"They'll have a lot to think about," Andrew joked.

"Be serious," she said. "I am mortified."

Andrew looked at her. It was true. She had unusually large nipples. They were like small cannons. They rose in centimeters when fully extended. They made a stunning appearance trying to push through her blouse. Extremely attractive. He held her in his arms, holding her out of sight behind the tree.

"Your breasts are very, very beautiful. I love the 'extensions.'"

"Don't just say that to make me feel good."

"Remember, we promised never to lie to each other. I spoke from my heart."

"I'm sorry," she tried to apologize. "Whenever I'm excited they get that way. Even a stray thought will do it. When I play and sing, somehow the music does that to them. I wasn't aware until now how much of myself I was showing."

"What you showed was mind-expanding."

"I wasn't trying to show off or be saucy. It just happened. The rain seemed to do it."

"Hooray for rain," he joked.

"How can I face them again?"

"Easy," he said. He removed his shirt and put it over her. "There you are, safe and sound, back in your privacy."

She kissed him. Her lips were still wet, and Andrew felt a special tingling. "I'm glad you understand," she said. "In the future, I think I'll put large band aids over them."

"I would like it better without the band aids."

"You'll have to learn to do without," she smiled. "You know the boundaries."

*

All summer Andrew worked steadily on the Henry trucks, moving furniture, now under Edgar Henry, who had come home from the Marines some months before and replaced Lee. Edgar was six years older than Andrew, and Andrew never particularly liked him. But there was plenty of work. It seemed half the country was restless, wanting to move. He was saving money to buy a car, as soon as he could get his license next year.

He continued to spend all the time he could with Deannie. Several times he asked her to go swimming with him. She said no. "Do you have a bathing suit?" he asked.

"I have one," she said. "But I don't like the way it fits. I don't have a bathing suit body."

"I can take you to a couple of places where we can skinny dip. Very private."

She slapped him with a gentle caress. "You know the boundaries," she reminded him.

On occasion he took her downtown to see the big bands playing on stage in large theaters. Once he decided to take a large sour dill pickle with him.

"Why are you doing that?"

"I read somewhere that if you suck on a sour pickle in front of someone playing the clarinet, he will have to stop playing. His thoughts about the sourness will make him pucker up his lips."

"And you want to do that to Artie Shaw?"

"Just as an experiment. I want to see if it works."

"That's wicked," she laughed.

But it didn't work. The first show was filled and they hid behind some side curtains when the theater emptied. They got front row center seats for the second show soon afterward. Andrew took the pickle from its wax paper wrap, sucked it quietly but noticeably. But Artie Shaw played on, not missing a note of Begin the Beguine—either the greatest or one of the two greatest clarinetists of all time.

"Serves you right," Deannie said.

"Can you put up with my wicked ways?"

"I'll bring you around."

They traveled to Ontario one August weekend, to a folk festival in Goderich. Deannie brought her guitar and was invited to play. She made a sensational impression. The Celtic purity of tone when she sang brought a complete hush to the crowd, mostly Canadians, but some Yankees and Europeans.

"O'Demenon the Phenomenon" [headline], the Star wrote of her performance. "She has the voice of someone three times her age—weathered, haunting, authentically sorrowful... She has a purity of tone very comfortable on the ears. When she is through with a song, it is hard to imagine anyone else ever singing it again."

There were discussions of contracts and tours, but she quietly demurred. She said she was not ready.

269.

"Besides," she told Andrew. "I don't want to leave you. I think you've got a hold on me."

"Let me get past the boundaries, and I'll show what a hold feels like."

"I can't wait," she smiled. "We've got time."

*

Some of the old music aficionados had gathered around Deannie and held her in conversation for a long time. One of them told her, "You have a perfect folksinger voice."

"When I begin," she said, almost talking to herself, "Something strange happens. It's as though the song is holding me in a lovely, gentle grip. And it sweeps through my whole body. I love the feeling. I don't want it to release me... Every time it happens, I'm amazed."

"We could never get tired of you," they said.

In his relationship with Deannie, Andrew developed what would become a lifelong love for folk music.

Somehow it never occurred to him to record her angelic voice on his wire recorder. He felt no need to do it. He assumed her voice would last forever.

*

After that restful summer, Andrew came back into school with pent up energy. He was moving into the top or near-top positions in a number of clubs and had joined the staff of the school newspaper. His role as Coordinator of the Citizenship Education Program gave him unusual range of latitude in trying new things. This included finding and inviting outside speakers, and arranging class assemblies in the Auditorium. The chess club

270.

he had organized was functioning well under Jiggety's leadership. He took part in plays in the dramatic guild and had become its president. In one of his first plays, his entering line was "What in the hell is going on here?" In practicing his line, he found himself in a number of amusing incidents when it was heard out of context. Deannie liked it so much, she would ask him from time to time "What in the hell is going on here?"

Andrew decided it was time to try something bolder. Although there were a number of ethnic and racial mixtures in the school, people tended to congregate in kind, except in sports. Andrew thought he could change the dynamic. With Mr. Holtzen's approval (and the principal's okay), Andrew formed the Interracial and Intercultural Society and became its first president. Among other things, he had read about the incident in 1939 when Marian Anderson had been denied a chance to sing at Constitution Hall, and had to sing instead at the Lincoln Memorial. The stimulus in him was strong. Prejudice must be addressed. Old grievances must be redressed. His Society could not do all that but it would at least be another step forward.

Once he had officers in place, and with their enthusiastic consent, he organized the first interracial and intercultural dance, in the gymnasium. He found he had a gift for organizing, a natural ability. Streamers, balloons, fruit punch, snacks, big band records, name tags, publicity, everything. He planned and put it all together well and it was held on schedule toward the end of September.

As president, he welcomed everyone, encouraged them to mix and get to know each other, then as the music began, he selected a partner for the first dance. He walked across the floor of the gym, where everyone was clustered more or less in kind, and asked "Peaches" if she would dance with him.

Peaches, otherwise known as Sylvia Manono, had skin the color of deep indigo, with intriguing hints of a yellowish hue. The hint of yellow was not so much a color tone as an impression captured only by a quick glance. If you tried to look directly at it, it would go away. But the shadows were visible, made even more colorful within the depth of the indigo foundation.

Peaches was tall and attractive, full of life. She had an outgoing personality and a wicked sense of humor. She had styled her hair especially for the dance. And wore her favorite clingy red dress.

"I thought you'd never ask," she laughed.

"I couldn't wait to get over here," he joked.

"Groovy," she said.

The first number was One O'Clock Jump. Peaches moved so well with the music, Andrew was already beginning to learn things from her. And when it was done and he began to walk her back to her seat, she stopped him.

"Not so fast, mister man. You the man. You can't go away til you slow dance with me."

"I like your boldness," he said.

"That's me. Big and bold. Sassy, too!"

"And full of life," he smiled. "We're going to get along fine."

The next dance was Dancing in the Dark, by his old friend Artie Shaw. And once more, at a surface level, they moved well together, but Andrew felt a certain sense of stiffness in her, almost an unwillingness to relax. He thanked her. "Terrific," she lied. And he walked her to her seat. The ice was broken, and couples were becoming mixed all around the floor. After that Andrew and Peaches became good friends, a relationship filled with warmth and laughter.

Andrew saw Kuki doing a jitterbug with one of the hip cats. They all wore zoot suits. If she saw him at all, she ignored him. Zoot suits with a reet pleat, they called it. Knee-length jackets with heavy shoulder pads, high-waisted pants with baggy knees and wrapped tight around the ankles, shiny shirts with overlong collars, a wide and short tie, two-tone shoes, and watch chain dangling to the knee. Both outdoors and indoors, they wore flat-top porkpie hats with very wide brims. Kuki had seemed to gravitate to that crowd. For Andrew it was a whole other world. Many of its inhabitants were reefers or pot heads, but Andrew tried to make sure no one would be smoking dope in the school. He saw none and didn't smell any and assumed they had not.

On his way to the other side of the gym, after dancing with Peaches, he happened to walk past Miss Whittle, who was one of the chaperons.

"I see you're moving up in the world," she said. He detected an unmistakable edge of ironic disapproval in the way she said it.

But the dance was a success. Barriers—at least here in this place and for this moment—seemed to loosen a bit. Everyone said they'd had a good time. There was even an article about it in the Detroit News, with a photo of Andrew dancing with Peaches.

Deannie liked it too. After Peaches, Andrew danced with one

273.

other dark beauty, then all the slow, sensual dances with Deannie. Glenn Miller's Moonlight Serenade, String of Pearls, Frank Sinatra's ballads, they all made her swoon, she said. "Falling–in-love music," he said.

*

The following month Joe invited Andrew to go hunting with himself and two friends from work. They would drive North to Oscoda and hunt in the pine forests along the AuSable River. Only for the weekend. Andrew agreed, and Joe loaned him an old Winchester rifle and ammunition.

Joe had a 1940 Ford and the four drove north with all the windows closed, more than a three hour trip. The problem was as Andrew quickly learned, the three adults were smokers. They puffed and puffed the whole way, only occasionally opening a window for a few moments, or when they stopped for gas in Standish. The smoke was heavy, oppressive. He did not know how they could stand it. But they carried on in conversation without mentioning it. Andrew kept counting the minutes until this would all be over. As the junior member of the group, he felt he had no right to ask them to ride with a window open. Smoking seemed like such a deadly pastime, he wondered what would drive people to do it.

And when at last they drove inland to a cabin they had reserved along the river, Andrew came out into the cleanest air he had ever breathed. Laden with a moist pine scent, cool from the night October winds, the air came into his lungs like a rapture. His lungs felt so delicate he did not know how he could contain it. He stood among the pines for quite a while, letting his lungs adjust, recovering, feeling a new sensitivity he had never noticed in his lungs before. He thought this would be the kind of air he would breathe for all his life, if the choice were his.

Hunting requires strategy, stealth, patience, keen observation, a sensitivity to wind direction, a desire to kill. Andrew found he had a natural instinct for the first five, but he had no desire to kill. He did not need the meat. He had no family to feed. Why put a bullet through the heart of an innocent deer minding its own business? It did not seem like a fair fight. The deer could not shoot back.

He did not express his reservations to Joe and the others. He thought it would not seem manly. They were all in a jovial mood, with no apparent concern for the welfare of the animal. They would sit in wait for an attempt to kill. They drove to the drop off point, then fanned out in individual directions, agreeing to return to the car before dusk. If anyone made a kill, he would fire three shots to assemble the others for help.

Andrew deeply enjoyed the comfort of the pines, strong and enduring through rain and snow and sun and wind. He breathed with expanded lungs to capture the pine-scented smell of the crisp autumn air, and the pungent aroma of the forest floor as it gently turned what fell to it into new layers of rich, loamy soil. He felt a whiff of eternity in that endless cycle, earthy and very real.

His whole being seemed very much alive in the quietness and serenity of the wooded trails. The way the wind whispered through the pines created a melancholy sound, a quiet moaning, searching for expanded meaning.

The sound of the moaning wind reached deeply into his spirit. The trees sheltered him from its October bite, but not from the images it evoked—on one hand a terrible sense of loneliness, on the other hand a sense of profound connection... to what, he did not know. Being alone in the north woods, at least for this little hour, played across his mind in poignant memories, and a heightened desire to engage with the higher mysteries of the universe, to find a larger universal perspective.

If there is a God, he wondered, can I find him here, along these empty trails? And that wind—is there somewhere in it some brief, compelling trace of his voice? Andrew, you are far from everything. You are here in the woods with only Me beside you. Why do you hold back? Rest your mind and spirit. Be still and know that I AM. All else is secondary to this one eternal truth. These thoughts raced through his mind almost as a fleeting shadow. If he took a moment to let it sink in, it was already gone.

The clouds were overcast in a way that said winter is coming. Andrew worked his way for a considerable distance up along a ridgeline, angled down, found an animal trail, and positioned himself downwind in a secluded place. The fresh surroundings continued to stimulate his mind. It was as if all the engines in his brain were turned down to a low hum, so thoughts could race and play and dart about until he caught one and nurtured it into ripening fullness.

His mind turned to Zeedie for a while. He loved her. He wondered for the thousandth time why she would not love him? The sigh of the wind through the needles of the pines gave no answer.

He thought of the Cameron farm. Clara had sold it, auctioned everything, and moved to Belgrave, a town even smaller than Lucknow, to be near her brother's family. He thought of Eileen, and the mystical word she had left on her pillow. If she could not come to Detroit, how could she go to Ireland, which was even farther? He thought about how close they once had been, and her emergence into such magnificent womanhood, made even more attractive by all the freckles, and how it had changed everything. He pulled the memory of her body into his mind, its dazzling fresh beauty in the sunlight along the river, the firmness of the grip of her hand around his. Would he ever see her again? Kismet.

He thought of Laura, how beautiful she was, how positive about everything, how crushed in the wake of her parents' divorce. She must be living in Vermont now, he thought, living the life of a country girl. But the memory of her soft velvet legs wrapped around his neck came back to him, and that sweet sensation, like a love torch. A once-in-a-lifetime experience? He wondered. There was a mystery there, but one that seemed gone forever.

He thought about Deannie. The purity of her voice, the sweet innocence of her character, the chemistry between them. She was a new high moment in his life. He was happy with her, happy just to be in the same room with her.

And his mind returned to the passions that once drove him to declare a quest to turn around the world. War was such a monstrous invention. Millions upon millions of lives lost or maimed forever, families destroyed. And all for what? He wondered, are there always good sides and bad sides in a war? Or is there a blending mixture?

In the war just ended the answer was clear. Hitler and his allies had to be stopped. Had he succeeded, he had planned to move every male over the age of 12 out of England, to someplace deep within Russia, surround them with barbed wire and machine guns and starve them to death. Then he would have sent his "Supermen" to repopulate the English islands. He would have used atomic weapons against the United States. He would probably then have done to American manhood what he had planned to do with the English. And then attempt to create a "master race" with the women who were left.

So, Andrew thought, it is not that every war is wrong. Sometimes the situation is black and white. Sometimes you just have to fight for your life, fight to preserve what has enduring value to civilization. Maybe the better answer is that we have to somehow engineer a real and lasting world peace. So that war is no longer such a natural inclination. His mind turned again to thoughts of how this might be done. There was going to be a United Nations organization, but they were already fighting among themselves and may be doomed. There has to be a better way…

He was so lost in thought he had not noticed that a 10-point buck, coming from an upwind direction, was idly grazing on some winter berries hardly 20 feet in front of him. He had been so quiet where he sat the deer did not notice him and had not picked up his scent.

His first instinct was to lift his rifle from his lap and kill the deer, but he did not move. A second, more powerful thought, danced across his brain. Enjoy the beauty of watching this unaware creature grazing in its own natural domain. Why kill? Why bring an arbitrary end to his animal's life for no reason other than to experience a brief sense of power? He had no need for this kind of power. And so for a while as the buck nibbled bushes in front of him, he simply enjoyed watching nature in its course.

And then a shot came whizzing by his head, inches above him, striking bark off the tree where he sat. The shot had missed the buck, but frightened the animal so thoroughly the buck took off and was out of sight in three quick giant leaps. Joe rushed up near Andrew. "I didn't see you," Joe said.

"You almost killed me," Andrew laughed, and showed him the splintered tree.

"Jee-sus, I'm sorry. You were so well hidden."

"Upwind, too."

"Couldn't get a shot?" Joe asked.

"I decided not to shoot," Andrew said.

Joe showed signs of uncharacteristic aggravation. "But that's why you're here," he almost stammered in incomprehension. "That was a 10-point buck!"

"Maybe hunting's not my natural skill. If we needed the meat to survive, I would have made the kill."

"But we needed to drape him over the roof of the car," Joe said, still agitated.

"You can still do that. You've still got tomorrow."

Joe seemed to settle down, then began with some hesitance in what he wanted to say next.

"Andrew, I want to change the subject."

"Okay."

"I saw the <u>Detroit News</u> last month, that picture of you dancing with a spook."

"Oh, you mean Peaches."

"Whatever you call her. Have you thought about what it means? Are you giving any thought to your future?"

"As a matter of fact, I am."

"Well, don't be a schmuck."

"Joe, I like you and respect you, but I don't think you should tell me who I can dance with and who I can't dance with. I started the Club to promote understanding."

"Andrew, I'm only thinking about your welfare."

"I appreciate your concern. I really do. But I have my own life to live."

Joe's expression turned to sadness, his eyes cast down. When he spoke his words were barely audible in the brisk October wind. "You're heading for outcast road."

Upon arrival home Sunday evening they found the Henry home next door had been firebombed during their absence. The Henry home and trucks had been destroyed. One life had been lost, a woman friend (Blackie) who had been asleep in an upstairs bedroom. The fire trucks had poured so much water on the house Joe and Jessica were renting next door that it survived with only blistered paint and some water damage.

Bubbles the cop was still investigating. The Henrys had scattered. "They had a run-in with the Wheelers Union," he said. "You don't run in with them unless you're ready to take them out.

They're too strong to take out, at least for ordinary people."

*

The next year was filled with the warmth of his new friendships and occasional parties, ice skating, trips downtown to see big bands, and an ever strengthening closeness to Deannie. As close as they already were, there seemed to be enlarging realms in which they found satisfaction with each other. The one boundary line that had not moved was the constraint she placed on his hands. "What in the hell is going on here?" she would joke. Or "I'm not ready for that," she would say. "Don't you know I will go insane if I can't have my way with you?" he would joke. "I'll visit you in the outhouse," she would laugh.

It was a productive year. In the following semester, Andrew was told, the school was going to create several advanced math and science classes for him and about ten other students. Andrew continued to get straight A's. He began speaking on the radio on behalf of the Citizenship Education Program. He became president of several clubs in which he had not yet attained that goal. He found an after-school job in a local drugstore. And by June, when he had saved enough money, Joe taught him to drive and Andrew bought a 1941 Mercury with 150,000 miles on it for a hundred dollars. Joe taught him how to keep it running, basic automotive mechanical skills.

In June the first reports of UFO's filled newspapers and airwaves. Among all his friends and associates it was the singular topic of discussion. Kenneth Arnold had seen nine disc-shaped objects in the sky as he was flying over the state of Washington, and they moved in ways superior to any known technology.

Other stories rapidly followed. People were either seeing things or something new was in the skies. Andrew decided to reserve judgment. If he saw one personally, unmistakably, he would believe. Until then, he would only take in information.

He joined the Royal Astronomical Society, then formed an astronomy study group in school, and was able to borrow a telescope. He became a member of the Detroit Engineering Society and thought he might become an engineer.

The thought of UFO's did not disturb him. From as far back as he could remember, he had assumed there were countless other planets in the universe that were populated by living, sentient beings. To think otherwise, that in this immense creation—only a tiny part of which is visible to us—that we are the only intelligent beings, that, in his reasoning, would be the height of arrogant conceit or stupendous ignorance.

In June, as school ended their junior year, the group met for a party. Everyone had different plans for the summer. Deannie would sing, but otherwise stay near Andrew. He would go with her when not working. His car now gave him freedom to take her places, even to the rippling sand beaches up on Lake Huron, and she had at last consented to swim.

Brundi would work all summer in the woods of northern Michigan, manning one end of a huge cross-cut saw ("the misery whip," he said). Brundi had broken up with Cynthia. "She was unfaithful," he told Andrew. Aram and Anna would be away all summer at a special music program in Connecticut. Jiggety and Poppy planned to go to Arkansas and Mississippi to visit relatives. Cynthia would spend a lot of time on her father's boat in Grosse Isle, while he built a large house on the riverfront.

In saying goodbye for the summer, Jiggety took Andrew aside and said, "I never got around to analyzing you."

"What makes you think I need analysis?"

"Everybody needs analysis."

"Jig, I really like you, but I think you're a little cracked."

"I've spent more than a year and a half working with you, beating you at chess, observing you—you want all this to go to waste?"

"Jig, I'm your friend, not your patient."

"Sure, but Poppy's my friend too, the best friend I have in the world. I analyze her all the time." Poppy smiled broadly. "She helps me understand the Chinese mind. With Poppy's help, I will become an international whiz."

By now Cynthia had come near. "What's up?" she asked Andrew in her provocative style.

"Same as usual. Nothing." Andrew said.

"What a waste. Do something useful," she laughed and walked away.

Deannie now came over and took his arm protectively. "What's Jig trying to do to you?"

"He wants to look inside my mind."

"Only professionally," Jiggety said. "Nothing personal. I am an excellent judge of character. I can look right into people's souls. I want to show you how you look to a trained mind."

"Then you must judge that I must be thinking I don't want you climbing around inside my head."

Jiggety laughed. "Andrew, I don't have to go inside. All the scaffolding is there. I can work from the outside. Peek inside through the windows."

"Do you think you can find <u>me</u> in there?" Deannie laughed.

"Deannie," Andrew smiled. "You already fill half my mind. How could he miss you?"

"Why don't you let him give it a try?"

"I think I'm outnumbered," Andrew said. "Jig, do your damnedest, but if you break anything you're responsible for all repairs. Take your best shot." Several others came around, including Cynthia.

And Jiggety did. "I'll skip right past the obvious stuff, get right down to the meat. Andrew, you are a man of contradictions. From a psychological viewpoint, you are a mess of complexities. You are an Alpha Dog, but you come across as someone inwardly relaxed. You're intense and passionate, but you try to hide it. Some of it shows through. You're gregarious, and yet reflective. You're idealistic, but you are also a practical realist. You're precise, but you're comfortable with ambiguity. You're a born planner and organizer, but you don't have a clue yet about how to plan your life. You're thorough, but I don't know if your thoroughness is a blessing or a curse. You see how messed up you are?"

"You're missing some important things," Brundi broke in.

"Brundi, my friend. Stand in line. Your turn next," Jiggety said.

Jiggety continued. "If I had to say it in one sentence, I would say you have a penetrating intelligence and you are trying to penetrate the unknown—you are engaged in a relentless pursuit of <u>meaning</u>. You're always searching, exploring, trying to push past the limits. You're an all-or-nothing guy—at least that's what I've observed. I think you're the kind of guy Teddy Roosevelt had in mind when he said, and I quote, 'no man is worth his salt who is not ready at all times to risk his body… to risk his well-being… to risk his life… in a great cause…'"

"And here's something else," Jiggety added, "This is such a wild contradiction it must drive people crazy. Most people are locked into a single paradigm—the inability to see reality except through a specific, habitual frame of reference. But you, my friend, you can come into a discussion with five paradigms at once. You're like the cowboy who can ride, rope, and shoot. This sometimes scares people."

There was a natural pause and Brundi stepped up to the head of the line. "Jig, if you're trying to wrap Andrew in a psychology cocoon, there are a couple of other things you'd better add."

"Fire away," Jiggety said.

"He hates suck-ups. He hates to see someone sucking up to power and authority. He hates to see the suck received. And hates people who walk around with a sense of entitlement. He'll never cut in line."

Cynthia interrupted. Looking at Andrew, she said, "Sounds like you should be going out with me, not with Deannie."

"Why?" Andrew asked.

"I've got more fire. I'm more complex. I'm more a major risk."

He looked at her eyes more closely. There was a teasing, engaging expression. "Deannie burns with a deeper flame," he said. Then added, "And her songs reach into places you have never touched."

Cynthia would not be distracted. "In the breast of every Hungarian is a fire, and a need to dance around it with fallen angels."

Andrew smiled. "There's more poetry in your soul than you let on."

Deannie took his hand. "You know what you've both left out?" she asked both Jiggety and Brundi, pointedly ignoring Cynthia.

"What?" they asked.

"Andrew has a warm spot for underdogs. He has a sense of fairness that seems to include every creature, human and otherwise. One day he was coming up a driveway and didn't know I was watching… it was after a rain and there were these gleaming little small puddles evaporating in the sun. And worms, I didn't know where they'd come from, but they were just there in the sun, dumb and drying, their little bodies dying. I could see their soft pink skins already hardening and becoming brittle, the air was so clear. And they didn't know what to do. And every moment they were edging closer to the point of no return, just lying there dumb and motionless…"

"I watched Andrew. He bent down. He gathered them gently on some fallen leaves he used for scoops. About 20 of them. He placed them on some wet soil, then he used the leaves to scoop water. He sprinkled them. Then he dug into the soil with his fingers to cover them with a nice moist blanket."

Andrew felt awkward, increasingly uncomfortable. "I'll

have to get to know this guy," he tried to joke. Deannie squeezed his hand.

*

It happened in late October, on a particularly windless, sunny afternoon. From the diagnosis to her death took only eight weeks. Deannie had developed a very rare and aggressive form of cancer. She had no warning signs, only that she suddenly felt weak and not herself. She thought she had the flu. The cancer was so rapidly spreading that even a second and third opinion could not alter the prognosis or its swift outcome. "Are you sure?" Deannie and her parents, then Andrew, asked over and over again.

They think it's called Wagner's disease, Deannie explained. "The auto-immune system gets all screwed up. It doesn't know which is friend and which is enemy. Usually you die within a few weeks, after they discover it."

The doctors were sure. In the handful of reported cases, this form of cancer had never been arrested or reversed. No one had lasted longer than eight weeks. You go four weeks feeling pretty normal, then it's a one-way roller coaster ride to the bottom.

Andrew quit his after-school job and ceased all extracurricular school activities so he could spend as much time as possible with her. Deannie had become stoically calm, but he knew she was inwardly shaken. In the first two weeks she showed no outward sign of the disease. She told Andrew she might have one or two more good weeks before the disintegration. He held her a lot, caressed her, and they talked about nothing in particular, or just sat quietly together reading.

"You know what's really strange?" she told him, "I feel okay inside right now. If you were to tell me I'll be gone by Christmas, I'd laugh you out of the room ...Nuts, isn't it?"

"Sure is."

"But I don't feel like singing any more ...I guess that's a sign."

"Deannie, I'm not a praying man, and I don't even know if this is prayer, but every day and every night I say to God if you have any leftover angels please send them to Deannie. She sure could use some help. You must have a spare angel or two."

"I'm not much with prayer myself," she said. "I don't even know what to pray for. I can't ask God to spare me. That would be selfish. I'm sure he's got more important things to do."

"Right now, I can't think of anything more important than you," he said.

"I just had a crazy idea. My parents are going to be away for two days. They're going to Boston, to see one more specialist. They know you'll be with me here, that I'll be cared for if anything goes wrong."

"I won't leave you. I won't even go to school."

"Well, here's my crazy idea... My uncle has a place in Belleville on the lake. It's a nice place. I've been there a number of times. It's winterized but he doesn't use it after October."

"And you're suggesting...?"

"I know where my parents keep the spare key."

"Deannie, I don't think you're crazy. I think you're a genius."

The week before Thanksgiving he drove her to the cottage. It was nicely furnished for year-round living and had a large fireplace. Andrew opened the flu and built a fire. Deannie had never drunk anything alcoholic before, but as she opened a bottle of her uncle's wine she told Andrew, "I'm feeling bold today."

"How bold?" he grinned.

"Bolder than you think."

They sat on the couch holding each other close, in front of the warming fire, slowly sipping the red wine. Deannie became more talkative. "You know," she said, "last summer when Jig and Brundi were trying to analyze you…?" He nodded. "They left out a couple of other things…"

"Tell me."

"There is an aroma of friendliness about you, as natural as the air you breathe."

He kissed her gently. "I'd like to think so but I don't think everybody would agree with you."

"To hell with everybody," she said, startling him. She had never before uttered even the mildest form of curse.

"Do you think the wine is talking?"

"No. I'm feeling a nice warm cozy sensation, but the wine hasn't got to any place important yet."

He poured them both a second glass.

"I'll tell you what else," she said. "Jig and Brundi are males, so they wouldn't know this, but any woman would."

"I can't wait to hear what you're going to say next."

"You have kind of a relaxed masculinity …sure of itself but not waving any flags about it."

"You are most gracious."

Her thoughts now became more serious. "Do you have a plan for your life?"

"I don't have a plan, only a vision."

"I thought you might have everything all planned out."

"I'm not sure I want to plan my life too carefully. I'm so driven, so methodical, I'm afraid I might succeed," he laughed. "And that would be the greatest danger of all. I don't want to shut off possibilities, or narrow the options too closely."

"I was thinking about us."

Now Andrew became reflective. "Deannie, I'm going to tell you something I have never said before… to anyone. I love you. I never said those words before."

"I was hoping you'd say that. I love you with all my heart. I wanted to hear you say it first."

For some time they held each other in a warm embrace, kissing, stroking arms and neck and shoulders. And Andrew gently began to stroke her breast. She did not push his hand away this time. "I'm trying to respect your boundary lines, but I just can't help it. I want to be so close to you."

"I don't know where the boundaries are anymore. All I know is I don't want you to go insane when I die," she joked.

She let him unbutton her blouse and unsnap and remove her bra. And as he had once seen in the summer rain, her nipples, unusually long and large, extended fully into his lips. They were warm and delicious to taste. He took them in his mouth by turns as she stroked his hair. "You can spend all the time you want there," she breathed. And somehow as he moved alternately from her breast to her lips, he began to say things that made her laugh. Highly topical humor, puns, ricocheting puns, funny observations, sensuous humor, all intermingled with the bold sensations of his exploring lips.

"You make me laugh so much I'm afraid my face will crack. I'm not used to laughing this much."

"Laughter is the best medicine."

"Andrew, you're wicked. But I love your mind. Your mind dances with humor."

"What else?" he grinned.

"I love what you're doing to me."

He moved the large couch pillows to the floor in front of the fire and she found a soft blanket. By now they had each finished two glasses of wine. With their heads on the blanketed pillows he continued his explorations, removing all that concealed her last privacy. And as he did so he felt her fingers unbuckling his belt. Now he was certain of the outcome.

He remembered what Sondra Whittle had taught him about the other ways. He stroked her gently for some time, holding her close, until she released. She released so hard he thought for a moment she had become convulsive, but she recovered.

"You know just what to do with me," she said when she relaxed again.

"I'm just warming up," he said, holding her close, kissing her swollen lips. "The best is yet to come."

His drugstore job had enabled him to purchase condoms in privacy and he had adopted the habit of carrying a package just in case. He reached into his pants pocket and with one hand began to unfurl one. When she saw what he was doing she put her hand over his. "Don't," she said. "I want to experience you, not the mask of you." He put the condom away.

And now they lay in close embrace again and he stroked her everywhere, her head and neck, her cheeks, her back, her loins and all that was in between, all the while sucking at her breast and lips. "You make me feel I was born to be caressed," she whispered.

"And I was born to be your caresser," he said softly. And then he took her hand from its movements along his sides, and placed her fingers over him.

"You're firm as a rock," she whispered.

"I've wanted so long to be inside you. To be as close within you as I can possibly be..."

"I've wanted to feel your love within me ever since I've known you."

And she guided him, then let go and wrapped him in her arms. And he moved slowly, gently for a while and looked deeply into her startled and dancing Morning Glory blue eyes.

"I didn't know anything could feel so beautiful," she said.

"I feel a power deep within you."

"I can't talk anymore," she said. "I just want to close my eyes and feel every inch of you. Every blessed inch."

And she closed her eyes and held him in tight embrace. And he began gradually to increase the tempo of his movements, trying to adjust himself to the rhythm and intensity of her breathing.

And after a time, when he knew she was close, he was careful not to let his passion ride into her too hard and scare her off. He moved within her breath by breath, holding back his impulses, until at last she gasped. "I'm a goner!" And only then did he let his passion move with strength and soon explode into her.

She responded with a convulsive force, but this time it did not scare him. He could feel her energy almost vibrating beneath him. He held himself above her on his elbows, letting all their flesh touch, but so as not to crush her with his weight. The convulsive energy of her flesh against him was utterly sensual.

"Help me find a place to land," she whispered as though she had no breath left. And he held her tightly until she landed.

And for a long time they lay in each other' arms, touching and caressing, kissing... "You took me all the way," she whispered. "It was everything I hoped it would be."

"I can't describe how beautiful you are in love."

"Do you think anyone has ever loved this much before?" she whispered dreamily.

"I can't see how that would be possible."

"You're my first, last ...and only."

"You're a beautiful love," he said.

"I've never been happier."

*

And for another week, in which they reveled in their new level of awareness and closeness, the two of them talked endlessly, and from time to time would repeat the vows of their interwoven love. And then, as the doctors had predicted, Deannie's body began to disintegrate rapidly.

"I'm too young to be this old," she said once, but otherwise accepted her condition with a valiant and resolute calmness. And Andrew stayed by her side. Her parents had moved her bed into the living room, and he slept on the couch beside her. The speed of her wasting away was almost beyond his comprehension. Just a week before, she had been so brilliant, so vibrant. And in her uncle's cottage, she was so alive and tender in her love no one would have believed she was this close. She was losing weight very rapidly. Her face had suddenly become gaunt, almost haunted looking. But the sparkle never left her eyes. Toward the end, as he stood beside her bed holding her hand, she whispered to him.

"Do you think we could have made a life together?"

"We would have made a beautiful life together." It was all he could do to hold back tears. She was so calm, so stoic, he felt he could not let her see him break down."

"Do you see any angels?" he tried to ask as casually as he could.

"I'm not sure what angels look like," she whispered, but now with great effort. "I guess they'll have to hunt around until they find me."

"I gave them your address." It was his last attempt at humor.

And he caressed her quivering body until it gave up it's beautiful life. She died Christmas Eve.

Where was Christ? he wondered. Why is the beauty of her voice lost to the world forever? Who stole her innocence from the world? Why?

*

Christmas came and went. The funeral was a blur. New Year's Eve was a hazy fog. He tried to take solace in poetry. He turned to Tennyson.

"But oh for the touch of a vanished hand,
and the sound of a voice that is still . . ."

But it could not bring relief from his sense of loss. He took long walks alone, and sometimes with Aram, Brundi, or Jiggety. They tried to lift his spirits, but he was in a distant place for a while. He treasured their friendship, and knew they understood because Deannie had been their friend too. They mourned her death with him, but he had found something deeper with her, that their mourning couldn't reach.

And now as January plunged on, he went back into his classes, and resumed his extracurricular activities.

On a cold and desolate mid-January day Cynthia asked him if he would go for a walk with her after school. The skies were gray and a light snow was falling, and they walked together for some distance before she spoke.

"I want to talk with you because I came across a poem. I know you have a poetic heart— I wanted to share this one with you."

"Who's the author?"

"I don't know. All I know is it's an old poem."

"Tell me," he said.

And she turned so that her words would not be lost in the bitter air. And he turned to face her. She spoke:

"Beauty is only altered,
never lost.
And love,
before the cold November rain,
Will make its summer
in the heart again."

295.

He kissed her on the cheek. "Thank you. It's very beautiful."

"That's all," she said. "You can walk me home now."

"You are a good friend."

"Will you get over Deannie?"

"It will take a while. We became very close. I can't hear a folk song without images of her floating through my mind. I can't breathe without her in the background of my mind."

"Let me be your friend while you recover."

He removed her glove and held her hand in both of his.

"Cynthia, I have a feeling we are going to be friends for a long time."

"That's what I want," she said. This time she kissed him on the cheek.

*

In late January Joe fell ill with a renewed attack of rheumatic fever. This time, because a union was now in place at the plant, he would not lose his job. And as before, he would not receive any form of compensation while he was out. The illness was to last for months.

Jessica still worked, but her wages could not alone support the family. They might have scraped through, but all the medical bills and medications overwhelmed their ability to stay afloat. By mid-February, when the duration of the illness seemed clear, Andrew decided to act. He did not consult them, but knew what he had to do. He lied about his age and took a job on the afternoon shift at the Lincoln-Mercury plant. The Ford Motor Company was still in a state of imbalanced transition since the death of Henry Ford the previous April.

It was a poignant moment for him because his radio speaking engagements were now enlarging, and in addition to his responsibilities as president of a number of clubs, he had become, with Aram Kanajian, co-editor-in-chief of the school paper. Despite all the time he had missed while attending Deannie, he still had managed to maintain his record of straight A's, even in the several advanced math and science courses which had been especially created for a number of the top students.

So, in one sense, he was riding on top of his little world, the brass ring in hand.

But in a different sense, he was considerably troubled within, anxious about Joe. He really loved him and wanted to see him well again. He gave Jessica his whole pay envelope (payment was always in cash), except for five dollars he kept for food and transportation for the week. Jessica told him his weekly contribution would keep the wolf from the door. "When that wolf comes scratching at your door, it smells like his paws got stuck in his droppings," she said, keeping her language moderate. But Andrew wanted to do more. What?

As a last resort he decided to try to pray. He still wasn't sure how to do it. His prayers for Deannie had been rather offhand and casually stated. Now he began to wonder what he had done wrong. He thought maybe he should be more formal. Do you use the more affected speech of the ministers? Do you have to close your eyes? Could He hear you if you just whisper? Or speak the words quietly within your mind? What if you have no words, don't know exactly what to say? Can He hear your

thoughts, read your mind? Can He just <u>know</u> what you need?
Then why pray at all? Why make petition when He already
knows what you want to ask? Are some prayers better than
others? Are some pray-ors better than others? Are some things
better to pray for than others? Should we even be praying for
<u>things</u> at all, or something else? This whole business of praying
was very confusing. But, beyond the confusion what held him
back further was his remembered experiences with prayer. He
had once prayed ardently for a bicycle. God sure had taken his
time. God must have decided he should keep walking for a while
first, stretch his legs. Maybe God has a great sense of humor. Or
maybe God is truly wise and knows things we are not capable of
understanding. Andrew remembered in one of the books he had
read, someone wrote that if we had a God small enough for our
understanding, He would not be large enough for our needs.
There was some comfort in that thought. Maybe God knows
what he's doing after all.

But why, Andrew asked again in his mind, why did God not
send an angel or two to help Deannie? She was so innocent, so
pure of heart—surely she must have deserved a little help. The
angels never showed up. Maybe they got lost. Maybe it was me.
Maybe the way I prayed was too much like a passing
conversation. Maybe I should have tried to speak in a foreign
language, like the priests. Maybe God doesn't understand
English. Maybe my prayer was inadequate. She would not pray
for herself. She didn't want to be any trouble. There are so many
really bad people in the world, why not take one of them instead
of her? And now here is Joe, sitting on the cliff. Are you going

to pull him back or push him over? Andrew inwardly apologized for this last thought. Whatever he knew about God, he knew enough to know God doesn't go around pushing people off cliffs. "God," Andrew whispered, "If you are a God of love, please start loving…"

In the back of his mind he felt a certain sense of shame that he would resort to prayer. There was a lingering suspicion that if you engaged in prayer it meant you were throwing in the towel, admitting defeat, showing the world you did not have the guts and stamina to tough it out all by yourself. Prayer was for weaklings, a crutch. He hated to make such a visible statement about himself. But then he thought if it does no good, at least it can't hurt. He was still confused about the eyes. He thought he should close his eyes if he prayed. But what if anyone saw him with closed eyes in the daytime? They would <u>know</u> what he was doing. To be safe, he thought he should make his prayer as brief as possible, make sure nobody would see him.

He went out into the alley behind the house and found a place where several 50-gallon open drums were filled with garbage. He looked carefully around to make sure no one could see him. Then he ducked down behind the garbage drums, shut his eyes, and said out loud. "I hope he gets better… Please make him better." Afraid of discovery, he rose quickly to his feet and walked back through the alley as though nothing had happened.

*

He set into a rigorous schedule. School from eight in the morning til three in the afternoon. Forty-five minutes by streetcar and bus to the Lincoln-Mercury plant. Punch in at four. Work the shift til twelve thirty. One hour to get home. Take a bath. Sleep three hours. Study two-and-a-half hours. Begin again.

The plant assigned Andrew to the maintenance department, where he met Tom Wharton. Tom was partially crippled, used crutches, but could work sitting down, which is where they put him. He handled the routine paperwork for the department and generally worked with several large ledgers and scheduling books. He was one year short of retirement at age 65.

Andrew quickly learned Tom was a poet in his spare time, his "real job," he said. "But the pay is piss poor." Tom had a heavily weathered face, a full head of gray hair and gray beard, and watery blue eyes that always seemed ready to bear tears. There was a perpetual strain in his voice, but you did not notice it when he told stories. He had a lot of them. One day soon after he started, Andrew sat with Tom at lunch break and listened to his story.

"I left Detroit in 1899. I was 15. I whaled the Atlantic for three years. I joined an exploration party in Brazil. We went into what was then the far reaches of the Amazon. I personally killed the largest sawfish in the western hemisphere. I have its long sawtooth bill hanging in my living room. I went to Paris and spent four years trying to become an artist. I was told my paintings would suck the life right out your wallet..."

"What does that mean?" Andrew asked.

"Don't know. Never could figure it out. All I could tell for sure was painting was not my natural gift. So I gave that up. I went to Africa and became a hunter. I drank a lot of whisky and published some of my poetry in British journals. Can't even remember their names. Really obscure. Then I worked on the Panama Canal for two years. This was during the Great War, the war to end all wars. I worked my way on a freighter very slowly across the Pacific. I spent five years in India in search of my soul. Couldn't find it…"

"Maybe it wasn't lost," Andrew joked.

Tom continued not responding to the joke. "I was 38 years old, didn't know what I wanted to do… so I came back to Detroit to see if I could find a new footing. I took a job at the Ford Rouge plant. Thought I'd stay for about a year. Worked on the assembly line for 20 years. I never planned to stay permanently. Only long enough to save enough money for a new start. But before you know it you get into a rut. You've got steady pay, and you remember how tough it is in the world outside. You drift along year after year…"

"If you started with Ford how did you get over to Lincoln-Mercury?"

"In 1942 I was run over by a drunken taxi driver without an operating permit. Took all my savings. They said I could sue, but it wouldn't do any good. He didn't have any money."

"I get it. That was during the manpower shortage."

"Yep. Everybody was off to war. Ford let me come over here and gave me a job where I could work sitting down."

"Are you still writing poetry?"

"Never stopped. I keep piling it up with the idea someday I might get it all published."

Andrew probed. "With all the adventure and excitement in your life, how could you take a monotonous assembly line job for 20 years?"

"That's the sixty-four dollar question."

"I want to know how you think about it."

Tom chewed on a bologna sandwich for another minute, sipped some black coffee out of his thermos, and seemed to be staring at something far away. "I'm not ignoring your question. Just thinking about it a little bit. I'm not gonna give you a bullshit answer. I'll try to tell it the way it plays in my mind."

"You seem to have a philosophical look in your eye."

"I was trying to think like a poet, not a philosopher, but here goes..." He finished his coffee before he spoke. "This is where men come when they're defeated, when they're broke and hungry and scared to reach. They come here to get some money, get ahead. Hardly anyone comes with the thought of staying forever. They don't feel defeated on the morning they apply for work, waiting in the pouring rain on Miller Road. The idea consumes them gradually. Every year it's less of a struggle. And after a time there's no other life within their reach. The plant becomes their purpose."

Lunch break was almost over, but Andrew asked him to continue, until the whistle blew. Tom continued. "All the bloody battles to organize the plant---oh! They were worth every broken head. We have some protection now. But with politicians talking about a recession, everyone fears a layoff. So the object is to survive, gain seniority. High-seniority men can survive all but the worst layoffs. You don't tilt at windmills or make waves. Seniority is security. Security is that lovely mermaid voice, singing on the banks of a dirty river... This is where the iron mermaid sings with a throat of steel—I wrote that once, in one of my favorite poems—'she can consume a thousand years of living flesh in a single gulp...' I even tried to write it a different way, but it keeps coming out sexual. When I think of Ford I think of sex. I can't help it! Those iron thighs, those gray-green whispering loins, that smoky voice, that siren song that lures men to their pleasure and their doom..." He wanted to continue, but Andrew interrupted.

"Tom, did you finally become cynical? Could your poetry not pull you out of cynicism?

"'The plant corrupts the spirit not by what it does, but by what it doesn't do. The plant is neutral. It holds no value, no moral purpose. The snake that worried Adam may have worried Henry Ford but not his plant.' That's another thing I wrote. In the plant the only worry was of Ford himself... Henry Ford would hand you a shining rose while he holds a stopwatch over you as you're trying to take a shit. He would give you a garden to grow vegetables, but wouldn't let you leave the line for a break even if you had diarrhea and were trying to hold it in. Sure, he's dead now, but his plants are still an extension of his mind. Working here is like working inside his mind..."

"I'll be out of here in a few months," Andrew said.

"Best of luck to you," Tom said. "Just remember, Rule Number One—nurse the job."

After that, Andrew often ate lunch with Tom, gathering Tom's recollections of a life that had not yet found its purpose. He enjoyed his nine-o'clock-in-the-evening lunch breaks with this crippled poet, dying by inches at a time.

One night he brought Tom Wharton the first 10 pages of a story he had begun to write. He hoped Tom, with all his vast experience and worldly wisdom, would tell him he had a natural gift for writing. The next night Tom handed back the 10 pages with only a five-word comment.

"Write about what you know."

Tom's words sank deep within Andrew's soul.

*

Cynthia began coming over on Saturday nights, the only night not occupied with deadlines. Andrew liked her and did not discourage her visits. She was also pleasing to the eye. She was a good conversationalist, always interesting. He liked her fire and zing, even her raciness. Her father had bought her a new car and she liked to show it off. She had a way of dressing that would show a lot of long legs when she was getting out of the car. She knew men liked to see a fair amount of flesh, especially if shrouded in a bit of mystery.

All through the spring she came over week after week on Saturdays. Sometimes Andrew would take her to a movie. In warmer weather in June they would go on drives in his car, find a quiet place in a park, and talk, or take a long walk. They talked about many things, but Andrew held back when she tried to talk about their relationship.

"We don't have a relationship," he told her. "We're friends, very good friends, but we don't have a relationship."

"You're only saying that because you're still hurting over Deannie."

"I loved her."

"Get over it. Life moves on. Talk about it. That's why you have me. Darling Andrew, you idiot, I'm here for you. Don't hold back. You have this goddamn habit of not letting on when you're hurting. Open up with me. I'm laying it all out for you."

"Let's just take this a step at a time."

It became increasingly clear to him as spring wore on, that Cynthia's visits had a more determined agenda.

"How would you like a hot, flaming love affair with a virgin?" she whispered in his ear one evening when they were parked and talking in his car.

He laughed. "From what I know, the only guys who <u>need</u> virgins are idealists, romantics, and guys who aren't sure of their masculinity."

"You forgot one type," she said.

"Which one?"

"You forgot to mention guys who are born explorers, who constantly need to investigate every new mystery, peek into every nook and cranny."

"I'm a born explorer," he smiled.

"So there you are."

"But I'm also trying to learn self-control."

"Don't practice self-control on me. That's not my thing. Fuck self-control."

"Cynthia," he laughed, "you know that I know you're not a virgin."

"Did Brundi tell you that?"

"You've pretty much said it in your own words."

"Andrew, you idiot!" she joined in laughter, "don't you know

I have the power to revirginize myself?"

"Now I'm really curious. How does a girl revirginize herself?"

"Simple if you know how to do it. I just close my eyes and tell myself nothing ever happened. I go into a little bit of a trance. Takes about 20 minutes— the important thing is what goes on in the trance. That's the secret technique. It changes your whole attitude about yourself. It wipes the slate. Cunning, ain't it?"

"You can do all that?" he smiled.

"It's like getting a face lift. Then I'm good as new. Brand spanking new. Ready to give it a go all over again. I <u>know</u> how to be fresh. I know I feel like a virgin to a man."

"You have an amazing mind."

"That's not the only amazing part of me. I was born with nature's gift. Can't take credit for it. You may be pleasantly surprised." She paused. "I'm sure Brundi would have mentioned it."

"Brundi's not a talker," he said.

"Aren't you curious?"

"I'll take your word for it."

"Chicken!" She kissed him hard on the mouth, open lips, just a hint of tongue. "Come join me at the party," she pouted. "Play with me."

"Cynthia, I like you as a friend. That's all."

"Next, you're going to just dump me. Abandon me..."

There were actual tears in the corners of her eyes. This puzzled Andrew. He had never seen this in her before. She seemed so sincere.

He hugged her and held her close. "I told you, I have a hunch we're going to be friends for a long time. How could I dump you when we've never crossed the line?"

She snuggled in his neck. One thing about her, he thought, she is voluptuous and very sensuous. She has a way of conveying her sensuousness so you feel awakenings within yourself. He hoped she wouldn't notice what she had done to him. "I heard about Miss Whittle," she said softly, wiping her tear-wet cheek against his neck. She brushed her hand against his arousal, only the barest, lightest touch. It seemed she wanted him to know that she knew what she was doing to him.

Andrew's first reaction was to deny it. He had assumed no one knew, no one at all. He had never spoken a word. But he quickly rejected the thought of denial. Lying about age on an application to get a job was one thing. Lying that would puncture the integrity of a relationship, any relationship, that was something else. He decided he would not become that kind of liar.

"What did you hear?" he asked tentatively.

"I want some of what she got."

"How do you know about Miss Whittle?"

"Women talk. They can't help it."

"But how did you find out?"

"I have a knack for being in places where good conversations are going on. That's one of my talents. There's something you don't understand about women: women talk. Especially to women who are alert and alive. That's me."

"Cynthia, I think you will go far in life."

"I won't take no for an answer."

"One step at a time."

"Andrew, my darling idiot. I'm already ten steps ahead of you. When are you going to catch up?"

*

In early May Joe recovered and went back to work. Andrew decided to continue working. The pay was good. Once Joe's wages resumed, money for school would be needed. He could build up a nest egg. By then Andrew had been accepted at University of Michigan. He had rejected three scholarships because the applications asked how much his father earned and he thought it was none of their business. But he accepted one that did not ask this question. It would pay tuition, room and board. He would enroll in the school of architecture in September. He had an idea buzzing around in his head.

One Saturday afternoon, after Andrew and Cynthia had enjoyed a late Polish breakfast with Joe and Jessica, Cynthia asked him about Joe's health.

"He's got a problem heart. Most of the time you'd never know it. But when it kicks up, it kicks hard."

"Want to know something?" Cynthia asked.

"What?"

"I'm really juiced by Joe."

"My God, he's 37 years old. In three years he'll be 40. He's an old man."

"Yeah, but I like older men. He really juices me."

"You're weird." Andrew pondered her remarks. He thought she was a bit off in the head. In his mind all sex life ended at 40.

You just hung it up on the wall after that. Forty was old age.

Cynthia just sucked on a red lollipop. By mid-May she chastised him. "You haven't asked me to the Prom."

"I'm not going to the Prom."

"Everybody goes to the Prom."

"I'm working that evening."

"You're a real bastard. You lead me on then pull away. I bet you're no fun in bed either."

"I never led you on."

"You didn't kick my ass when I led you on. Same thing."

"Your mind works in the most fascinating ways," he said.

"You know what? I'll get somebody else to take me to the Prom, then screw the hell out of him when it's over."

"To each his own."

"Doesn't that make you jealous?"

"It would if we had a relationship, but we don't have a relationship."

Then she made a bold proposal. "Marry me!"

He laughed. "You're just saying that because I'm hard to get," he joked.

"Don't overrate yourself. I could have you any time I want. Marry me and you'll never go hungry. My father is making a ton of money."

"Cynthia, I have hungers you never dreamed."

"You didn't even ask me if I love you."

"I don't want to know," he said.

"Well, I do. So there." She kissed him gently just under his ear. "I'm trying to decide," she said, nibbling on his ear, "should

I become a woman scorned . . ." she paused, thinking about it.

"No. I've decided you're an idiot. You don't know what you're missing. Maybe I'll just write you off as a lost cause. But I'll always love your voice and imagine how it would sound saying certain things to me."

"Sounds very final," he said.

"Final as you want it to be," she smiled sweetly, kissed him with a consuming hunger, and pushed her tongue deep into his mouth and rolled it around. "From now on I'll just have to call you kemo-sabe," she said.

Then she left to work up a date for the Prom.

*

Cynthia's visits had helped him shake off the trauma of Deannie's sudden disintegration and death. He told her that and thanked her for her friendship. Except for his almost nonstop schedule, life had come back into familiar patterns. Jessica worked, kept the house in order, and never seemed to tire of finding new creative ways to make salty observations. Joe had readjusted to his work routines, but his last episode with illness caused him to think more than usual about mortality, about what comes next. One Sunday he asked Andrew, "Do you believe in God?"

"No," Andrew quickly responded. Then thought for a few seconds more. "No," he repeated. "Maybe a God who keeps the universe running, but I don't feel any personal connection."

"Well, you should believe," Joe said.

"Why?"

"It doesn't cost you anything. You don't have to do anything.

Why take a chance?"

"I'm too busy right now to think about God."

"Your funeral," Joe tried to make a joke of it.

*

By June, Andrew was feeling the exhaustion from the pace of his last few months. Somehow he had managed to get to work on time every afternoon. Somehow he had managed to continue his academic record. Somehow he was able to discharge the responsibilities of his extracurricular activities. He had achieved everything he had set his mind to after the sum-es-est epiphany. He was one of the few authentic "Wheels" in school. It was everything he had wanted. I should be feeling on top of the world, he thought. I've had it all there, in my hand. Achievement after achievement. But all he could feel was exhaustion and a sense of emptiness. Somehow, out of this experience, small as it was in comparison with real world problems, he had learned a lesson that would last him throughout his life. He had lost the need for personal glory ever again. He had lost even the slightest desire for fame or mortal status. He had lost all ambition for power. And this realization stirred deeply within him. With no need for power or glory, ever again, he felt a stunning new sense of freedom.

He was grateful for the friendships he had found, and all of those with whom he was especially close—Brundi, Aram, Jiggety, and Cynthia—vowed they would try to keep in touch after graduation. He went to graduation ceremony with gown over his blue jeans, and then immediately to work. He hardly thought about the Prom.

311.

For all he had learned and read, his education was still quite circumscribed. He had never heard of supermarkets, Boy Scouts, tennis, golf, skiing. He had never contemplated the existence of the world of financial exchanges. He had barely any consciousness of religions beyond Protestant sectarianism, Pentecostalism, and Roman Catholicism. He had only minimal familiarity with cultures outside of the United States. So much of the world was still foreign to him. So much of life experience was still hidden behind the veil.

And then Tom Wharton's story of his life and adventures lingered in the back of his mind like a haunting melody. Why would someone gather all that experience and, like an old wounded lion, just come home to die? Tom didn't think big. And as Andrew reflected, his own mind was not thinking very big right now either. As he grew up, the worlds of finance, of corporations, of opera, of business, were so alien to him it might have been another universe. None of this inhabited any part of the realms of his consciousness. Except for the Ford Motor Company, which seemed to be its own universe, no thought of corporations or big business finance ever drifted through his mind.

Somehow, Andrew knew only the basic outlines about what he did not know. He would have to expand his mind, become a real thinker, unlimited by circumstance or surroundings. He reflected wistfully on his boyhood dreams. What particularly troubled him was that he knew he was losing sight of all Kenneth had taught him, obscured in confusion of the tides of emotion that seemed to consume him.

And at the same time, the Cameron restlessness grew profoundly within him.

*

He continued to work through the summer at the plant, right up to his entry into the university. To enlarge his savings, he worked as a day laborer for the O.H. Frisbe Moving Company, moving furniture. Just as he had done on John Henry's trucks before that business had been destroyed. O.H. Frisbe was a casual friend of John Henry, and John had always referred all of his long distance trucking business to him.

On Sundays, Andrew usually spent time with Cynthia. Neither of them went to church. They shared a disdain for what they saw as hypocrisy, deeply rooted and pervasive. Instead, they would hike or ride bicycles or swim. Cynthia had a rather stunning look in short shorts or a bathing suit and had an elegant taste in clothes. Her long, well-shaped legs and athletic body seemed to give her a presence larger than ordinary.

Sometimes Andrew would drive to Cynthia's place on Grosse Isle, where her father kept his yacht. At their direction, the skipper would take them to Lake Erie or to Lake St. Clair to swim. It was on one of these excursions when Andrew saved her life. She had been caught in a treacherous patch of water that seemed like a whirlpool or undertow. Cynthia was showing signs of panic. Andrew swam with all his strength to get to her, then held her head above water until he could bring her to shore.

Cynthia coughed quite a few times, and tried to calm her agitation, but she was all right. She had inhaled only a little water. And when she was recovered, Andrew helped her back to the yacht, where they proceeded home. Wrapped in comfortable robes, she snuggled into his arms.

"I owe you my life," she said.

"Not for a moment. It was no big deal."

"It was a big deal for me," she said.

"You're too pretty to drown. I just can't see you as a corpse."

"I would be an exquisite corpse," she said.

"Yes, I think so."

"You're part Indian, aren't you?"

"Yes, Cherokee."

"Well, I once read that Indians have a very long tradition. If you save someone's life, that person belongs to you forever."

"I never heard that," he said.

"Well, it's true. Whether you like it or not, you can't deny the tradition of your ancestors. I now belong to you. Forever." She smiled and kissed him just under his ear.

"What am I going to do with you forever?" he asked with a laugh.

"I'll tell you where to start."

"Cynthia, my dear, dear friend, here's how I want you to spend forever..."

"How?" she asked.

"Like a beautiful, colorful, slender, long-winged spunky bird, flying gracefully through the universe. Your wings will make you forever free."

"You're no fun," she pouted. "Right here, right now, I've just confessed to you that you own me."

"I don't own you. I could never own you."

"Andrew, my dear idiot friend, whether you like it or not, I'll always feel a special obligation toward you. Don't you see? I'm yours whether you want me or not. Our lives are now intertwined in some mystical way."

"I feel a deep sense of friendship for you. That will never change," he said.

"Just hold me close for a while," she said. "Shut off that engine of your mind and enjoy me."

*

In September he began his studies at the University of Michigan, and quite unexpectedly, resumed the broken relationship with Laura Boutin.

#

About the Author

Paul Snider grew up in the back streets and alleyways of Detroit and, alternately, on an apple farm near Georgian Bay, Ontario. He moved fifteen times before he was twelve.

Photo © 2017 Jonah Levy

His religious life has often been checkered, with patches of light and shadow. During the Korean War he was what has been described as "an atheist in a foxhole." Nevertheless, he survived the war with two purple hearts.

Years later he learned he was not an atheist at all. What he had been denying all along was the clouded, inconsistent, man-made image of God.

As he continued the search for knowledge of God's higher ways, he met a woman with a shimmering spirit. She told him what she had been taught. "Everything you need to grow is already around you, and within you."

There seemed to be a deep truth in what she said. This was the beginning of his rebirth.

Paul is the father of seven, husband (to Mary) of 59 years, now retired from a business career, and living in Illinois.

With his beloved Grandpa Cameron. Lucknow, Ontario, 1938.

www.ingramcontent.com/pod-product-compliance
Lightning Source LLC
Chambersburg PA
CBHW060520180626
46817CB00002B/431